Mama's Gone

by

Leopold Borstinski

FEBRUARY 1997

1

ZING. ALICE FIRST heard a whizzing noise and then felt a sharp movement of air—way before she saw anything. And then it was all too late. She turned to her Mama sat to her left as the woman's head hurtled backward. The red circular mess where an eye once was. The blast of brain and skull that splattered the wall. Bobby threw himself toward Mary Lou to protect her from the assault, but there was no point.

He scurried over and lay on his dead wife as Alice hit the deck. Nikolay drew his revolver almost before the bullet flew through Mama, Alice thought. Lara Mikhailov dragged him down to the floor. Nobody in the room was above window height and there had been no fourth shot.

"Anyone else hurt?"

Three shots, one dead. A professional hit for sure. Worthy of the great Arnold Roach, may he rest in peace. Alice held her snub nose ready for action and Bobby cradled Mary Lou in his arms, rocking them side-to-side in the first moments of his grief.

Alice glanced at Bobby and looked at Nikolay. Had his gun been out before the zing? Couldn't be certain of anything right now. Events unfolded around her and she felt completely estranged from them. Despite the body lying near her feet, she didn't believe Mama was dead. She saw it was true, but it meant nothing to her. Like the world stopped still and she carried on breathing—only she continued on the sidelines as everything flowed ever onwards.

Nikolay's bodyguard, Mikhailov edged to a window and cautiously inched her head to spot the sniper. Nada. Nikolay Markov spoke to her but Alice couldn't discern a single word—still trapped in her time-slipped bubble. His mouth moved again but his expression became more aggressive. Angry.

"What just happened?"

"We know nothing of this. My mother's been killed. You think I'd do that? To my Mama?"

Alice found a pistol lying in her hand, which she must have taken out of her handbag. An unconscious action. She glanced round and Bobby had let go of Mary Lou, holding a revolver. Someone would pay for killing her Mama.

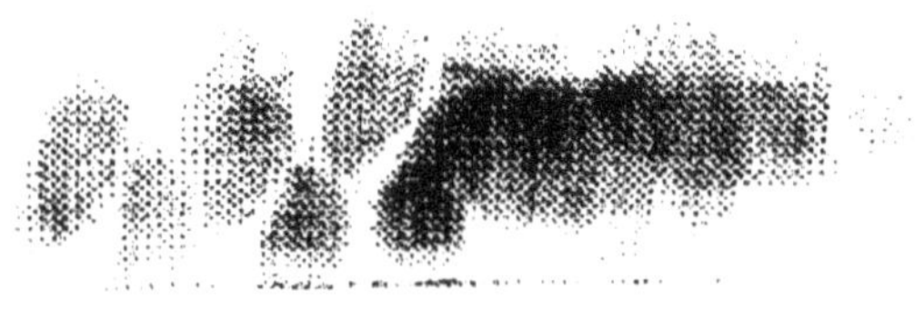

2

FATHER CARMOODY BABBLED on and, even though all his words were extolling his Mama's virtues, Frank wanted him to stop. To just shut his pie-hole. He had no right talking about his Mama because he didn't know her. How was anyone taking this man in a frock seriously?

"Mary Lou Lagotti, may she rest in peace, was a mother, a wife, a businesswoman. But above all she was a human being who died in tragic circumstances. She leaves behind two beautiful children—Frank Jr and Alice —as well as Bobby, her dutiful husband."

Mutterings and nods from the congregation echoed the priest's words.

"She joined our community nearly thirty years ago and she quickly became a fabulous contributor to our local charities. As her children got older, and her business activities thrived, Mary Lou grew as a force for good in Palm Springs."

More mutterings and Frank heard his sister sob again. She had done her best to keep it together as the assembled throng entered the building, but now her salty tears were annoying him. Again. He was tired of her and the way she acted as though everything was about her. This was Mama's funeral: not another place for Alice to be the center of attention.

Frank looked round at the sea of strange faces. Who were these people who'd turned up in his Mama's memory? They shouldn't be here. This was a private moment. He didn't want Alice or Bobby there either, but he had no choice. He put up with them because they were family. As for the rest of the congregation? Fuck them and the horse they rode in on.

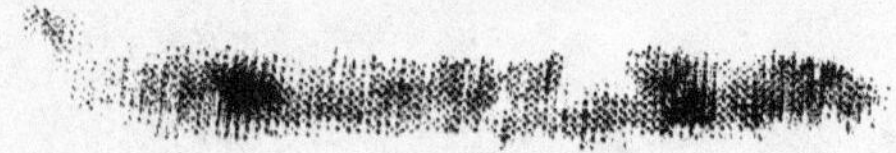

ALICE HAD NO memory whether it had been yesterday or last week when a person or persons unknown shot her Mama. Everything was a blur. People talking around her, at her, about her. But nothing seemed real. Like a movie playing out in her head—only with actors stood in front of her as the folks she knew—apart from the priest who'd popped out of a hole in the ground almost before Mama stopped breathing.

A gasp of air and another wave of sadness washed over her, engulfing Alice in a deep melancholy. Bobby held her hand but gave her no solace. Nobody could. She wished she had a partner—somebody to be with, who'd hug her and convince her everything would be all right. But she was alone as she stared at the sealed coffin. Although she wanted to confront the reality of her experience, she couldn't bring herself to think about what was in the wooden box. That was a thought too far. Even contemplating the wooden box itself made her want to cry again.

She tried to turn round to see who was here and staring at her, but that required her to let go of Bobby's hand and she didn't have the mental strength for that. Better to ignore the throng behind than lose her lifeline. Her connection with the living.

The priest droned on and each word continued to have no impact on Alice at all. She barely focused on what he was saying, so engrossed in her personal misery.

The sound of glass and the thunk of the bullet whizzing and landing in her darling Mama. Alice was assaulted by another wave of tears.

1973

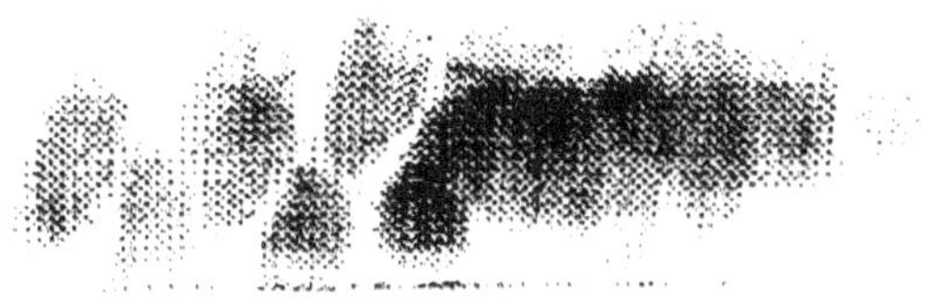

3

MARY LOU SETTLED into her new role as the business partner of Pasquale and Fabio, representatives of the West Coast mob. The previous year she'd proven her worth taking out a local heroin dealer and also whacking a made man from the East Coast outfit, Charlie Pentangelo.

Now she had full control of the Palm Springs trade, Mary Lou wanted to stretch her reach further than the Watts district of South LA. She recalled one of her earliest conversations with Pasquale and thought today was a good time to mention it. The three were sat in an empty warehouse, all cars parked round the back so any passerby could be forgiven for believing nothing was happening.

"Business is going well, wouldn't you say?"

"Sure. Profits are up and stable."

"I was thinking about Hollywood."

"They make great movies there."

"Last year, you talked about an opportunity we could work on together."

"I did."

Pasquale smiled as he teased Mary Lou. The prospect appealed of being the main supplier of cocaine to the movie moguls and their minions. While it might not generate the sizable profit afforded by selling small bags of brown crystal to the impoverished and desperate in the projects, there was kudos attached. And sideline businesses could arise servicing the needs of the rich and famous, whose tastes and interests were traditionally esoteric and often illegal.

"I'd like to crack open the Beverly Hills safe with you."

"And how do you know I've not pursued this with anyone else?"

"My people have asked around and no one has mentioned your name. So either somebody is dipping their beak in this trough or you are very discrete. I reckon it was worth asking."

Pasquale grinned and glanced at Fabio, who returned the favor.

"Would be great to break ground with you on a new venture."

"Good news. After the first year of operation, we should stick to our fifty-fifty split. On this occasion, I propose funding the start-up out of my end, so I would like sixty per cent of the profit to cover those costs."

Pasquale sat and stared at her for thirty seconds. Then he leaned over and whispered with Fabio awhile. They finished discussions with a mutual nod.

"Mary Lou, you make me laugh. With all due respect, when we first met, you demanded terms because you were putting your sweat on the line. Now you seek an accommodation because you have made money with me and want to protect yourself from unexpected financial downside."

She remained silent because Mary Lou understood she should let Pasquale speak until he was finished before responding. This three-piece suit with olive skin in front of her was one of the most powerful men this side of Vegas.

"And, to be honest, I'd seek the same if I was in your position. Tell you what, I'll lease you back the labs, equipment and people. That way, you make the financial commitment you already seem keen to invest. However, we share the risk because they will be my resources until you pay me off after the first year. That is how I believe partners should behave and it is how I would like you and I to do business, Mrs. Lagotti."

Mary Lou hoped Pasquale would play ball, but she hadn't expected this level of generosity. They shook hands and the deal was sealed. Now she could measure the high currency she held in Pasquale's eyes.

HAVING RETURNED TO her four-bedroom Palm Springs mansion, Mary Lou played with the twins for an hour before she left them with the ever-capable housekeeper Irma and headed to the Country Club. She sat in her usual booth with her back to the wall, so she could survey the entire room with one glance. The red leather furniture was fading but none of the patrons seemed too bothered.

The place prospered because it catered well for its diverse community. There were the ladies who lunched, their men who talked business when they weren't in LA tending to their commercial interests or fucking their mistresses—and the occasional golfer.

Milton Frazzini sat down opposite her just as a waiter delivered her coffee.

"I'll have one of those too, Pete."

The man had been the first to take her criminal talents seriously when she'd hit town after Alice and Frank Jr were born. They'd prospered together—Milton was an effective completer but had a poor track record for succeeding with his own projects. With Mary Lou's brains and his organizational skills, they managed an extensive area of LA's heroin trafficking.

Once Pete left the vicinity, Milton wanted to find out about the morning's conversation.

"We've got the green light to open up Beverly Hills. And the terms are better than I ever expected."

"Hollywood? I thought you had your eye on San Francisco."

"No, you made that suggestion and I nixed it. I've told you before, don't confuse our business with your dick. If you want to visit your latest piece of tail in San Francisco then knock yourself out or tie her up—or whatever. But do it on your own time."

Milton always blushed when Mary Lou talked about his extramarital sex life. Thankfully, this was a rare occasion. It was her job to understand the weaknesses of her key people, so she needed to know what he was up to when he was away from Janet and the boy.

Funny thing was that while Milton was off shtupping his floozy, his wife had something going with a local lad: Pete the waiter. She'd been letting him into her bedroom for over a year now. As a concerned neighbor, Mary Lou kept an eye on the goings and comings of Oakcrest Drive.

"The time isn't right for us to hop over to a strange town. There's plenty of money to make nearer to home. Besides, I thought you might like the Hollywood Hills. It'd give you a tremendous opportunity to mix with all those A-listers."

"Huh?"

"Where there are stars, there are producers. And where there are producers, there are…"

"…girls who'll do anything to get into the movies."

"And that's your kind of girl, Milton."

"I can't help the fact I'm attracted to the desperate and needy type."

"Your words, not mine."

"But you're not disagreeing."

Mary Lou grinned and let out a small laugh which Milton echoed. This would be a fun ride.

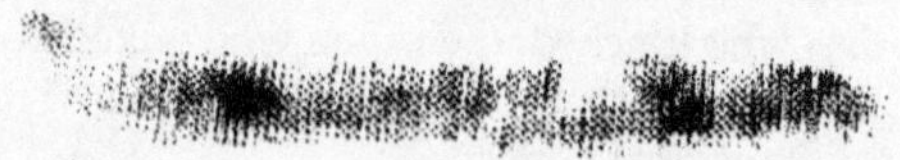

MILTON LEFT STILL smiling and Mary Lou waited for Bobby Trevisan to show before ordering any lunch. As if on cue, just as her stomach rumbled, the man walked in and sat down beside her. He squeezed her knee as he kissed her hello.

"Kids okay?"

"Reckon so, but I've been in the summerhouse all morning. No raised voices and no sign of Irma, so all was fine."

Mary Lou gazed round the room and rested a hand on his thigh. They had been together a year and she trusted him with her children's lives. Now she was busting with excitement, but Pete arrived with their menus, so she waited until they'd given their orders.

"We've got a new gig. It's all been arranged with our friend from the Hills."

A euphemism for Pasquale was always best in a public place—even one as private as the Country Club.

"Great! What's the plan?"

"I'll tell you when I have it figured out. Minimum we need is to liaise with Fabio as there's new product to process and locations to scout: we're running the studio snow express."

Bobby smiled and planted a kiss square on her lips. They had been investigating, plotting and planning for this caper over three months, day and night. Finally, it had come good and received Pasquale's blessing.

The incumbent suppliers had grown lazy and relied on the movie producers to supply the dope to the stars, but the studio system was falling apart and a new breed of film maker needed a new type of drug dealer. The Lagottis would go straight to the young brat pack and their enormous propensity to party and imbibe a cocktail of intoxicants. Bobby would resolve any disputes with the old guard using a high caliber revolver. You can take the man out of the mob, but you can't take the mob out of the man.

The Lagottis and Pasquale were as aware as anyone that drugs were just the beginning. The parties needed hosts and Milton was the guy to supply the right quantity of girls, eager to break into showbiz. Those that didn't make it onto a studio lot could be encouraged to deliver a performance or two in the underbelly of Hollywood and its porn palaces. Get the distribution right and even an average hardcore product could generate as much as heroin. No small feat.

Mama's Gone

BOBBY PLACED A call to Milton after lunch and they met in the summerhouse forty minutes later. The drapes overlooking the pool were drawn for privacy to separate domestic and business life. The fifty-by-twenty-feet space was a mix of comfortable easy chairs, couches and formal working environment. Mary Lou installed a desk near her secured walk-in cupboard and armaments storage. Next year, she told herself she'd install a safe—for the guns and the money. Until then, Mary Lou was the sole owner of the key to her secret wardrobe.

Coffees poured and cigarettes lit, they set about organizing the snow express.

"Fabio's runners will serve us well at the get-go until we've made our own contacts. They'll know the cool places and the most valuable party hosts."

"The next task is to organize the parties. Create some happenings. And that's where you'll come into your own, Milton."

"What do you need me to do?"

"The thing you do best: find some willing girls, who want to hang with the celebrities. And don't mind what they get up to with them when they're there."

Milton's expression was thoughtful for a spell and then his eyes widened as he got the joke. He loved to run call girls because he allowed himself to taste the merchandise which he never did with narcotics. The man lived in a moral sewer, but he had his principles. Whores, booze and gambling were fine but drugs were for the birds.

"Bobby, I want you to keep an eye on our heroin trade. The last thing we need is for that to turn to shit while we're growing new shoots near Burbank."

"Sure. Just don't push me out of the story."

"I won't. Only we mustn't take our eyes off the ball. We'll all share the prizes."

He nodded consent although Mary Lou hadn't asked his permission. This was her show and she was running it. The two had found a way of sharing a bed together while she wore the pants outside the bedroom. It helped that she was a successful bank robber and he was a washed-up mob killer. Both Mary Lou and Bobby had pasts they couldn't forget or escape from—no matter how hard they tried.

"The next week will be crucial. We need to deal firmly with any objections we may encounter. Better to put them in the morgue than leave some hopped-up hippie to complain we're stomping all over his territory."

"I'll take care of incidentals."

Bobby inhaled deeply and stubbed out the remains of his smoke. Despite what he told himself, he still enjoyed killing people and Mary Lou got it. So did Milton, who always showed him the utmost respect—no matter what the circumstances.

"Once we've established a toe-hold, we'll need a couple of girls to keep the good times rolling and to make sure our new friends buy their gear from us."

"It'll be my pleasure to run that end of things."

"Just remember we don't care how much hooch our whores drink or how many lines go up their noses. But their job is to get the guests to purchase our product and to do whatever they are asked. They can't say no to any request, no matter how debauched: church girls travel home in body bags. Capiche?"

"Understood. I've run this racket before. I'll be on top of it all."

"Are there any you won't be road testing?"

Bobby laughed and raised an eyebrow.

"Not unless they're under sixteen. I don't judge our customers but I will not fuck kids."

"A true gentleman."

"Let's get back to business."

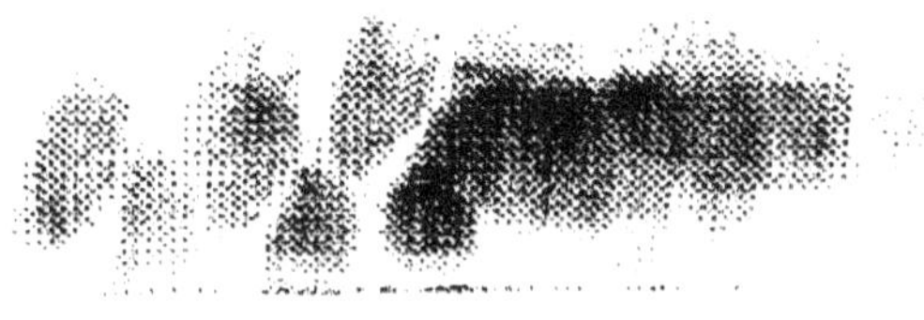

4

FRIDAY WAS THE first chance to put the operation into practice. Fabio's people and product were in the right hands at the correct location as an all-night party was in prospect. Hank Milana was celebrating the wrap on his latest offering: a gritty portrayal of New York street life shot on a back lot in Burbank.

Independently financed, its executive producer had returned to Manhattan, which meant Hank was in charge of the festivities. Lucky for him, Milton was on hand to keep the booze flowing and the lines cut, ready for snorting. He was a natural.

Although Hank balked at the initial price asked for the snow, he relented after two free samples. The deal duly sealed, the guests could enjoy themselves the way only young acting egos can. Milton watched the action from afar—never mix business with pleasure. And despite his base desires and the writhing mass of naked bodies before him, he did not partake.

Don't get high on your own supply, for sure. Don't ball your own ass when someone else is paying the bill. Watch, enjoy and learn what you can about your customer and their friends. That way, there'll always be another party.

He lost track of where his two hostesses had got to about an hour before, but Milton could be sure everything was fine because his eyes never left Hank. And if that man was happy then Milton was happy too. He saw Hank was happy because the artiste was snorting a line off the bare ass sticking up from a couch. The wink was a clue and the bear hug made him certain.

A glance at his watch told Milton it was four in the morning. He yawned and stretched his back to get more comfortable in his chair. With no notice, a woman fell on his lap, rolled off and danced in between his legs. Her groin was at head height and the only thing she wore was a smile. Milton kept his professional cool and tried to look past her rhythmic hips and maintain his vigil on Hank.

Each time he regained a line of sight, she moved so that her pubes were the only things he could see. He placed a palm on each hip to stop her movements, but she misread his actions and pushed herself into his face. This was one horny hippie.

Milton shrugged, stood up and took her by the hand. He walked up to Hank who was lying on a bean bag with someone's lips around his dick.

"Adam, meet Eve."

He positioned the woman so Hank's mouth was six inches below her navel. As he turned back to his chair, Milton saw the two had worked something out.

"The things we do for money…"

DOWN THE ROAD, a month later, Mary Lou and Bobby contemplated the expanse of a faded hotel on Sunset Boulevard. The realtor busied around them so he was desperate to get the property off his books. They did their best to ignore him and concentrate on the potential of the crumbling beauty rusting and aching under their feet.

Mary Lou's idea was simple but brilliant. If you own the venue where the exclusive gatherings take place then you don't have to worry about finding the next party: the soiree comes to you and you control everything that you pay for within a known environment. Besides, spending dough on a heap on Sunset Boulevard could only increase the value of the real-estate. Whatever happens, they win.

Soon they supplied cocaine to four parties a week, although Mary Lou viewed this as just one tip of the snow-capped iceberg. The hotel was big enough for them to run five or six separate events at the same time—but that was way into the future.

For now, they'd renovate the first floor with its ballroom: convert into an amazing party space and a reception area and restaurant, which could become an enormous bar and chill out zone. Security in the grounds and scrutiny of all who entered the Palace would mark out the place as the number primary location for the cognoscente.

Mary Lou gouged the realtor on price and two weeks later, the venue was theirs. One month of intense building activity supervised by Bobby and the former hotel was ready for business. By throwing an incredible quantity of men at the problem, Bobby had fit out the first floor—and converted the second into a series of offices and, what he liked to call, relaxation rooms.

Stood in one of these boudoirs, Mary Lou wondered why he had bothered. He smiled and led her to a clock hanging on the wall.

"Look right in the center of the dial."

His finger pointed to a black piece of glass. She was none the wiser and followed Bobby out of the room, into the corridor.

"Notice anything different from when we were here before?"

"The cockroaches are gone?"

"Yes, but there's something else: the rooms are smaller. Look."

He took her around the rooms, dragging her first to one wall and then off to the adjoining surface in the next chamber. Eventually, she saw it.

"Why have you thickened the walls?"

"To make a hidden corridor. That way we can move around the place without being seen."

"And what's that got to do with the clocks?"

"We've hooked up a cine-camera for each room."

Mary Lou smiled, but let Bobby carry on his explanation.

"We're getting the famous or the nearly famous in our orbit. But in a while, the powerful and the influential will want a piece of our action. Then we might find it useful to have an edge if you see what I mean."

SENATOR TEDDY PRESCOTT enjoyed the high life and the various perks offered him as a representative of the Californian people. He split his time between Washington and Los Angeles. Like so many Americans, movie stars were magical superheroes to him and he grabbed every opportunity to mix in their circles.

As a Republican, he fought a hard campaign on a pro-guns and anti-tax ticket. The right to bear arms against the British without paying for the privilege proved irresistible to voters and he won by a wide margin. This was back in 1970 when Sharon Tate's killers were still unknown and Vietnam continued to rage.

With a beautiful blond wife and two extraordinary children, the Prescotts were a wholesome group, projecting the family values electors liked to see. Five months after they opened the Palace, Milton called Bobby around six in the morning with news about Senator Prescott.

"We have a situation and need you to deal."

"Can it wait a couple of hours?"

"No. You better come over as soon as you've got your pants on."

"Understood."

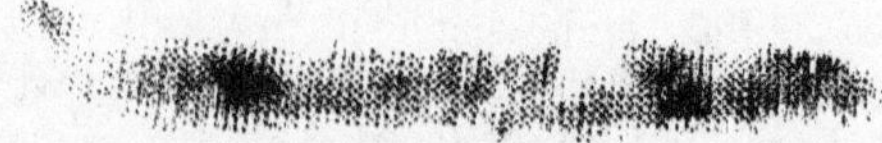

BOBBY STOOD AT the fisheye lens staring in at the room. He watched and waited, with Milton hovering next to him. After three minutes doing nothing, he stepped out of the hidden corridor and entered the scene of the crime.

"Hello Teddy."

The senator sat on the edge of the bed, a towel covering his lap. Milton made sure no one had offered him any clothes to wear. Best to keep him feeling vulnerable until Bobby arrived.

"Can you remember what happened here?"

His hand indicated the bloody mess lying on the floor on the other side of the bed.

"We were fooling around and everything was fine. I don't…"

Bobby walked round and picked up a beer bottle, holding it upside down, so red dripped off the neck and onto the wooden flooring.

"Looks like you were partying quite hard."

Prescott's eyes glanced at the glass container and tears welled up inside him. Bobby placed the object between Prescott's feet so he couldn't avoid its reality. The blood followed its natural course downwards and dribbled over the whole surface of the glass and onto the floorboards.

Then Bobby returned to the body and kneeled down to study it more closely. The girl lay face up, arms by her ears. Bruises around her neck, shoulders and head. And a tremendous amount of scarlet over her groin. There was no way to tell if she'd been unconscious when she died or whether she had struggled against the monster until the end. All her clothes were strewn over the floor and Teddy's were folded neatly on a pile on a chair. Bobby noticed the mirror and razor blade on the bedside table, but there were almost no crumbs of powder visible.

"She's in quite a mess, Teddy. She disrespect you?"

"No, not at all. Lizzie was a wonderful girl."

"Then what went wrong?"

Prescott looked up at Bobby with a quizzical expression. A shrug and more tears.

"You have nothing to worry about. I am here because I want to help you."

"Thank you."

"We will tidy up this room first after you've gone. It'll be like she never was here. That you were never in her bed and that you two were never together."

Teddy's body juddered as he turned his head to glance at Lizzie one more time. The towel on his lap fell to the ground and Bobby walked away. Once he'd closed the door behind him, he instructed Milton to give him the film from the camera.

"What would you like me to do with Teddy?"

"Set Prescott free and get Fabio's cleaner in as soon as possible."

"Okay."

"And next week, pay Teddy a visit and ask for a donation for the girl's funeral."

"Funeral?"

"I want you to remind him of what happened and that we have not forgotten. There'll be no burial. You know better than that. Dump her body in the desert."

"She'd been with us from the start. Great piece of ass, popular with the clients and sure could get them to pay for snow."

"Thanks for the eulogy. He must be out of here in the next thirty minutes. She needs to be out of here by lunchtime. Discretion is key in these situations right?"

"You betcha. By the time the rest of the guests wake up, this will be just a bad memory for Teddy."

"Damn straight. And sorry if I was grouchy when you called. Don't enjoy being woken up in the middle of the night."

"De nada. I figured some things are more important than sleep."

"Say that again. What was Prescott doing, the fucked-up whack-job?"

"I have told you, Bobby: I do not judge. Some behavior goes on under this roof, you wouldn't believe. The depravity I've seen…"

"I can only imagine—and that's enough for me. You keep the cine-reels, though?"

"Some of them might be sickos, but I'm not stupid. Of course I do."

"Good man."

BOBBY VISITED PRESCOTT at the family home a week before Thanksgiving. The place stood in vast private grounds in Malibu. Tailored lawns and adobe-style buildings. A butler answered the door and led him into the library. He settled into a brown leather chair and made himself comfortable.

When Teddy Prescott entered the room and saw Bobby lounging near his books, he almost popped a blood vessel.

"What are you doing here? Our business was finished a long time ago."

He remained seated and beckoned for Teddy to join him. The man wasn't used to mortals acting this way in his own home.

"I'm pleased to see you again too, Teddy. From what I hear, you haven't fucked any underage girls with any bottles lately. Or hasn't word spread fast enough yet?"

Bobby removed an imaginary piece of fluff from his knee. Mainly to give the senator a minute to collect himself. Prescott slumped on a nearby stool.

"There was no need to send me the film of my actions. I regret what I did in a moment of... passion and I paid handsomely so the child could be taken care of properly."

"Save the protestations for the voters. Or your wife."

Teddy's eyes flitted at the closed library door and back to Bobby.

"I am not here to chat about the past. What's done is done and I'm not in the mood for nostalgia. Let's talk about our future."

"What do you mean?"

"You are a powerful man, an honorable man. A man of influence—in California and other states like, say, Nevada."

"So?"

"My wife and I are about to take over a casino in Las Vegas and we do not want any trouble from the Gaming Commission. You can help us."

The blood drained from Prescott's face and he glanced at the door again.

"Before we talk turkey, why don't you offer me a beer..."

1994

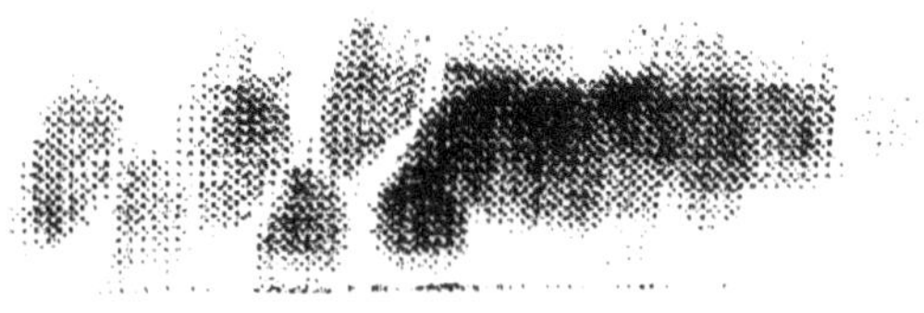

5

THE TWINS CAME home from their very separate schools and OJ Simpson stood trial for murdering his wife. While the latter fact consumed the nation, Mary Lou couldn't wait for her babies to return to the nest.

Bobby drove to collect Alice from Berkeley while Frank made his own way back from San Diego State. The boy only carried a suitcase and a backpack. She filled the car and trailer to the brim. Thanks to good packing by Bobby, there was just sufficient space left for two people to squeeze in between the boxes, bags and cases.

"What have you got in here?"

"My life."

He nodded, shrugged and set off for Palm Springs. On arrival, Alice threw herself into Mary Lou's arms.

"Mama, so good to see you. I've a thousand things to tell you about."

"And it's great to have you back, but Frank's home too. Arrived an hour ago…"

Alice took her attention off her mother's face and glanced round the hallway. A case and backpack lay in a heap near the kitchen door. Her gaze floated into the living room until the sprawling mess of her brother filled her vision. He blinked acknowledgement in her general direction and she offered a half-smile.

Mama led her onto the family couch and continued to hold her hand while Frank carried on with his tales of school. The anecdotes were tedious and, at least twice, Alice reckoned he was making it up as he conjured a mix of urban myths and other people's experiences. She couldn't bring herself to imagine him studying, going to lectures or doing anything which might involve effort. In her head, she'd wondered how the hell he'd graduated at all. At her darkest how, she even thought Mama had paid San Diego State to get him through at all.

At that same dark moment, a flush of pride filled Alice's heart because her degree had been earned through hard work, commitment and deep resolve. And it was a better school too.

She waited patiently until Frank ran out of steam. She knew Mama did not approve of interrupting her firstborn male child. Alice's four extra minutes on this planet counted for nothing.

All this time, Bobby sat silent in an easy chair. He'd been a member of this family for over twenty years, but sometimes he didn't feel a part of it at all. This afternoon was one of those moments. Before Alice could get into the full swing of her story, Irma appeared from the kitchen with a tray piled high with coffee and cookies.

Even though she was only the housekeeper, she kept a special place in her heart for those two bundles of joy. Not that they hadn't caused their poor mother grief over the years, especially the boy. He was a tearaway when he was a teenager—not much better now, only he had more money to get himself out of trouble without Mrs. Lagotti having to step in and save his scrawny ass.

TWO DAYS LATER, Frank grabbed his things, kissed Mama on the forehead and told her he was off to New York for a while. Mary Lou offered to drive him to the airport, but he declined.

"I don't like long goodbyes and you'll cry if you take me there."

After the taxi whisked him away, his mom sobbed. Once her eyes had dried out, she walked through the conservatory and onto the patio. Alice was floating on an air mattress in the middle of the pool, so Mary Lou sat on a sun lounger and watched her darling daughter soak in the rays.

"What are you going to do?"

"Lie here until dinner. Dunno."

"That's not what I meant. Frank's just left."

"He'll be back."

"For New York."

"Oh. That boy sure has a mind of his own."

"Am I going to lose you too?"

"You haven't lost Frank. He just doesn't know how to settle down anywhere."

"And you?"

"I'd like to grab this summer if I can. The next time I have this much vacation will be when I retire."

"Okay darling. You deserve that if nothing else. Then what?"

Alice slipped off her inflatable mattress and swam to the edge nearest to Mary Lou. Then she hauled herself out the pool and sat opposite Mama.

"I want to work with you and Bobby."

Mary Lou stiffened and shuffled on the lounger.

"What do you think we do—apart from making a few investments?"

Alice laughed and wrung the excess water from her below-the-shoulder length hair.

"Investments. Please? Frank and I aren't stupid. All the discrete conversations in the summerhouse. The men in dark suits who go through this place like it's their office. And Milton? Do you know what the kids at Montgomery High used to say about him?"

"Come with me."

They strode past the pool and into the summerhouse where Bobby sat, working at the desk. He swung round at the noise of the door opening.

"Alice wants to work with us."

"Do you have a résumé?"

"Be serious. And she says the kids have known about our business for years."

"And what is it we do, Alice?"

"Heroin and cocaine mainly. At least that's what you guys talked about most before I skipped off to Berkeley."

Mary Lou stared at Bobby with gritted teeth and he looked right back at her.

"Are you a cop?"

"No. What makes you think I might be with law enforcement?"

"You'll understand why later. You're correct, we started with narcotics but we used some of those profits to diversify into… other realms."

"Such as?"

"Prostitution and gambling mainly."

Alice whistled out of respect. She and Frank figured out the drug angle when they snuck up to the summerhouse and eavesdropped on the conversations going on inside the taboo building. But she hadn't realized how busy they'd been while she had been away.

"Like I said: I want to help. I'm smart and I could drive the business forward."

"You've been talking about having someone to assist with logistics. She could start there and we can see how she handles herself."

Bobby nodded. He knew this wasn't a discussion. Mary Lou had decided and this conversation was informational only. He thought it a good idea, but his opinion was not sought. So he didn't offer it. Alice always had a sensible head on her shoulders and was bright as a button. Frank would be a better choice to deal with a Mexican stand-off but he doubted if either had fired a gun in their lives. Mary Lou had wanted them to have a normal childhood and not get involved in their criminal ways. Something had changed her mind, clearly.

FRANK TOOK A limo from LaGuardia to a chichi hotel in SoHo. The decor comprised white walls and floors with every piece of furniture made of transparent plastic. He dropped a C-note on the concierge before he hopped up to his suite so he was guaranteed delivery of a girl and a snort or two of cocaine within an hour of tipping the bellboy.

Having fucked her twice, he got bored with the skirt and sent her packing—with a respectable gratuity because she'd been good while she lasted. That left the rest of the pile of coke for himself and he cut sufficient lines to keep him going until morning.

Once room service had delivered his breakfast, Frank called down to the concierge to arrange for more female companionship. The two hookers kept him amused for the entire afternoon but he got bored again. Up to some designer stores on Fifth Avenue and back to the hotel bar to see if his new threads attracted the right kind of woman: easy to impress with big tits and few opinions of her own. The venue was full of his target market because so many rich, dumb men with high libidos and few social skills inhabited these kinds of drinking holes.

With a credit card, which had never received a single payment from him, Frank soon found himself surrounded by adorable asses. The only question left in his mind was which one to pick for tonight. He felt like going clubbing and didn't want to be let down by a girl with poor rhythm. He chuckled to himself when he realized when he brought her back to his suite he didn't want her to have poor rhythm there either. Fuck-a-doodle-do.

The vintage champagne flowed and the chicks hovered around the rooster. Bubbly conversation continued into the evening as every now and again he popped into the washroom to take another hit of his snow. Each time he walked away from those short skirts, he risked some cock taking over his flock of fuckables.

As predictable as the rising sun, when next Frank returned he found some Latino hunk stood by his ice bucket entertaining his ladies. The guy didn't yield an inch and carried on talking as though Frank wasn't there.

"Hey, bud. You're in the way of my champagne."

"You can take it in a minute when I've finished telling my friends about what went down last week in the studio."

"No one wants to hear. Move on, buddy. I need to get to my drink."

The ice bucket was on the bar and the bartender maintained a watchful eye on its contents—Frank looked after those who looked after Frank. The barkeep listened in to the conversation between the men but said nothing. Just carried on cleaning the whiskey glass in his hand.

The Martini Bar in the Courtney Hotel was renowned for two things. First, as its name suggested, they mixed a mean martini. Second, all the waitresses in the bar wore the same uniform: a light gray one-piece cotton-and-lycra body suit which had long sleeves to cover the servers' arms but no legs. Every crevice of the women's bodies were on view.

Just as he uttered his last words to encourage the Latino to step down, a waitress hustled by and the guy stopped paying attention to Frank and stared at the woman's crotch. There was something about the shape of her thighs and roundness of her ass that made him want to see more. Big mistake.

Frank grabbed Julio's hand that held his champagne glass and twisted it behind him. This caused Julio to turn and face the bar and Frank seized the hair at the back of his head and push his skull down onto the bar. In one smooth action, the barkeeper snatched the ice bucket and its contents off the clear plastic surface a quarter of a second before Julio's forehead smashed down on the unforgiving hardened material.

The women surrounding them screamed and scattered to leave Frank alone to assault Julio further. Red gushed from his head and the bartender leaned forward.

"Mr. Lagotti…"

Frank pushed Julio's skull into the bar more and looked up.

"I think the gentleman has received your message loud and clear. Why not let him go now?"

"Are we through?"

Saliva, blood and a tooth left the mook's mouth and a brief nod showed consent. Frank released him from his grip and pushed his body further down the bar away from his perch.

"How do I look?"

"I'd say you should pop to the bathroom. Looks like you might have a spot or two of dirt on your shirt. By the time you come back, I'll have set up another bottle—on the house. None of the last one was lost, but it may leave an unpleasant taste in the mouth, anyway."

Frank did as he was told and returned with a smile on his face and a white ring around his nostrils. He swigged a glass of champagne and then took stock of the room. A quick check that Julio had left and Frank collected chicks again. Trouble was, his heart was no longer in it and by the time the bottle was empty, Frank decided to leave.

"What entertainment can you offer me this evening?"

"Chilled or high octane?"

"Do I look chilled?"

The concierge smiled and picked up the phone to reserve a table in the VIP area of an '80s Old Skool club night.

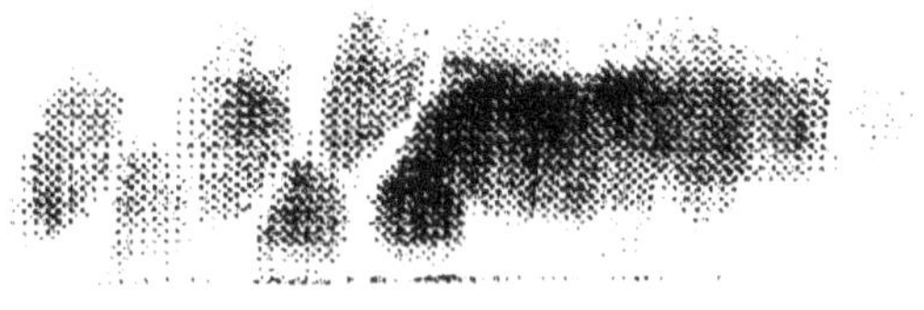

6

THE PHONE CALL came through direct to Mary Lou. Although not inevitable, she couldn't remember a time when Frank hadn't asked for help to get himself out of a hole.

"Hi Mama."

"Hi Frank."

"I'm in a spot of trouble."

"Where are you and what's the problem?"

"They got me on intent to sell."

"Where Frank?"

"Ninth Precinct."

"Manhattan?"

"Yeah. How long since you were arrested?"

"Just got here. They processed me and then I demanded my constitutional phone call."

"Say nothing but be polite. I'll send someone over to sort this out."

"Thanks Mama."

Mary Lou hung up the phone and sighed. That boy never learns. What did I do to deserve him? Then she thought back on her life for a moment, shivered and realized the answer. Dragging herself to the present, she called a New York attorney and briefed Harvey Knight on the situation.

"It's a pain but can you get him out of there today? I don't want Frank spending a night in a police cell."

"Will do. You know the best thing for him might be to find out how the other half live."

"He's my baby."

"Who is old enough to sell narcotics to an undercover cop"

"Just free him and spare me your lectures on child rearing."

"Not a lecture, but the finest legal advice I have ever offered you—the small fortune you've paid to cover the amount of my time I've spent extricating him from law enforcement holding facilities."

The silence on the line meant Harvey's words hit home.

"Get him out, Harvey."

FRANK STARED AT Harvey across a precinct table. As ever with the boy, there was a story and an excuse.

"I was at a party on Avenue A."

"How d'you hear about it?"

"A pickup in my hotel bar… We were all relaxing and laughing and having a good time."

Harvey nodded. He understood what a good time meant to Frank.

"And I was sharing the coke. Everyone was doing a line. Nobody seemed bothered. Then one black bitch asks if I can get some for her. Now I'm always willing to oblige a young lady in distress but I don't know her from jack shit. So I play it cool and tell her I'll help her if she helps me and we leave to find somewhere more congenial to conduct business if you get my drift."

"Was there anywhere to your liking in the apartment?"

"Truth was the only place to be alone was the bathroom. So we go to it and afterwards I ask her how much she wants to buy. With her scrawny ass still sat on my dick she asks for four 8-balls. I tell her I can get that weight to her tomorrow. She pushes to have it there and then, and encourages me by getting on her knees and sucking me off."

"And you relented?"

"Couldn't think of a good reason not to help the skank out. She showed me the green and we hopped over to my hotel. Up in my room, I took out the snow, she had a taste and just before I thought we were done, she pulls a gun and a badge from fuck-knows where and makes me assume the position. I swear thirty seconds later we were joined by the rest of the squad. Was a set up, man."

Harvey's legal pad had filled up with notes.

"Did she instigate the sexual intercourse or did you?"

"Me, but she didn't object."

"And the oral?"

"All her own work. My plan was to ball her back in the hotel."

"And you did not try to ask for money until she mentioned it?"

"Yessir."

"I assume she never spoke of her chosen career."

"It was a party. Who talks about how they earn a living?"

"Interesting they haven't charged you with any sex crimes. Protocol should have stopped her from fucking you. The drugs charges: we can make them go away. A quiet word with the man upstairs if due process can't extinguish their flame. I'm more worried about why you were part of a sting… How long you been in town?"

"Couple of days. No more."

"No disrespect but have you got into any other trouble since you arrived here?"

He stared and struggled to remember. The amount of cocaine coursing through his veins meant his memory was not operating at full speed. Harvey waited. Frank tried to wind back time and listed his activities after landing at the airport: girls, drugs, booze—and not much else. His blank expression spoke volumes.

"Any altercations?"

"Huh?"

"Fights?"

Frank shut his eyes for ten seconds and thought some more. Then his eyes flashed open wide and he smiled.

"Not a fight exactly. I mean, I can handle myself."

He described the hassle with Julio while Harvey continued to take notes. Anyone stood over Harvey's shoulder would have seen he had drawn a perfect cube underneath his legal assessments of Frank's situation. He put his pen down and closed over the pad.

"Frank, sounds like you made a mistake, dear boy. From what you say, I think you had a tussle with a well connected New York family. They have extensive narcotics operations across the Five Boroughs and enough reach to get the cops to set you up. Chances are the woman was theirs and not a real cop. You sure she was black and not Hispanic?"

"Now you ask, dunno. What's the name of the family she's with?"

"Don't worry about that. If I were you, as soon as you're out of here, check out the Courtney and leave town. You do not need the mob breathing down your neck."

"Fuck-a-doodle-do."

DESPITE HIMSELF, FRANK left his hotel and headed off to JFK. He had no idea where to go but he was certain he'd had enough of America. What was the world coming to when you found yourself in jail for banging a girl who wanted some snow? Besides, the Latino had no right to take over his women —and it didn't matter what tribe he came from.

So a trip abroad made sense. At least for a short while. And wouldn't Mama be pleased if he returned with a new business partner? He and Alice figured out all about the narcotics trafficking and Frank reckoned that was something he could turn his hand to as he understood the product intimately —cocaine anyway—and handled himself well when cutting deals. Frank'd got a skank to suck him off for the price of a few 8-balls only last night.

With his limited knowledge of world geography, Frank chose Spain as his destination. It was close to Africa but Europe sounded a lot more civilized. Once he'd wrapped his head around the idea that his dollars were no good to him, he discovered the joys of being an American abroad.

He could be as obnoxious as he wanted, provided he kept a smile on his face because the local muchachos had no idea what he was saying. Frank used as little of his own pesos as possible and slapped all he could on his credit card. Only the small bars and drug dealers demanded cash. After a few weeks, he hopped from Madrid to Barcelona and then onto Seville. Then he bumped into a bunch of kids who were heading to Marbella and he hitched a ride with them.

The days of hardcore Balearic beats had faded, but that didn't mean there was no life left in the clubs. With a different music scene, to the ones he was used to, came a distinctive drug of choice: ecstasy. You would be forgiven for thinking the west coast student communities would have embraced the tablet that made you want to hug anyone who moved. But no. There was more money to be generated from powder than tabs so organized crime wasn't too interested—including the Lagottis.

Frank was in his element though: dancing beyond dawn, off his head on drugs, surrounded by semi-naked women. When he wasn't fooling around with them, he was fucking them and if he wasn't doing either of those two things, then he was asleep. A twenty-four-hour party person.

Three months since he hit the southern coast and all he had to show for the experience was a sore dick and intimate knowledge of every ass in the neighborhood. He woke up one Thursday to find his face by someone's bush. Frank looked around and saw he was in a bedroom but he had no idea where he was or who owned the pubes near his lips.

He gave them a quick lick but was swatted away like his mouth was some kind of fly. His feet were on a pillow and somehow he'd turned round in his sleep. Or they'd both crashed out half way through playing. A dirty grin spread across his face.

Frank was thirsty, so he hauled his carcass off the bed in search of liquid. The studio apartment offered him a sink in the bathroom and another in the kitchenette. There were foul dishes piled high in the kitchen and spent needles lying next to the toilet. He took his chances with the sink faucet and glugged back several handfuls of water.

Then he turned around to check out the devastation from the night before. The girl wore only a blue bra with yellow polka dots and snored loudly. Frank walked over and moved her head so it was resting on the mattress and the noises abated. That helped him think more clearly. Almost before starting, his attention wandered off as he noticed the roundness of her tits peeping out from the sides of the skimpy underwear.

What was he doing? He had told himself he would forge a new connection for Mama but all he'd achieved was a heavy dose of sex, drugs and rock 'n' roll. He needed to get his head in the game. Frank opened the fridge as an auto-response to his stomach rumbling. The girl mumbled something foreign and rolled over face down.

There was nothing to eat except raw vegetables and butter so he gave up on breakfast and turned his attention to the bush on the bed. She was stretched out like a starfish and he scratched his balls for no good reason. He felt his hard-on and decided not to waste it. Frank considered taking her from behind but experience taught him he'd need to wake her up to get an orgasm out of the coupling. Nah, too much effort. Instead he jerked himself off while standing over the girl. A gift of love for when she surfaced.

That night he took the ferry across the Mediterranean Sea and docked in Tangiers. If he couldn't make some solid contacts here, what was the point?

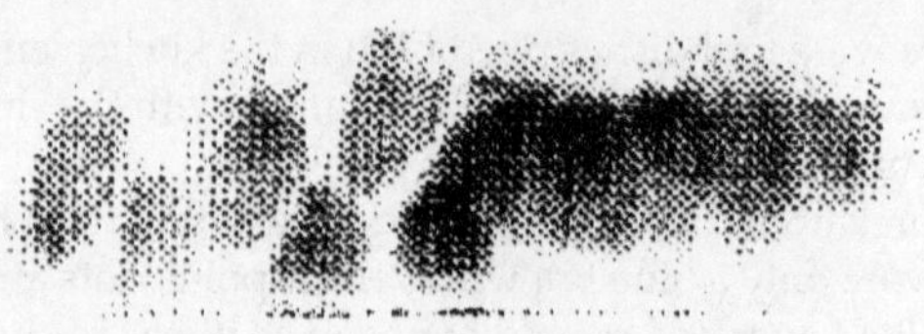

7

IN SEPTEMBER, ALICE and Bobby headed off to Vegas so she could learn about the family business. Running a casino was a huge undertaking and competition was fierce. A decade before, the mob had left the strip, ceding control to the entertainment corporations. Off the main drag was a different story. Footfall might have been lower but gambling margins were sufficiently high to make it a profitable venture. The opportunity to launder cash from their other operations kept motivation up during the occasional month when takings were down.

By Thanksgiving, Bobby allowed Alice to spend two days a week alone at the helm. The initial response from senior staff was disdain thinly disguised as utmost respect. They saw the daughter of the boss dropped on them and what had she done to earn the role—apart from the advantage of nepotism and privilege.

The third week at the Lady Fortune Casino, trouble came knocking at ten at night. Alice was sat in her office to check the day's takings before the evening shift was over. The phone rang and five seconds later, she picked up.

"We have a code blue."

A simple phrase to describe one problem: someone was cheating and the person on the other end of the line was stood on the casino floor.

"Where?"

"The poker tables."

"Down in a minute."

Alice headed straight to the surveillance room where closed-circuit TV monitors were laid out, row upon row. There wasn't an inch of the gaming spaces that didn't have a lens aimed at it. Sat in front of every monitor was a guy staring, watching, waiting for some behavior that was out of the ordinary.

"Talk to me."

"See the john in the blue baseball cap?"

A quick scan of the screen and focussed attention where the finger pointed.

"He has two different signals. A usual tap on the baize and he gets the top of the deck."

"Like everyone else."

"Watch. Once or twice, fingers from his other hand rest on the table and out come cards from the bottom."

Within five minutes, Alice saw for herself.

"How much is he up?"

"Hundred thousand so far."

"Let's keep this civilized. Go down onto the floor and invite him to our VIP room. Offer to help to bring his winnings along. Then meet me in the auto shop. I'll be down in a short while."

Alice walked over to the internal phone fixed to the wall next to the door. She dialed reception.

"Page Naldo Friscelli and tell him there's a car needs fixing."

Bobby had introduced Alice to Friscelli their second day in Vegas. They spent only fifteen minutes together but Bobby assured her she could trust Naldo with her life. He was the quietest, most grounded human she had ever met. Every pore oozed strength. Ten years younger than Bobby but she could tell there was a special bond between the two mobsters. This meant Naldo would be true to his word when he offered her undying allegiance.

As Alice entered the auto shop in the basement of Lady Fortune, she was hit by the stench of motor oil. A wide variety of tools hung on the walls and in the middle was sufficient space for three vehicles to be worked on at the same time. Right now there was a solitary chair and one man wearing a blue baseball cap, sweating profusely.

Alice walked toward him and everyone heard the clink of her heels on the tiled floor. She stopped four feet away from the john, forcing him to look up at her.

"How much has he won so far?"

"Hundred and fifty grand by the time we got to him."

"The dealer?"

"On her rest break."

"You've been a lucky man today, haven't you?"

Alice hadn't moved her head from staring at the guy during this conversation, but her change of tone showed who she was now talking to. He nodded in reply and swallowed hard.

"Get this lucky guy a glass of water. He can hardly speak with all his good fortune."

Beat.

"We like winners at the Lady Fortune. It shows our customers that anyone can succeed. Young or old, rich or poor. It's the American dream."

Alice circled round the chair, returning to her initial position. Even more sweat as she kicked the leg of his seat.

"But casinos only thrive if they are fair to everybody and everyone plays fair… Did you play fair?"

His eyes, filled with fear, widened further than either of them thought possible. Naldo stood by the entrance, a position he'd held since Alice entered the room.

"What did you say? I can't hear you. Did you play fair?"

Another hard swallow but no sound came out of his mouth. He glanced at Naldo and back to Alice.

"See, we've been watching you and know you haven't been playing by the rules. So we know what you've done. The question is whether you are man enough to admit it. That will determine what happens next."

"How long you know the dealer?"

"Four years."

"How long you been coming here?"

"A week."

"How much you made in total?"

"Nearly a million."

"Congratulations. The smart thing was not to take too much on any particular day. The dumb thing was to continue coming back."

"I figured little and often would keep us under the wire."

Alice nodded and patted the john on the knee. Then she idled over to Naldo.

"I don't want to see his face in Vegas again. Same for the dealer. And give a five thousand bonus to the guy who spotted them. Then I'll fire his ass because he took too long to do it."

Naldo nodded and Alice left the room without looking back. That afternoon, he drove to the desert with a spade. His trunk was empty when he returned.

Mama's Gone

VEGAS WAS AN unreal town at the best of times and Christmas time doubled the insanity of the place. Like a bad smell on the sole of her sneakers, Frank appeared at the Lady Fortune in early December.

"Mama told me to come and help you over the vacation season. So here I am!"

"She never mentioned it. What makes you think I need you?"

"Hey, don't give me that sisterly look. I'm here because Mama asked me. If you've got nothing for me to do then I'll hang for a while and head off in January. No big deal."

"Is Bobby aware you're here?"

"How the fuck would I know? I can't read minds."

Alice gazed at the bedraggled heap of a brother stood in her office and sighed.

"Listen bro'. I've got things covered. Nothing personal but we don't need your… talents… here. Stick around for sure but keep clear of the cops. And that's real important in the casino: any issues and we lose this license to print money. Do not fuck this up. We can give you some chips if you want to chance your luck—only we get them back out of your winnings. If you have any."

"Don't mind if I do. Can you comp me a suite too?"

"A room, not a suite. They're for the high rollers. Not lifelong losers."

A smile crept across Alice's face as she enjoyed the moment. Frank appeared untouched by her putdown.

WHEN FRANK AND Alice weren't competing, the twins got on fine. With party season in full swing, she introduced her brother to the few friends she'd made since hitting town and he returned the compliment by getting them invites to the coolest gatherings in the city.

Their first joint attendance was in a penthouse owned by a dude Frank met the night before in a champagne bar. When the twins arrived, Alice surveyed the scene in the living room and didn't want him to leave her hip. So many people and such a buzz. It was overwhelming, but not for Frank who thrived in this atmosphere. Almost before she'd exhaled, he blazed a trail straight to the makeshift bar on the far end of the room, introducing himself to what he hoped would be his first liaison.

Alice stood transfixed, trying to decide where to go. While Frank's degree was a miracle, Alice earned hers by studying every night when she wasn't working to pay her way. Mama had helped, for sure, but she didn't believe her college place was a right just because she wanted it. This meant she spent scant time at frat houses or sorority parties with commensurate fewer social skills than her younger brother.

"Overwhelming. Isn't it?"

Alice's head nodded in agreement before she had a chance to see who she was talking to. Tall, dark hair and cute lips. The guy's body was well-toned beneath his blue designer suit and Alice smiled at him.

"Shall we get a drink? I'm Tom."

Without another word, he held her by the hand and they zigzagged over to the bar where he ordered a martini for himself.

"Cosmo, please."

She reckoned he was only ten years her senior and conversation flowed into the night with a healthy mix of dancing and smooching to while away a few hours. Before long, they were leaving the apartment block.

"Fancy a nightcap?"

ALICE AWOKE WONDERING what she was doing beneath silk sheets. Then she recalled the two hours between leaving the party and falling asleep. Tom had been much the same as the other men she'd slept with. She didn't hold it against him as she hadn't experienced an orgasm with them either. Alice was thinking sex was overrated for women, despite what the glossy magazines said.

The guy was still asleep, out for the count. Something about the feel of the sheets on her skin made Alice stop for a second and enjoy the sensation over every part of her body the silk touched. Her stomach, breasts, a knee and crotch. She turned to look at Tom again to make sure he was definitely sleeping.

She moved her hand down between her thighs and did to herself what he failed to deliver. Then she scooted out of bed, grabbed her clothes and went home to shower and change for work.

THE NEXT EVENING, Alice and Frank entered a different apartment but she couldn't say if she was staring at the same people. Plucking up more confidence than the night before, she wended her way round the chatting drinkers hoping to make eye contact with someone long enough to start a conversation. She also was on the lookout in case Tom was here.

A red dress caught her attention which was attached to a smile.

"Just got here?"

"Uh-huh. I'm Alice."

"Samantha, although everyone calls me Sam. I don't know why I introduce myself as Samantha because I prefer Sam too."

The entire sentence came out in one nervous breath and ended in an embarrassed giggle.

"What does a girl have to do to get a drink at this party?"

Sam took Alice to the bar and they both ordered cosmos. She enjoyed watching the woman sashay her way over to a space near the balcony. They peered outside, but it was too cold for anyone to want to stand out there. The red plunge dress swooped down at the front and almost was open to Sam's navel, so Alice thought. Her eyes lingered on the sight longer than politeness allowed.

Conversation and cosmos flowed through the evening and Alice couldn't help feel jealous every time Sam received attention from the many male suitors. Even Frank flitted by at one point. As guests left, Alice touched Sam on the arm and suggested: "Fancy a glass of wine back at mine?"

"I thought you'd never ask."

SAM'S RED DRESS lay underneath her panties on the floor of Alice's bedroom. When the older twin woke up, she realized what she'd known for many years, but had refused to acknowledge: dicks didn't do it for her. She rolled over to face Sam and stroked her stomach just enough to rouse her from her slumber. A sleepy smile in response and Alice leaned in to kiss her newfound lover.

They met up every night for the next week but Alice ensured she kept her word to Frank and they both accompanied him to the slew of parties he'd gained invites to. She understood her brother believed his chances with women improved if they saw him entering the party with girls who were obviously friends. Softened his image and made him a safer prospect.

The bubble burst on Alice's Saturday night when the phone rang two minutes after Sam went down on her. Three in the morning, according to her watch.

"Yes?"

"Hi. I need your help."

"You sure pick the worst of times, don't you?"

Alice picked up the call only because it might have been the casino needing her urgent attention. A brother bleating was a different story altogether. She positioned herself with her back leaning against the head board and her legs apart, knees up. Sam took the hint and carried on where she left off.

"Huh?"

"What's the matter, little boy? It's the middle of the night and you've woken me up."

"I wouldn't want you to panic or anything but I'm in a lovely home with a revolver pointing at my head. Turns out the woman I met at the party earlier has a husband."

"And he is the one with the gun?"

"Yep. He's a reasonable guy. If we wire him compensation, he won't shoot me in the balls."

As soon as Alice talked about firearms, Sam stopped her stroking and scurried to the bathroom. Some family conversations best stayed private. Alice watched her leave the room with lust and disappointment that their fun was over.

"Answer me straight, okay?"

"Yep."

"Do you believe him?"

"Yes."

"Any other option for you to get out alive?"

"No."

"How much?"

Alice heard a muffled voice in the background name a six-figure sum.

"Tell him I'll wire it over as soon as the banks open."

"But it's Saturday, sis'."

She grinned at the fact that the time with Sam had made her forget the day of the week. And at the fear in Frank's tone.

"Don't think you can charm your way with the couple until Monday morning?"

"No."

The husband's voice got louder.

"Only joking. I'll send Naldo over with the money. He'll be with you in less than an hour. The man will resolve the issue. He always does."

"Thanks. Is this guy reliable?"

"He'll follow my instructions to the letter."

An audible sigh and Frank's relief was palpable.

"We can talk about how you got yourself in this situation in the office, young man. Swing by—sober—in the afternoon."

"Sure thing. And thanks again."

One phone call to Frescetti and he agreed to take care of everything. Alice lay there and grabbed a pillow to inhale Sam's scent. Her fragrance filled Alice with butterflies.

"Come out, come out, wherever you are!"

The bathroom door opened a crack to reveal a hand and half a head.

"Is it safe?"

"Always is, my darling."

"I don't like guns. They scare me."

She pouted and leaned back on the en-suite door to close it. Alice beckoned her over with a first finger and Sam lay on top of her, between her legs. They hugged for five, maybe ten, minutes until the tension left Sam's body. Then Alice giggled, placed both hands on the top of Sam's head and pushed down until her tongue resumed its earlier work.

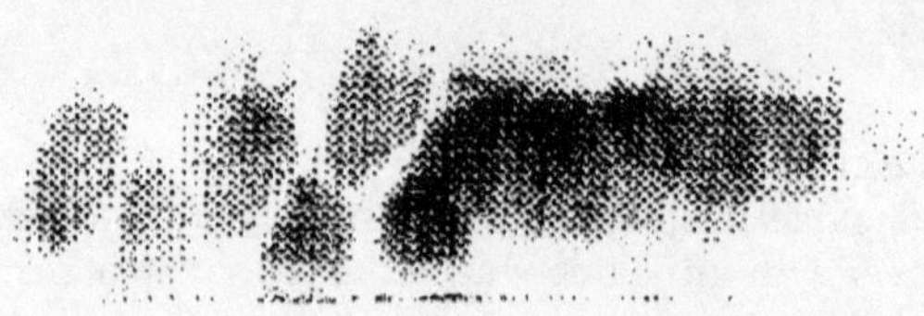

8

NEW YEAR'S DAY approached and Frank still hadn't left. Alice didn't mind as much as she thought she would, but on one of Bobby's occasional trips to town, he could see she was happy. Hence more relaxed about her annoying baby brother.

"You met someone?"

"What makes you say that?"

"No reason. There's a glint in your eyes or am I mistaken?"

"Don't know what you mean."

Alice pursed her lips and waited for a second to produce a dramatic pause. Bobby waited for the payoff.

"Sam."

"And when will you take Sam home to meet your mother?"

"We met at a Christmas party, so it's way too quick for anything as serious as that. Too soon for you too—before you ask."

"Shame. Anyone who can put a smile on your face is always worth meeting."

"Leave things be for now."

"Back to business then. We have been encountering resistance in LA and have traced the cause to a neighbor of yours."

"How so?"

"The beneficial owners of the Ace of Spades are chiseling into our heroin trade. There have been skirmishes but nothing heavy yet. I'm making you aware because these matters can blow up in your face mighty fast."

"Are you concerned enough to want to stick around?"

"Concerned enough to fly over but you kids must stand on your own two feet. And you stopped clinging to your mom's apron strings years ago."

"Seen Frank this trip?"

"Landed and came straight here. Besides it's before lunch so what're the chances of the boy being awake?"

Alice laughed and Bobby smiled. Now they worked together, he was far more open about his opinions about business or the family. Her memories growing up were of Bobby being the most taciturn human she'd ever come across. Maybe he chose the time and place to mouth off. Pas devant les enfants.

Bobby stayed in Vegas long enough to share a cocktail with Frank but left before any heavy session could get going. This made Alice less secure as she felt as though Bobby rushed back to circle the wagons. She canceled leave for all security guards and put them on alert for any potential crisis.

Half an hour after Bobby departed she got Naldo to bring Frank up to her office before he was too wasted.

"Did he mention something to you?"

"Nah, chewed the fat then hopped back to Palm Springs."

"There could be problems about to hit us. Until it's over, stay in the casino. Get the concierge to order in what you want, but don't leave the building."

Frank sat straight in the chair. A serious expression ripped across his face in a way Alice had never seen before.

"How bad?"

"Not sure but important enough for Bobby to take a day trip. There's shit going down at home too so we need to be careful."

"You might not believe me but I want to help. Tell me what and I'll do it."

"Forgive me, Frank if I don't jump up and down with glee. Your track record involves snorting and whoring. Neither of these qualities are in high demand right now."

"Give me a chance. That's all I ask."

"I will bear you in mind if the opportunity arises. In the meantime, stay sober and make yourself useful helping Naldo and his crew. Follow his instructions to the letter then who knows what'll happen."

THE ATTACK CAME the following day when an armored van left the Lady Fortune on time laden with used notes. Bad news was: it never reached the bank. The Lagottis had been robbed of a little over three million—or a week's take.

"Make enquiries. We need to know who did it, who is holding our money and where it is held. No actions, no reprisals against any suspects. We stay calm and serve our revenge like a fine white wine."

"Smash the neck and gouge their faces out?"

"No, Frank. Cold. We serve it cold once we find out everyone involved along the trail. If we act too early then the other perpetrators will fly to the four corners of the country."

Her brother nodded consent but Alice was not convinced. She gave Naldo a look as if to instruct him to keep special close to the boy.

"This doesn't mean we should appear to sit idly by. Can we please hire out-of-town experts to set a fire in the basement of the Ace of Spades? Nothing to destroy the building but enough to cause a modicum of chaos and a lot of inconvenience."

Her other thought was that if the money was still inside, they'd have to keep it safe and move it immediately. It's much easier to follow three million dollars in one vehicle than chase down batches of fifty thousand—or worse.

TWO DAYS LATER and Alice entered the auto shop to see Frank pounding a man's head to a pulp with his fists. Blood splatter and teeth littered the floor. Naldo looked on but did nothing. Three others in his crew sat around sipping beer.

"Stop this frat meeting right now."

Frank held his arm back but did not land another blow. Naldo passed him a towel and he tried to clean up the guy's face.

"I thought my instructions were clear. And I expected better of you."

A dagger-eye glare at Naldo. Then Alice strode in to take her place next to Frank. She looked down at the man: hands and ankles bound with electrical cable. An oily rag stuffed into his mouth with tape stuck over it. His nose the only outlet for his noisy breathing. Despite the violence meted out, he was calm. Alice thought he'd be hyperventilating, but no. Naldo had the measure of him. The punches were just to keep his mind occupied until she arrived and squatted down so her head was the same level as her captor.

"I want you to listen carefully when I say these things to you."

The guy stared straight at her with hate burrowing into her skull. Then he blinked and the edge to his manner abated. He maintained eye contact and his breathing rate increased a touch.

"You are here because your father and the rest of your family stole from us. This is not acceptable. The good news is that we have recovered our money and each of the individuals involved in the theft have been liquidated.

"Before they died, each of them confessed to their part of the crime. You need not worry on that account because we all know you did not commit the robbery. And we will not torture you into confessing to something you did not do. We're not the Feds, after all."

They all laughed and Alice discerned the corners of his mouth turning upward too.

"That's the good news: the money is back where it belongs. You, my friend, are our reparations. You represent the compensation we are owed for the inconvenience and upset caused by your father—and his kith and kin. We mean you no ill will."

Alice touched the guy's arm to show she understood his concerns and his breathing returned to its earlier pace. She stood up and walked over to Naldo who rummaged in his pockets and then resumed his original stance. She sauntered back and mopped the bloody forehead with Friscetti's handkerchief. Then she slid the material over his cheeks and soaked up the red still dripping off his chin.

A quick pull and she ripped away the tape over his mouth. The guy spat the rag out and took in mouthfuls of clean air. Alice dropped the reddened cloth onto the floor and clicked her fingers until someone passed her a beer. She let a few drops land on the guy's lips to moisten them and held the bottle so he could take two, no three, long glugs.

Alice took the drink away to give the son of the Huang family a chance to catch his breath. Then she switched the bottle for the revolver she'd kept in her other hand, pushed it in his mouth and squeezed the trigger. His brains flew out the back of his skull and Frank jumped with a start.

She put another slug in his heart and fired a third shot into his groin. Alice flipped the safety on and placed the gun on top of the bloody handkerchief. Perhaps for the first time in his life, Naldo smiled. His student learned fast.

As she walked out, she turned her head in Frank's direction.

"That's revenge served cold."

She strode back to her office and hopped into the shower—the facilities were extensive but not surprising as she worked and lived in a hotel. A call to Mama to let her know everything was under control, then home time.

Alice stayed in a suite on the twentieth floor so her commute was minimal. Sam cooked two bowls of stir-fried chicken with noodles. They sat on opposite sides of the dining room table, which felt like they were an ocean apart. She reached out to touch Sam's hand in between mouthfuls.

"What's wrong dear?"

"Nothing really. The food tastes great... I'm not that hungry, is all."

"Thanks but there's something up with you."

"Work. It'll be fine. Right now I'd like you to take me to bed and hold me."

Hand in hand, they scurried into the bedroom and slipped under the sheets. Alice nestled in between Sam's breasts and tried to exorcize the image of her first kill out of her head. The softness of Sam's skin comforted little that evening but Alice inhaled her fragrance and the demons floated away by the time they were both asleep in each other's warm embrace.

SHUN HUANG SAT on the other side of the table to Mary Lou in a nondescript meeting room in an anonymous hotel chain in the heart of Los Angeles. Also present was Bobby, Shun's brother and a bodyguard each. There was no need for the muscle for either group because no one would be stupid enough to attack these two bosses in the middle of peace talks.

"We have come here today to end the difficulties between our families. Both have suffered loss…"

"Some more than others."

"…but the important thing is for us to draw a line under all the unpleasantness and to move forward."

Mary Lou had spent a week of shuttle diplomacy to get Shun in the same room. The intermediary they'd used had convinced him the war must end and that Mary Lou was open to compromise. Word on the street was she'd ordered Shun's head on a platter—the work begun by Alice was to end with Mary Lou. The truth was Mary Lou didn't care whether Shun lived. She wanted him to stop muscling in on her drugs supply lines. Every day she wasted fighting him was more time when earnings were down.

"We are here to prevent more blood being shed. One of my sons died because of our differences."

"That is a lamentable state of affairs and I am truly sorry for your loss. If we reach an agreement today, I guarantee no member of your family'll die at our hands."

"Your word is important here because it is all you have. Without power or wealth, we are alone before our gods with only what we say to keep us on a true path."

"You have my word. But in exchange, I need to know you will cease your encroachment into my territories. You have carved out a niche for yourself here in LA at our expense and attacked my property in Las Vegas. You must put an end to both matters."

"My son paid the ultimate price for our actions in Vegas. Now I am left only with daughters. Your business operations and your children will be safe there—from our involvement."

"And what about LA?"

"We need to earn a living and our access to Chinese sources means our product is much cheaper than yours. I'm talking opiates here. Let me be clear: we are not departing the city just because we are inconvenient to you."

"I understand and respect that. Your family has done well in a short space of time. At our expense though."

Mary Lou stared at Shun while they spoke but Bobby made sure he was on top of the entire roomful of people. They had talked through their game plan for the meeting into the small hours sat in the summerhouse and then later in bed. Bobby had been told that Shun's brother wanted blood revenge and had been put in his place by Shun. The man might be a grieving father, but he was a smart businessman first.

"Yours is the biggest heroin operation in California. We were bound to nibble at the crumbs on your plate."

"What I propose is a way for you to consume a three course meal."

"I am here to listen."

"Build up your business by all means. If you open up territories we are not yet covering, then we can support you with the resources we have available. For that we receive twenty per cent of your turnover. In areas of ours which you now occupy I must ask you to share more of your good fortune because it has been gained off the back of twenty years hard work on our part. In these places, we will get fifty cents on the dollar."

Shun stared at Mary Lou for fifteen seconds and then leaned over and whispered to his brother, cupping his hand in front of his mouth to hide the movement of his lips. Mary Lou didn't bother to even strain to eavesdrop. She knew their plan and how she would respond no matter what he said. Bobby continued to survey the room.

"What would these resources be?"

"People, guns, processing labs. I could even get you some office space if you wanted."

This last comment raised a brief smile on Shun's face. He resumed his whispering and Mary Lou went on staring. As their conversation appeared to carry on for a while, she stood up and walked over to the coffee pot to get a second cup. By the time the mug was empty, Shun and his brother had finished their dialog.

"Under the circumstances, we are open to sealing a deal but the price you ask is too rich for us… Ten and thirty per cent."

Mary Lou picked up her coffee and pretending to take the last sip from it. She opened her clutch bag and applied lipstick using a makeup mirror. She saw the impatience in Shun's eyes.

"Twenty and fifty. Your family remains safe and we do great business together. And we both get to dip our beaks in the trough."

"Twenty and forty?"

Shun knew the money was to be made from South LA and other Lagotti territory. New areas would be harder to capture and he wanted an easy life. He was too old to spend a year or two fighting his way across LA, block by block.

"Fifteen and fifty. Take it or leave it."

Mary Lou placed the lipstick in her bag and waited for the whispering to subside.

"We agree."

"And five per cent ownership of the Ace of Spades."

The brother's blood vessels nearly burst out his temples but Shun showed restraint. He looked at his brother and stared at Mary Lou.

"Done."

The tension at the table dissipated with nods from all concerned and Shun walked round to Mary Lou so they could shake on the deal. With business settled, there was nothing more to say and everybody left. Bobby held back briefly to let the meeting room manager know they were done— and settle the check. Before they strolled out the lobby, Mary Lou told him to wait while she headed off to use a hotel phone.

"Just called off the hit on Shun and his brother."

Bobby smiled. They had taken the time to cover every eventuality. Cutting the head off the snake was one of many options they'd considered.

1995

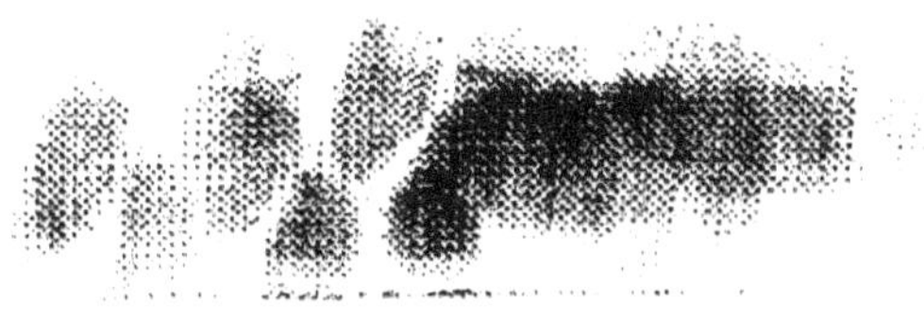

9

"YOU'VE DONE WELL here. Revenue is up and the place is running nice and smooth. You should come back to Palm Springs."

Bobby and Alice sat in her office in the early evening. She'd enjoyed being at the helm of Lady Fortune and had forged a comfortable life. Sam visited from Boston most weekends which meant Alice could concentrate on work but still fall into the arms of someone she cared about. And the sex was good too. Would she be able to recreate all that under the watchful eye of her mother? Besides, running a casino was fun and when there was an occasional spot of bother, she had shown herself she could handle it.

"Vegas is more my town. The bright lights. The buzz when you hit the streets. You can taste it. There's green coming out of every manhole cover. This is a moneymaking wet dream of a city."

They lounged on the couches Alice had introduced to the vast expanse of the office almost as soon as she'd moved in. Bobby missed a trick—she encouraged people to stick around and have informal conversations so they'd reveal more of what they were thinking. Alice was so much more than a black designer pants suit and red lipstick. That was all Frank saw—on one of the rare moments he was sober.

"It's a great town for sure and you can always visit it. No one's saying you should never come back. But you need to listen to me. Your mother and I would like you on the west coast. We have some issues in California and you and your brains must be here to sort things out."

"Mama wants me to return?"

"Yes. You can live in LA if you don't want to hang in sleepy Palm Springs."

"She asked for me? Not Frank?"

Thoughts of Valentine's Day holed up in the suite with Sam were evicted from her mind.

"I'm in. Let me know when I need to move. And you're right, I can't stay cooped up in Palm Springs."

"Until you get yourself sorted, you could use the top floor of the Palace."

"Who'll take over at this end?"

"No one could replace you, dear."

"Okay…"

"I'll go back to keeping an eye on things. We'll bring in a manager. And before that Frank can earn a day's wages."

"Don't spend too long in between trips if you want the place to be still standing."

Bobby issued another smile. She much preferred the adult relationship she had with him.

"And Naldo comes with me."

"Naturally. I wouldn't have hooked you two up if I thought you'd separate so easy."

Alice smiled now, realizing how important Friscetti was in her newfound world and the trust he'd been given to mind Alice Lagotti, daughter of Mary Lou.

THEY SAT AROUND the pool in the afternoon, tumblers of whiskey in their hands. In the five days since Alice returned to California, she had spent the first day unpacking. The thought of living in the Palace long-term was too weird to handle, even though she'd lived above a casino and hotel for months. Somehow that felt normal whereas in her childhood, it was somewhere to visit for sure, but Mary Lou never allowed the twins the run of the joint. There was something taboo in the woodwork.

As an adult she got the fact it was a glorified whorehouse and cocaine dispensary although nowadays the selection of narcotics was far wider than that. The prostitution continued, but the parties were drying up. New Hollywood wanted different nighttime escapes and shipping in younger girls wasn't the answer. Frank would be in his element though he'd fuck his way through the profits in his first week.

Then she flew Sam over and they pretended to be tourists around Beverly Hills, much as her mother had done decades earlier when Alice could barely walk. Days of sightseeing and nights of naked bliss. Sam was proving to be an essential part of her life.

"Would you think about moving west at some point?"

The question came out of the blue in the middle of horsing around on a couch in the living room. They both had their hands up each other's skirts while they watched a movie.

"Maybe. I'm doing well in Boston and my company only has a small practice out here. It would be like a demotion."

She was an account exec at a media and marketing firm: she needed to be where the clients were. Sam's finger continued its massage, having stopped for a moment.

"I'm not saying no, dear. Just it'd be a big move for me and, well, we've only been going out three months…"

Sam was right: Alice was moving way too fast. There would be time enough. Instead, she should lose herself in the moments they had together here and now. She closed her eyes and focused on Sam's first finger. When she opened her eyelids, she was back sitting with Mama and Bobby on a lounger by the pool.

"Palm Springs is quiet in the Winter."

"Gets cold at night though."

"Sure, but I'd forgotten how restful the town is."

"That's not Palm Springs—it's 20 Oakcrest Drive."

"Yeah. Only have happy memories of this place."

"What about Cindy?"

"Who?"

"A family friend, you might say. But it doesn't matter. You don't remember her and she's long since gone."

They each took a sip of their drinks, almost in unison.

"Tell me: why am I back on the west coast? Can't be to have another drinking buddy."

"Huang was a red flag to me. I know we have resolved them as a problem…"

"In the short-term."

"…but they represent a bigger threat to our organization."

"How so?"

"Entry into narcotics is getting easier by the day. Any fool with a bag of pills and some foot soldiers can take over a handful of blocks. Before you know it has happened, they control a district and you're fighting to retrieve what's yours. Doesn't mean we shouldn't fight for every inch we own, but as the struggle gets harder, more gangs will appear and it won't be like the good old days when five Families ran the country. We must deal with each bunch of sniveling upstarts one-by-one."

"So we must find additional ways of earning money before it gets taken away by the Feds. They are proving way too successful at getting stool pigeons to squawk."

"And what have you come up with?"

"Us? Nothing. We've been around too long. We need someone new to the game to introduce a touch of zing."

"Get Irma to mix me a cosmo. It'll be a very long night."

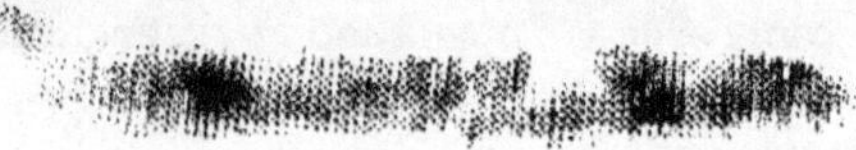

ALICE LEFT OAKCREST at six in the morning. By midnight the cosmos weren't cutting it for her so she moved over to vodka tonics. This made her chatty and giggly but nothing more. Mama and Bobby gave up by two because her conversation was slurring too much for anything to make any sense. So she flipped around the cable channels in search of inspiration. Three hours later, Irma came downstairs to find Alice dribbling on an armchair and called her a taxi.

When she woke up in the Palace, her eyes widened like a spark had been lit inside her. She rummaged round the apartment until she found a phone and dialed as shakily as her still-drunk finger would allow.

"Mama, I've got it. We'll reinvent the numbers racket."

"Don't say another word. Go back to bed—you've only had an hour's sleep—and come over this afternoon to talk this through."

The line went dead and Alice checked her watch. Mama was right. She got out of her clothes and sloped under the covers. Within two minutes of closing her eyes, she was sleeping like a baby, albeit a loud snoring infant that reeked of booze.

"YOU CAN BET your bottom dollar that everyone loves to gamble."

Mary Lou and Bobby sat in the summerhouse while Alice paced up and down taking occasional sips from her orange juice.

"The Lady Fortune proves it's true. Hell, Las Vegas shows I'm right. Americans will bet on anything. That's why before the war, they'd even bet on a number. That was all the numbers game was."

"Yes, but you know they rigged it?"

"Of course. Arnold Rothstein was behind all that, yeah?"

"Love the history lesson. This trip down memory lane is fabulous but..."

"Don't you see? Haven't you been watching the news?"

Bobby and Mary Lou looked blankly at each other. Had they been so caught up in their own little world to have missed a life-changing event? Alice waited as patiently as she was able for the penny to drop. When the two turned back to stare at her eager for a clue, she realized she'd have to wait until hell froze over before any flicker of recognition from her audience.

"California State is starting a lottery. Ordinary Joes will slap greens down on the counter of their local convenience store hoping to win millions. Instead of a shady dude writing their lucky number in a ledger, they'll walk round with a shiny piece of paper printed by us with the digits neatly circled."

The expressions remained the same: abject incomprehension why Alice was so excited.

"There's a load of security around manufacturing the tickets but the store owners won't care if the pieces of card are legitimate or not. They get paid by the Joes. Having real-looking lottery cards would be fantastic and we must have sufficient cash to grease enough palms in the right places. It'll be like we're printing our own money, only we do it through a network of retailers."

Everyone was quiet for a spell until Mary Lou punctured the silence.

"What if someone wins using one of our tickets?"

"Either the fake is good in which case the Joe gets his cash. Or it's not and the storekeeper takes the heat."

"And then word goes round they bought the cards from us and…"

"…and nothing. I'm talking about looking and acting like a wholesaler here. They won't know the difference. We charge the same as the real guys only our costs are lower because we're not using high tech printing presses or having to pay union rates."

"It's so simple, why didn't we think of it?"

"You've been doing this too long and don't drink enough cosmos."

"She has a point."

"About the cosmos anyway."

For the first time since entering the room, Alice slumped down on an easy chair. She drained her juice and slammed the glass down on a nearby table.

"Oops, misjudged the height of that."

Mama sent Bobby to the kitchen for a refill for Alice and a large pot of coffee.

"And cookies."

When both he and Irma returned with a bountiful supplier of drinks and munch, they worked through the fine detail. Planning a successful new venture was down to the small print. Alice's big picture made perfect sense but the little gotcha details would send them to jail.

Four hours and two plates of cookies later, they thought the master plan was one hundred per cent bullet proof.

"Let's sleep on it and go through everything again tomorrow. Do you want to stay for dinner?"

"No, I've got stuff to do. Thanks Mama."

"It'll only be a bowl of pasta."

"I mean for wanting me to be in on this with you."

"Silly. Apart from Bobby who else could I turn to in my hour of need?"

Alice shrugged then kissed her mother on the cheek before she left. Mama could have called Frank. That was the answer to Mary Lou's question that Alice didn't want to hear. And Mama hadn't said.

At home, Alice stepped out of her jeans-blouse combo and went back to bed. She so needed more sleep. Before she allowed herself to close her eyes, she put a call through to Sam.

"I've missed you."

"Me too."

"Would you like me to hop over to Boston this weekend instead of making you fly over here?"

"No. My house share isn't as cozy—or private—as your penthouse. Besides, I get a chance of glimpsing a cavorting A-lister at yours."

"That's the nicest way anyone's said you live over a whorehouse I've ever heard."

"I know you're embarrassed about it, but I think it's hot. All those people naked beneath us humping away—it's bestial."

"Tell me, what are you wearing right now…"

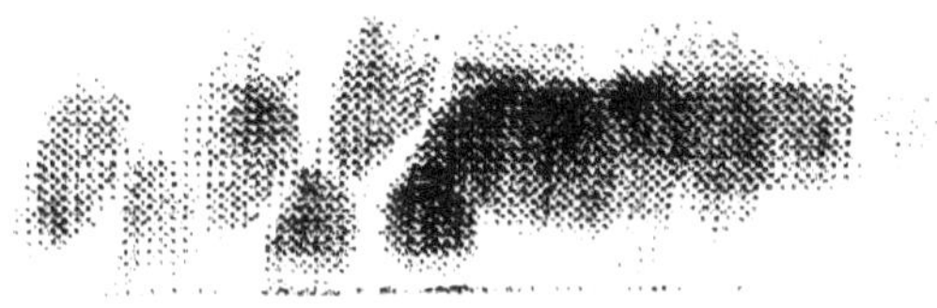

10

ONE INDUSTRIAL PARK is much like the next. Vast buildings made of concrete with no attempt by the architect to inject any beauty in the affair. Once constructed the block is surrounded by a car lot big enough to house the vehicles of all the poor saps working inside the gray walls.

The only planning that takes place is to ensure all the roads are straight —to maximize real-estate usage within each plot. No spare land is wasted on making space for a tree or even a small shrub. Nothing to make a human feel alive.

Another touch to alienate the worker ants is to encase the entire experience in barbed-wire fencing. Keeps uninvited guests out and prevents workers from escaping.

Such an enterprise was the Bakersfield Industrial Park, situated as its branding hinted at the intersection of the two highways where a community had grown called… Bakersfield. The park lay at the dirtier end of the tracks where no one wanted to live but when you lived in a nowhere town, you took any job under any circumstances that was going. This provided the best explanation why anyone worked at the concrete block with the name Bakersfield Printing on the awning nailed to the right of the main entrance.

Monroe Linwood spent twelve years at the plant before he met anybody associated with the Lagotti family. He was yet another guy propped up at the bar or playing the odd game of poker with the boys on a Thursday night. The first thing that made him unusual was the clever way he'd got all the local loan sharks to hold markers on him. Cards were not his passion but baseball kept him alive despite the anchors weighing him down like his dutiful wife and four adoring children.

A hop, skip and a jump later and Mary Lou held those markers and could make Monroe an offer, much as her step uncle had done decades before. Only on this occasion she wasn't intending to rob a bank.

"Thank you for taking the time to see me."

Monroe, Mary Lou and Alice sat around a motel room bed while Bobby and Naldo stood near the door. The place was packed and Monroe was nervous.

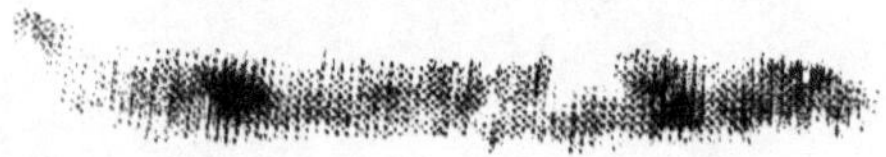

"SO'S WE'RE CLEAR: you owe me a lot of money. All the debt you have amassed with local operators has been bought up by me. This means I've paid off all your debt."

"Thank you ma'am."

"You are most welcome. That was your good news for the day. Now you need to come to terms knowing that every red cent you owe to me."

Monroe gulped because what Mary Lou said scared him and everyone staring at him had made him feel nervous from the moment he entered the motel.

"Do you know how much you have gambled away?"

He shook his head. If Monroe knew the amount, he wasn't going to utter it here. This woman knew the big number.

"Over one hundred and twenty thousand dollars plus chump change. Out of interest, do you have that sort of money to repay me?"

Another shake of the head.

"I thought not because if you did, I'd have expected you to pay some of it back to open a line of credit… Do you have a life insurance policy by any chance?"

"No ma'am."

"So you're not even worth anything dead to me."

Monroe's eyes lifted from the floor and opened wide in Mary Lou's direction. She let the idea of his death hang in the air for five seconds until the notion ran out of energy and landed on the carpet, soaking into the stained geometric pattern.

Mary Lou turned to Alice and Monroe shifted his attention accordingly. Alice's soft voice forced Monroe to strain to hear her words.

"Do you have fifty bucks spare each month?"

"Huh? No, ma'am."

"You see, if you paid fifty dollars a month, it would take you two hundred years to pay me back. And you can't even offer fthat much."

A tear departed Monroe's left eye and traveled down his cheek to drop onto the carpet and join the idea of his death.

"I sure am in a fine predicament and no mistake."

Alice offered him a cigarette from her pack. With a shaking hand, he removed one and put it between his lips. By instinct, he fumbled for a box of matches in his pants pocket, but found diddly squat. She picked up her lighter from the bed, flicked it on with her thumb and held the flame near the end of his smoke. Monroe inhaled and the tobacco caught fire.

"You have a way of sorting out this mess you've got yourself into. You must listen to what I have to say and decide what you will do."

She outlined the plan for Monroe to use his access to the printing shop to borrow a template for the State lottery cards just for one night. He had to walk out to his car with it and drive home on a particular day. Then not lock the automobile overnight, return to work the next day and return the plates.

"Do you understand what we expect you to do?"

"Yes I do."

"Will you help us and clear off your debts for the sake of less than an hour's effort?"

"Well ma'am. You've told me you won't kill me and what you're asking is mighty dangerous. One hour or no. So why don't we agree that I never place a bet again and leave it at that?"

Mary Lou responded without hesitation.

"You are worth nothing to us dead and maybe your family will shed a tear. But I promise you this: if you choose not to help then one by one your children and your wife will find out the many miserable ways to die. And I guarantee you will shed a tear because their deaths will be on your hands. Each and every one."

The guy swallowed hard, took a long drag on his cigarette and stubbed it out in the ashtray lying on the bed. Then he wiped his nose on his sleeve, cleared his throat and spoke with all that his dignity would muster—which wasn't much.

"Let me know when you want us to rip off the California State lottery."

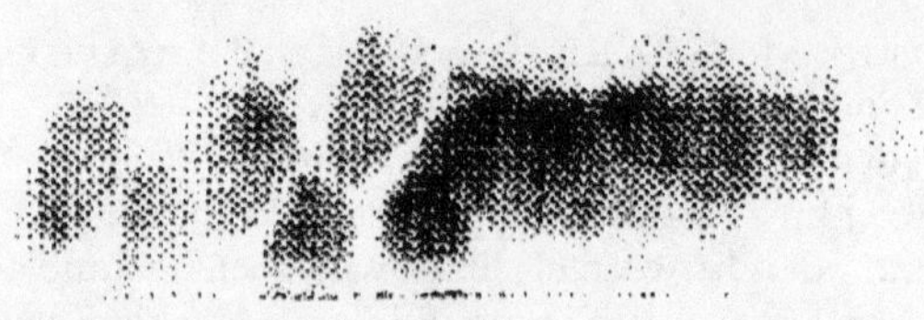

11

ALICE AND BOBBY were working together just like the first week at the Lady Fortune, only this time she wasn't so green around the gills. She was pleased Mama was entrusting her with the project and happy to be collaborating instead of running it all herself. It was good to have a trusted soul with whom to bounce ideas.

The lottery wouldn't launch until much later in the year which meant they had enough time to get everything ready. The biggest hurdles were to prepare the printing presses and to pull together a team of hustlers.

Alice scouted suitable locations to print vast quantities of fake lottery tickets and Bobby used his connections to find guys who could persuade without breaking bones. Any fool can threaten a storekeeper with a gun. It took brains to achieve the same wearing only a smile—and a three-piece suit.

While she traveled around the state, Alice also checked out various towns to live in. Sam might enjoy the sizzle of living in the Palace, but Alice thought she'd find more comfortable surroundings: Sunset Boulevard had seen better days. When she looked at Malibu for light industrial parks, she headed into the center of town to see if there were any condos of interest.

After two weeks on the road, she and Bobby met up in the summerhouse. Mary Lou sat in on the conversation so she could keep abreast of how things were progressing.

"The crew is forming slowly. Too many guys only know how to crack heads."

"I blame the violence on TV and video games."

"Hilarious. Is there anywhere to print the tickets?"

"Agoura Hills. It's on a main road route for our trucks—you have trucks, right? I could oversee the operation easily from Malibu, the other side of the Santa Monica Mountains."

"Say what?"

"I'm thinking of moving there."

"Let's come to that later. My memory of the place was that it's a sleepy hick town."

"Hick town? Yes. Sleepy? Not so much. Perhaps when you were a boy but I don't remember the moon landings, so who am I to say?"

Alice winked at Bobby, who smiled back.

"There's an industrial park away from the residential area. It's not exactly built up near there for sure, but its main street has a certain buzz about it. I mean a bunch of fellas wouldn't stand out in the local diner. They are enough out-of-towners waltzing around for them to pay no nevermind."

"Security?"

"Usual deal. We'd have to make our own inside any building so we didn't draw attention to ourselves on the street. If you want no one within a thousand feet, then we could buy farmland and station rancheros at the gate."

"Good work darling. Why don't you show me and Bobby the sights of Agoura Hills tomorrow and we can run with it or rule it out?"

"Okay, Mama."

"That's settled. Now tell me about Malibu."

"It's a cool place to hang out and it'd be somewhere I could call my own."

"Don't you enjoy living rent free?"

"Of course it's been lovely and I am truly grateful. Only…"

"…you don't want to hang onto your mother's apron strings forever."

"Right. And as fabulous as being on top of a cathouse is…"

"…you've had enough consorting with prostitutes on your doorstep. I understand. You realize we can't protect you as well outside our premises."

"True, but I'm sure Naldo will put together a crack protection detail."

"Sure, but at your expense as you are choosing to create the complication."

"Understood. And it's not a problem. It is an opportunity for me to have my own bricks and mortar."

AFTER THE FAMILY trip to Agoura Hills, Mary Lou signed off the venue. Then they popped by Malibu so Alice could show them the real-estate she was seeking. Nothing much in the scheme of things: beach-side residence with a pool, an untold number of bedrooms and sufficient space for live-in help.

Like she was reconstructing her childhood but relocating it for a sea view. With her success at the Lady Fortune behind her, Alice could afford to pay for this indulgence. Mary Lou and Bobby agreed to support her fulfill her dream. She might have run a casino but she'd never had the pleasure of dealing with realtors before.

That night, Alice returned to the Palace and found Frank in the main lobby. Up in the penthouse, she offered him a glass of champagne.

"Mighty kind, sis'."

"You're lucky to catch me in. I've been on the road these past few weeks."

"So I hear."

"Oh? Keeping tabs on me?"

"Nah. I spoke with Mama a day or two ago. That's all."

Although the pair were far from friends nowadays, Alice was pleased to see her brother. He reminded her of times gone by. Of messing around in the Oakdrive pool and playing in the park. The time before High School and the death rattle of puberty when the twins found they'd lost whatever special connection had been hard-wired into them at birth.

Deep down, Alice knew this pit of nostalgia was a displacement emotion for Sam. But warmish feelings about Frank were the best she had in the absence of her girlfriend in her bed.

"Anything in particular bring you to LA? I thought you had a casino to run now I'm not in Vegas to look after it."

She couldn't resist turning the knife in his side—it came so naturally to her as a reaction.

"Don't be like that, sis'. The Lady Fortune isn't much fun without you hanging around. So I was wondering if there was anything you were up to that I could help."

"Nope. I'm good thanks."

"Word on the street is that you're setting up a nice lottery scam. Certain I can't dip my beak?"

"Absolutely sure. And you mean Mama told you what we are planning, right?"

"Yeah, just messing with you. I'd love to be in on any new deal going down. For once I want to build something that the family can be proud of. Contribute. You know?"

"Yep, Frank but this isn't your party. You must find some other thing. Possibly elsewhere."

"Understood. Haven't been to the east coast for ages. Maybe I should try there."

"And I'll tell Bobby not to expect you back in my old office any time soon."

Alice let him stay in one of the guest rooms overnight. When she came home the following evening, he had vanished and left a note on the dining room table: "Gone fishing. F xxx"

MONROE TRAVELED TO work every weekday without fail. Even when his back played up, he appeared at the gates ready, willing and able. In the past, he might have sloped off to watch a baseball game or to try his hand at poker, but now he was a model, but nervous, citizen. His wife Laura noticed the difference within days and the kids enjoyed having their dad around to play with. This halcyon calm and joy persisted until June when the smile was wiped off his face one crisp morning.

He'd backed out the drive and was about to slam on the gas when he saw a dude a little ways down the street waving at him. The guy half stood under a tree and Monroe was lucky to spot him. He coasted toward the fella and wound down his window.

"Can I help you, bud?"

"Sure. You remember your agreement?"

"Huh?"

"The motel…"

A blank expression held for three seconds and then wide-eyed recognition of the name and his compact with the devil in a designer pants suit wearing red lipstick.

"Today you keep your word. Do what you must do at work and leave the item under the driver's seat."

"Don't lock up tonight, right?"

"You said it, friend. Do that and we won't see each other again."

"What if I can't get to the templates or they've put on extra security?"

"Then figure it out or we'll meet again. Look stay calm and think on your feet. Besides, any real problems and you can leave a note in the car instead. We'd rather wait one more day and obtain the item than you fuck things up for everyone. Capiche?"

IN HINDSIGHT, MONROE realized it was the easiest way to earn a hundred and twenty thousand dollars. How he sneaked out with the plates defied belief. His security pass gave him all points access and because they'd been printing cards since Easter, everyone had grown complacent. There were no checks, no metal detectors. Nothing his imagination had conjured up on his route into work.

When he got home, he parked frontwards in the drive as usual. The only difference was that he didn't turn the key in the lock before coming inside. The following morning the plate was where he'd left it but with an envelope containing a stack of bills.

He stuffed the greenbacks into his pocket and replaced the template early in his shift. They hadn't mentioned any payment on top of clearing the debt. Mighty stand up that Lagotti girl. The doofus used the cash as a massive beer and betting fund. The local bar had never known such trade and relations with his wife took a predictable drunken downhill slide.

Pumped with arrogance fueled by the ten grand donated by the Lagottis, Monroe shared his views on women, gambling and work to any barfly in his vicinity. This made him unpleasant but of no consequence to anyone. When his friends tired of his endless tirades, he needed more interesting stories to spice up their interest.

"Don't buy a Scratcher in November. I betcha there'll be fakes flooding the market before you can sneeze."

That Tuesday evening sealed his fate because two days later, he was visited at work by the local law enforcement. Monroe joined them for an interview at the sheriff's office and discovered the pleasure of an overnight rest in one of their cells.

Despite the genuine fear for his family's safety, Monroe spilled his guts to the detective because the secret burned him up inside. Anyway, they'd promised him that if he did the right thing, they wouldn't touch Laura and the kids. They had kept their word so far. Been stand up guys. And he had done what they asked—to the letter.

ALICE PICKED UP the phone, listened to the news from the other end of the line. Her face remained impassive and all Sam could do was know it was work and something serious had come up. She knew better than to stick around and popped back inside Alice's Malibu beach-side retreat and fixed herself another drink.

"He's been arrested for sure? Not just a person of interest?"

"Correct. From what I understand, he's given them a full and frank statement. During Prohibition, they'd say he sang like a canary."

"Have you seen the cop's report?"

"Not yet. Hope to do so tomorrow."

"Are they going to indict and how much has he provided about the people in the motel meeting?"

"Yes and don't know at this point. My contact said the confession was full and frank but he gave no details."

Alice sighed: she didn't need these kinds of problems screwing with them. Mama would not be pleased. She should deal fast because nothing gets better unless you make it so. To pretend Monroe hadn't squawked was plain stupid. What's done was done and she needed to put it right as quick as possible.

Sam wandered onto the balcony to see if Alice was finished with work and they could get back to staring at the stars and fooling around.

"Okay. Keep me informed as and when. Bye."

She stood next to Alice and placed a palm on Alice's cheek.

"Are you done?"

"Not quite. One more call and I'll be all yours. Won't take long."

Alice squeezed Sam's butt before patting it to encourage it to turn away and go inside. To reinforce the idea, she passed Sam her empty glass.

"Be a dear and mix me another cosmo."

Alice blew her a kiss and she padded to the cocktail shaker, ice bucket and assorted bottles in the living room. Meantime, Alice dialed a number she knew by heart.

"I've got an urgent job for you and nobody else. Monroe Linwood is breathing and helping the police with their investigation. Let me know when the cops find he's accidentally died in their facilities."

"And the family."

"Leave them be for now. They've suffered enough living with the motherfucker all these years. My contact is finding out what the police found out and he'll tell us whether Mrs. Linwood knows anything. If she does, she'll decide to hang herself with the shame and the grief. Okay, Naldo?"

Before breakfast was served, Monroe choked himself on shards of the sheeting from his bed.

ALICE SAT BOLT upright with a judder and saw Bobby's hand in hers. The priest droned on. She recalled the cold blast of air as the bullet flew into the room. The incomprehension of the meaning of the breeze. Then the sound of the shot and the gentle splatter of liquid on her face.

All she could do was close her eyes and squeeze Bobby's hand tight. The inner yell of pain consumed her again and she escaped from the present by thinking about the past.

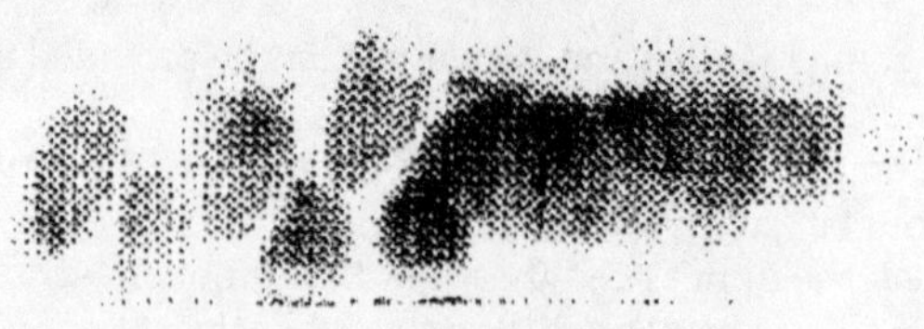

12

FRANK CHOSE NOT to head to New York after the trouble he got in there last visit. He had no desire to spend time behind bars again even if it was only a few hours. So he tried to imagine where he could go to chase tail and party hard.

A lascivious grin crossed his face as he remembered a town where three quarters of the population were students: Boston. Term time the place was awash with willing ass and out of season there was still more than enough to go round—if you had green in your wallet and snow in your pocket. You could fuck anything you wanted with that potent mix about your person.

At Logan, he told himself he'd keep his word to Alice and find a business opportunity to exploit. First, he needed to get a place to stay and free his mind from the grind of running that casino. He took a taxi to the Boston Merit Hotel and settled into a suite at the five star establishment. His bottomless pit of a credit card funded by his mom delivered the finest of room service meals before he sauntered out of the lobby that evening in search of female companionship.

Frank considered himself to be showing high moral fiber by wanting to go to a nightclub and buy tonight's pussy with cocktails and cocaine. In the past he'd have had a word with the concierge and stayed in his room. So he sat in the VIP area of a heaving club trying to pick out someone to impress.

The choice was phenomenal and Frank couldn't decide which way to look first. The problem would separate the contenders from the crowd. He left the safety of the VIPs and hit the bar. A group of five girls stood nearby and four of them he'd happily fuck. The fifth one had hair too short, so Frank'd let her suck him off if he had to. He ordered a bottle of vintage champagne, which caught their attention due to the flurry of activity associated with delivering and opening it. As planned.

"Would you like a glass? Sharing is caring."

The prospect of free booze could not be turned away and they eagerly agreed. Forty minutes later and they were dancing. Another quarter of an hour and they sat at his table in the VIP section. Conversation giggled, twisted and flowed until he decided it was time to find out who really wanted to party.

"Anyone fancy a little something to perk you up?"

Only Eileen was interested, who was Frank's favorite on account of her hot pants, round tits and hair down to her nipples, so he imagined. He ordered the others another bottle of champagne to keep them warmed up and led her away by the hand. Two Jacksons got the attendant to let them into a cubicle in the women's bathroom.

A kiss and a squeeze, then he put his finger to his lips and Eileen watched him cut a line and snort it up his left nostril. Then he set up a second and offered it to her. She nodded and held her hair in one hand and sniffed away. Frank smiled and they kissed some more. Then he pushed her downward until she was crouching below him. She looked up at him, grinned and undid his pants. This Ivy League beauty understood the meaning of a fair trade.

She stayed with him for twenty-four hours and then he got bored with her and the two friends who tagged along. The three enjoyed his snow and he pleasured himself inside all of them. The great thing about money is that everyone wants to taste it but even he understood pretty ass followed his green, not him, and the fun eventually faded and died.

A WEEK LATER and student tail stopped interesting Frank. There was too much chase involved with an educated female, besides which he was noticing a burning session when he took a piss. Antibiotics and abstinence were the orders from the hotel doc and that made sense.

This created a problem: he could spend his daytime looking for business opportunities, but what about the long nights? The answer came to him as he sped across town in a taxi—Chinatown. The handful of blocks known as the epicenter of Asian culture was not Frank's chief concern. It was the opium dens.

While his family had built its second fortune out of heroin, he hadn't considered the poppy seed as anything relevant to him, but his first foray with opiates in Morocco showed him how wrong he could be. The warmth inside was incomparable—like being blown by a thousand vestal virgins. Only better.

After a week, during which he hardly left his crib, the madam told him he had to go. His money had run out and his credit card was not accepted in this cash-only business establishment. At the hotel, he made his way up to his suite and phoned Palm Springs.

"Mama. I love you very much and I need your help."

"What is it now dear? Money or a lawyer?"

"Mama. I'll pay you back this time I swear."

"Do not make promises you have no intention of keeping. You are nothing without your word. How's Boston?"

"You having me followed?"

"Who do you think pays your credit card each month? Don't be silly."

"It's a great town and I got connections who can help with our business. Only…"

"…you need more green before you can close the deal."

"Speculate to accumulate, you told me."

"Throw my words back at me. Nice. So I'll do the same to you. I've said this before but today I mean it. If you're a man, you'll keep your promise. This is the last time you get any money from me. Just don't tell your sister. And you will pay it or I shall treat you like any other debtor. Capiche?"

Frank had no desire to sleep with the fishes and, perhaps for the first moment in his adult life, he told the truth.

"You have my word, Mama."

"I'll wire over the cash later today. Family discount: you get twelve months to return the capital and a tithe in interest."

FRANK'S TIME PARTYING in Spain had not been a total waste as he'd had the smarts to take the ferry to Morocco and investigate what the country had to offer. Local hashish was supplemented with opiates from Afganistan although sometimes it came from as far away as China.

He hadn't contacted the upper echelons of the trade but he knew well connected guys who'd deliver him a couple of kilos of product should he so desire. And they were keen to supply into the US as any entrepreneur would.

This created Frank's chance to take Mama's scratch and morph it into gold. He might have been to college but deep down he was a punk and he only took two days to assemble a motley bunch to push his wares onto the streets of Boston. While they sold bags of crystal on street corners, he looked to gain a foothold in the opium dens themselves.

During the first month, his crew sucked in several beatings as existing suppliers flexed muscles to show the new kid on the block not to fuck with them. But they hadn't met Frank before or knew what he was capable of. The boy had a spine of reinforced steel and he refused to back down. If some thug put one of his in hospital, he went out to find the guy and slit his throat personally. He never bothered checking whether the corpse made it to the morgue.

The second month was easier. His street team had found a groove and had elbowed itself into four blocks of turf to make a living. Wasn't much, but it was a good start and offered Frank his first scent of income in his life.

He felt positive about earning money for himself and this fed his desire for more. With a spark lit within, he found the grit to focus on securing an opium den. Like all narcotics businesses, they faced two main risks: hassle from the cops and supply drying up. Police were paid off to turn a blind eye to all but the most obvious indiscretions.

The owners of the dens usually were not the drug runners themselves. For reasons of tradition these were viewed as separate specialist tasks, but Frank didn't see it that way. He got himself basement rooms and decked them out ready for some johns. Via his street crew, he found a madam to run the place and some Chinese dudes to keep the peace. With payments to the Police Benevolence Fund, he was set to go.

The boy figured he didn't need to take over anybody else's shack because there was plenty of old men wanting to toke on a pipe. Why go to the effort of slamming heads together when you could start operations with no one noticing or giving you a hard time?

By June, Frank had three locations owned and two others supplied by his crew. Cash rolled in and he paid back half what he owed to Mama as a sign of goodwill and to show her he was making good on his promise. Besides, he knew soon he'd be asking his mother for a favor that didn't involve money.

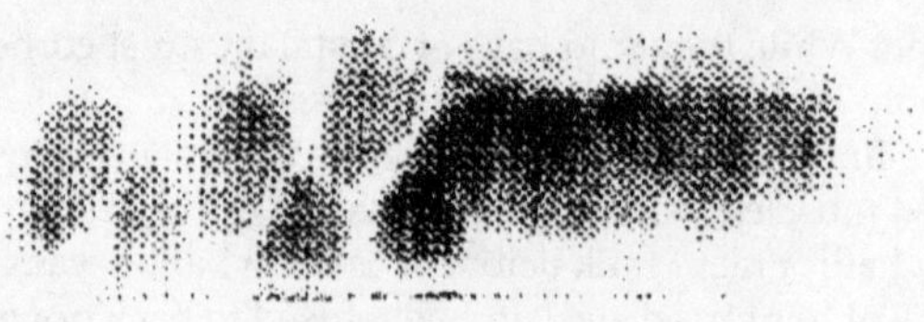

13

FRANK BELIEVED IN thinking big. The money from opiates would flow freely and coagulate in his pocket. But it wasn't enough. The most important thing to him was to be more successful than Alice. The cash coming out of Chinatown was a good start, but nothing greater than that. She took over a casino, so he needed to set up a gaming house from the get-go to show Mama how much better he was than the girl.

From where he stood in the reception area of one of his opium dens, there was a world of possibility opening up to him but it would not be in Boston. Betting on the east coast centered in Atlantic City so that would be his destination. He spent days treading the boardwalk in AC to find just the right establishment.

Any place whose name he recognized was of no use to him. Frank needed somewhere that attracted customers but wasn't too good at its job. That meant the management would be weak and ripe for a discreet takeover. He discovered his quest one block up on South Michigan Avenue where he came across a broken sign announcing the Lucky Nugget.

When he walked into the joint, he saw enough johns at the slot machines to believe the place wasn't too far from the main drag. Then he stood and watched roulette tables, poker and blackjack. There was craps going on at the other side of the room but Frank didn't have a nose for dice.

Card games interested him more because there was a skill in finessing your hand. The spin of a wheel or the flip of a numbered cube only required you to calculate the odds. An ordinary pack of playing cards held an infinite set of possibilities to be manipulated by a knowing expert.

Within thirty minutes of standing in the room Frank spotted four examples of card sharps at work. The owners were hemorrhaging money to cheats and their own stupidity. He looked round the ceiling to see how many cameras were operating, but either they were exceptionally well hidden or there were none; probably the latter.

Then he exchanged some chips—enough to get him invited to the VIP room on the second floor. A champagne bar at one end and a comfortable mix of different tables for the high rolling aficionado. Frank noted how the only women were dealers. If he ran the joint, he'd turn this area into a lap dancing club. Men don't just want to gamble their lives away, he mused.

A glass of complimentary sparkling wine inside him and he killed an hour at a poker table. The dealer had fascinating long bright pink nails which took his mind off the game. Or at least they would have done so had he not spent so much time staring at her fulsome cleavage.

Despite his preoccupation with her breasts, Frank stood five thousand dollars better off and gave her a purple chip as a tip which he dropped in between her tits. He cashed in his winnings and left the joint.

The next morning, Harvey Knight took Frank's call wondering which precinct he'd be heading to shortly.

"No, it's nothing like that. I want your advice on buying a casino."

"Is this booze talking, or worse?"

"No man. I'm deadly serious. I've found a place in Atlantic City but I need your help to buy it. Shall we meet up and talk things through?"

"That where you're based now?"

"Will be but nowadays I have business interests in Boston. If we pull this off, I'll move over here for sure."

"Can you get to my office for tomorrow afternoon?"

"Yep."

"See you then. Stay on the line and my secretary'll finalize the details."

"DOES MARY LOU know what you're up to?"

"Not right now but I wanted to be better informed before I speak to her."

"Good decision. Tell me what you expect out of the deal and then we can work out the best route to get you there."

Frank explained his idea to run the place but to own the joint too because that's where the real money was made. He didn't want a salary—he wanted income with capital growth. Harvey listened and sipped his coffee. This boy impressed him and was so much more of a man since they last met.

"Thing is, I'll need my name on the game license, but my past doesn't make me first choice, does it?"

"You are right. If the owners want to sell and you agree terms, the gaming license could prove sticky. But you are also correct in thinking your mother can help. When you speak with her, remind her it'll be worth dropping a dime to Teddy."

"Who?"

"Teddy. You don't need to know any more about him at this point."

"And financing? I've got some scratch but it won't be enough."

"How much?"

"Low seven figures."

"Congratulations. Last time we met, you didn't have a cent to call your own and I'd have bet on you floating down the Hudson before the month was out."

"Thanks, I guess."

"Don't take it the wrong way. You've done well. That's a positive and I'm recognizing that in you. If you were still the same mook cracking heads in five-star hotels, then you wouldn't be in this room today."

Frank nodded and thought how far he had come since then.

"If you think it'll help, why don't we phone Mary Lou now so she can tell you're serious."

"How does the call do that?"

"My meter's been running the minute you sat down. The cost of a long distance conversation is the least of your worries."

Harvey beamed at him because the joke was very much on him—but it was at his expense and one he could afford.

"Hi Mary Lou. How's tricks? You will never guess who I've got in my office…"

AFTER FRANK BROUGHT along three members of his crew, the owners of the Lucky Nugget decided staying alive was a higher priority than owning the casino. They exited their family business as quickly as they could so he bought the joint for next to nothing. Teddy Prescott pressed some flesh and the gaming license was safe when the Gaming Board met.

"Nice guy, Teddy."

"Yeah. You should have a beer with him sometime."

Frank couldn't tell if Bobby was serious, but he didn't care because the place was his. First order of business was to hire some watchers to keep an eye on the tables. With security sorted out, he set about being creative with the second floor.

The previous owners tried to attract wealthier individuals with limited success. The place wasn't upmarket enough for real high rollers and it suffered from being a block from the boardwalk where the serious action happened.

Frank understood what johns wanted in life: to bet a little, drink a little and to chase tail a lot—or as much as they could get away with if they were married. The Lucky Nugget would deliver all that an American male in AC could afford.

He was also sufficiently self-aware to understand the last person to run the joint on a day-to-day basis was him. He hated paperwork and was still learning how to keep people onside. His small team in Boston was one thing but a hundred or more in AC? You gotta be kidding. Leonida Acerbi came highly recommended by Mama who had hired him to manage the Lady Fortune four years ago.

"Personal circumstances prevented him from staying with us longer, but he was a great guy. Kept everyone in line. Motivated the dealers to keep the johns playing. Good fella all round."

"Spill. If he will work for me I need to know all about him."

"He left Vegas in a hurry. For reasons I never understood, Leonida started a relationship with the daughter of the Las Vegas sheriff."

"Straight out of a Roy Rogers movie."

"Don't get cute. The old man found out and wasn't happy about the situation. The next day when I heard, I didn't crack open the champagne either. Sheriff Redneck only discovered anything because his fair maiden confessed she was pregnant and Leonida skipped the state line the same afternoon."

"Wow."

"Turns out the reason she told her pop was because she couldn't figure out whose it was. She'd been spreading her legs for several guys all at the same time."

"And you still trust Leonida?"

"His judgment with women is flawed, but he knows casinos. And he didn't spill a single word about our operations to the girl."

"How can you be so sure?"

"First, we had no trouble afterwards. Second, we interrogated him when we caught up with him the following week."

NATURALLY LEONIDA WAS worth his weight in gold and drove the Lucky Nugget into a healthy profit within weeks of his arrival. Frank offered him one piece of advice before he started.

"Keep your dick to yourself. Do not go chasing ass in AC without checking out her family history first, you get me?"

"You don't have to worry about that. I'm a changed man—I got married to a stripper and have plenty of action at home, thank you."

Frank chose not to apply the same rule to his own sexual encounters. A pile of lap dancers within easy reach was too much of a temptation for him. Once the club was running efficiently—and it only took four weeks from launch, he spent an unhealthy amount of time on the second floor. The way he viewed it: he was paying the girls to show their tits and asses anyway, so he might as well enjoy the product.

After two nights, he decided that watching was for chumps and he bought a few hours with some of the prettier skanks. He saw how desperate they were for green and that they'd agree to anything he suggested if the price was right. He'd get them stoned to within a wisp of consciousness and then fuck them any which way he could conceive.

"Frank, leave the girls alone."

"I pay them. I tip them. The Nugget gets its fair share of the profit."

"Let's set aside the fact you're getting high on your own supply of women."

"Nicely put."

"Once you've spat them out, the whores are in such a bad state, they take a day or two to recover—and during that time they're not earning. I hate to say this to you, but…"

Frank gritted his jaw.

"…you're pissing on your own porch and it must end."

Leonida paused and let his words sink in. This could put his job—or even his life—in jeopardy, but the consequences of saying nothing were worse. If Mary Lou found out he'd not tried to stop Frank sabotaging his own joint, she would issue the hit on him there and then. No questions asked.

"Why not take a break from the Nugget and spend time in Boston? I'll look after everything here while you build up your business interests there. Or remind yourself what educated ass tastes like. When you come back, you can play on the first floor again."

"But not on the second?"

"No, Frank. We were making a lot of money there until you went through all the girls. To be honest, most of them will leave if we're not careful and word on the street is that someone'll die soon the way you treat them. I'm not judging, but I am trying to run your business."

Frank shook Leonida by the hand and gave him a brief hug.

"Thank you—for your honesty. Takes a brave man to say what you did."

"Just looking out for your best interests."

"I respect that. Book me a flight to Boston tomorrow. Looks like AC needs a break from me."

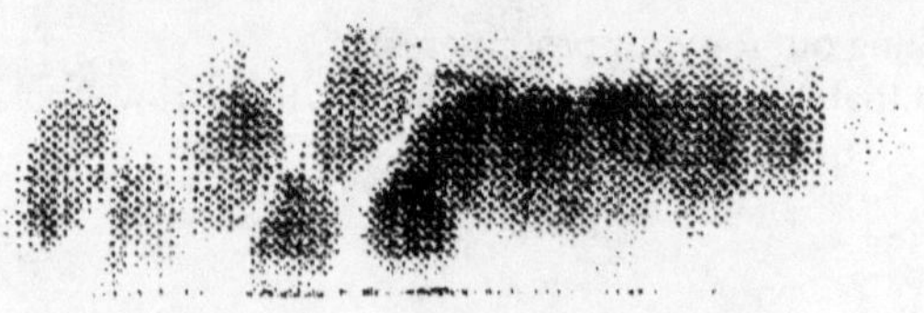

14

SOME WOULD SAY they had an idyllic life together. Mary Lou and Bobby split their time between home in Palm Springs and the hustle of the Palace in the crumbling facade known as Sunset Boulevard. It was like the inhabitants of Los Angeles had watched the film and lived its dream.

"I don't know what Alice was complaining about. This apartment is lovely."

"Until you step outside. Then you are surrounded by all the girls from Partytown USA."

"We might be married but you're telling me you have a problem going down an elevator with a bunch of drugged-up semi-naked hookers?"

"Me? No. I've always admired the female form in all its glorious varieties."

Bobby leaned over in bed and kissed Mary Lou on the cheek while stroking the tattooed rose beneath her navel.

"Just Alice isn't a middle-aged guy. She might have a different perspective."

"Kids of today: ungrateful. Pure and simple. When I was her age, I lived in a two-room apartment the size of a nickel. And was happy to be with a man who could afford the rent."

"Well, she's not with someone and was brought up in much better circumstances."

"I know but…"

The thought ebbed away as Bobby's hand left her stomach and went to find some other fun. A giggle and two deep sighs from Mary Lou showed it had succeeded.

NEXT DAY IN the summerhouse, they talked about business and the difficult trading conditions.

"Trouble is: the days of receiving protection from the mob have long since passed. I can't remember when we saw Pasquale or Fabio last."

"I heard they retired to Florida."

"No kidding. I thought both would die in California."

"Maybe they will, but they're enjoying games of penuchle with their old comrades in arms. Miami-Dade County is where capos go to rest."

"I've still got one or two more projects before I hang up my hat."

"You've plenty of successful years in you yet."

"Tell me about it. I'm finding new ideas hard to come by—Alice will save our bacon."

"And without a mob behind us, every muchacho for miles comes biting at our ankles."

"They don't play by the rules either. Instead of taking out a street dealer, they whack the boss. What kind of way is that to live?"

"If the rats and cockroaches won't get you, then your own fellas will. The Feds have been far too good at getting stool pigeons to blab."

"And once they start, you can only stop them with a bullet."

"Sometimes I wonder why we bother having a house phone."

"We never have a conversation on it in case the FBI has it tapped."

"Worthless piece of junk."

Mary Lou was right to be cautious. Too many fellas who'd built up worthwhile operations served life sentences thanks to the testimony of those they thought they could trust. The Feds had turned underlings against capos and capos against bosses.

While she and Bobby had never risen through the ranks—they were so far from thoroughbred Italian—they had created a sizeable organization. Not having to pay their tithe helped the bank balance, but they spent considerably more than ten per cent on security for their empire.

Without the safety net of the mob, finding a reliable partner was hard. Ventures popped up and fell apart all too easily as mistrust or deceit revealed itself. Narcotics was fraught with danger.

Drugs had been the most profitable part of the business for years, but was populated with the most unstable and untrustworthy characters. This meant pieces of the jigsaw would break apart with a moment's notice as someone was taken in for questioning or got plain greedy. Mary Lou and Bobby spent a disproportionate amount of their time keeping all those plates juggling in the air. It was tiring and they both knew they were too old for that caper.

In Mary Lou's head, Frank was the perfect guy to manage the narcotics operations, but she needed to wait for him to grow up more before she could let him take over the reins. Alice had the temperament to flourish with all the other parts of the business. She had every faith Bobby and Alice would run things very well. Gambling, prostitution and their other rackets would thrive under her stewardship.

But Mary Lou wasn't ready to give up and head over to Boca Raton just yet. Knowing the lottery gig would succeed was the first step and figuring out how to replace narcotics revenue with something safer was the second. After that, she'd have to see. Besides, she didn't want to hand over a doomed business to Frank. Perhaps he could make it thrive. He had street smarts and had a better idea than Alice of how the ordinary Joe thinks.

BACK IN THE Palace, Mary Lou and Bobby took advantage of what the city offered. They checked out a show and dined in some of the most pretentious restaurants on the west coast. The money continued to roll in and Frank's call about the Lucky Nugget made Mary Lou think her son was finally growing up. Even Bobby had to admit the guy was something.

"I'm surprised to hear myself say this, but the boy has done right by you for once. He has actually given you some of your cash back."

"Half of our money."

"And not only does he look like paying the rest but he's got sufficient surplus to fund the purchase of his own casino."

"Wonders will never cease."

"And some. I bet it'll put Alice's nose out of joint."

"I haven't told her yet. She needs to have total focus on the lottery gig. That's big news for us too."

"For sure. More states'll legalize gambling because they are desperate for money. What Alice is doing in California, we can replicate across the country. Frank opening up an opium line on the east coast is our first narcotics venture on the Eastern Seaboard. Your children are something else."

Mary Lou grinned from ear to ear.

"I know. I'm very proud of them."

Then she burrowed under the sheets until Bobby's breathing became deep and rhythmic.

Mama's Gone

MONROE LINWOOD WEIGHED on Mary Lou's mind. While she was pleased with the way Alice handled herself at the situation they'd got to within a few hours of a knock on the door and a troop of Feds tipping hats and thrusting a search warrant in her hand. Too close for comfort.

There was only one thing to do: a top-to-bottom security check on everyone in the organization. And no exceptions. They'd begin with narcotics, the weakest area, and move on to prostitution later. Mary Lou sent Bobby on the road to interview anyone peddling, manufacturing or managing the various operations along the Californian coast.

Nothing. Their call girl rings were a mix of high-class hookers in a place like the Palace through to much cheaper options for the working man, who'd rub their tits for twenty bucks and the promise of a shot of tequila.

The locations were diverse and diffuse. In LA, the model created on Sunset Boulevard was replicated although renting apartments in a cheap condo served a cost-effective means of delivering the girls to the johns. This required someone to run each apartment or an entire block for those with the right skill set.

Bobby began in the Palace because he had a soft bed to sleep in overnight. As he expected, everyone was clean. When he moved away from the confines of Beverly Hills, the story changed. He found apartments run by a dude called Coby Ingham.

They hadn't met before and Coby had a self possession Bobby hadn't come across for quite some time. Almost like the guy felt protected by an unseen hand and wasn't the least bit bothered about his line of questions. If that hand was cloaked in an FBI leather glove then they were in trouble.

Bobby called Naldo as he was round the corner looking after Alice. Within an hour, Coby was bundled into the rear of a van and taken to a special location out in the desert. A person could scream until their lungs burst out their mouths, but no one would hear them call. This place was remote as hell.

By the time Bobby and Mary Lou arrived on the scene, Naldo had the guy tied up with electrical tape—wrists and ankles—with a hood over his head. The shack was replete with shelving attached to two of the walls. On the shelves were the full gamut of DIY tools that looked as though an electrician, carpenter and plumber had stowed away all the equipment they might ever need.

When the couple walked in, Naldo nodded at them and pointed at the hooded figure in the middle of the room. His wobbly chair only added to the sense of foreboding Coby felt. Mary Lou grabbed a stool and positioned herself in the far corner so she could observe proceedings. Bobby dragged a small wooden table and stopped when he'd placed it in front of Coby. He sat down opposite him and gave a hand gesture for Naldo to remove the hood.

As soon as the material was off his head, Coby blinked four or five times and tried to get the measure of the room. Before he had time to focus on any individual, Bobby slammed his fist down on the table to attract Coby's attention. He was startled and gave a little jump. Other than that, he stayed cool.

"How long you been running the girls in your apartment block?"

"Dunno. Two, three years. I don't know why you're treating me this way. I've always delivered on my numbers."

"This isn't about money."

Coby stared right though Bobby, trying to figure out what gives. He looked askance at Naldo and then he noticed Mary Lou. Neither gave anything away and both turned their heads toward Bobby. Coby refocused on the man sat opposite.

"What is it about?"

"You, Coby. This is about you."

"Huh?"

"Let's start with the basics, shall we? Are you a cop?"

"No."

"Are you a member of any law enforcement agency?"

"No."

"Are you working with any law enforcement agency, local or federal?"

"No. Look, whatever you think I've done, you're wrong. I wake up, I check the girls are fucking the johns, I sort out any problems. I sleep. That's my life. Period."

"Coby, you are too generous. You must spend some time outside your rat hole. I mean, how d'you eat? Do you have a girlfriend? You go to the movies occasionally."

"Of course I eat. And I've got a steady."

"Right. So don't tell me all you do is work because that's not true."

A stone cold stare boring into Coby's soul.

"Only speak the truth in this room, understand? You lie, you die."

Coby's eyes widened. If the circumstances of his arrival hadn't rattled him, then Bobby's words sure did the trick.

THREE HOURS LATER and Coby was singing like there was no tomorrow. Bobby accused him of skimming the proceeds of the block. He admitted to it. Was he feeding information to the cops? Yep. To the Feds? Sure. The fact he had electrodes attached to his balls might count as coercion in a court of law, but the shack was not a duly constituted venue exactly.

All the while, Mary Lou sat impassively watching Coby while Naldo earned his bonus. Red trickled out of Coby's right cheek where Naldo had made an early incision. His wailing was too loud and Naldo moved on to a different body part. No one wanted a headache from all that noise. A fingertip lay on the floor in a large pool of blood. Naldo had strapped each wrist to the armrests of the chair before he got the shears out.

When Coby regained consciousness, they gave him a glass of water and took out the electrical equipment. He admitted everything: the Feds, the skimming. Everything. Bobby reckoned he'd have sung to the assassination of Abraham Lincoln if he was given the chance but Mary Lou interceded.

"Let's finish up, gentlemen."

Coby dribbled toward Bobby, who thought he discerned a smile of sheer relief. Unfortunately he misunderstood Mary Lou's instructions. Naldo kicked the chair over, whipped out a pistol and shot him once in the head and once in the heart.

"Now we know."

Bobby wasn't so sure. He felt Coby was hiding something but by the end the guy was singing to every suggestion put in front of him. Naldo and he were an excellent team at extracting information from people but this didn't sit right. As a mark of respect to Naldo, Bobby helped him destroy the body and clean up the shack ready for their next visit—whenever that would be.

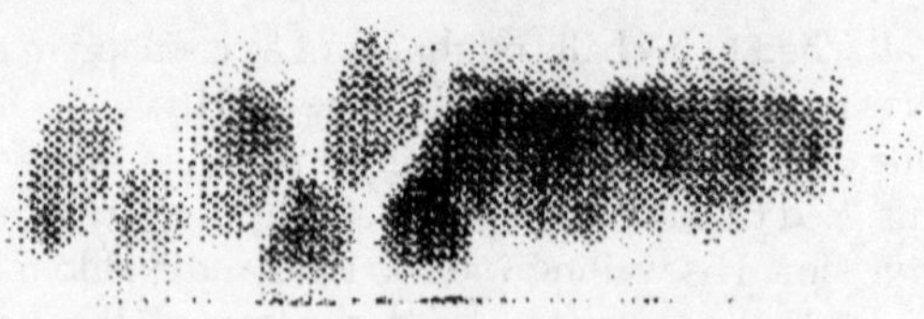

15

COBY WEIGHED ON Bobby's mind. Not so much his death—that had been almost inevitable the moment Naldo dragged his sorry ass into their desert hideaway. Bobby kept playing back the confession in his head. Over the years many men had admitted all sorts of misdeeds to him. Mainly they told the truth and occasionally they would lie. Or rather, they might utter an untruth at the start, but Naldo's persuasive techniques encouraged them to change their story—at least by the time a pair of pliers or a scalpel had been applied.

A few brave men lasted a little longer but not much more. Coby had been different. He'd fixed on claiming his innocence and only broke down just before his end. His behavior wasn't consistent with his words. Bobby feared they had made a mistake although Mary Lou was satisfied: she'd found her canary.

The guy had something to hide but maybe it had nothing to do with Feds. What if his only sin had been to shtupp the odd girl in his block? Or even every one of them. Might he have held back that information thinking it would be better to admit to that than have his dragon-wife find out.

The only promise Bobby had made was that lying would get him killed. If Coby thought he was giving up a story Bobby wanted to believe then it wouldn't have appeared as a lie and Coby'd have survived. Only Bobby didn't tell him the truth. A tangled web.

Mama's Gone

WHEN HE NEXT met up with Alice in her Malibu apartment, Bobby voiced his concerns.

"You got to be kidding, right?"

"No."

"You reckon you coerced a confession out this guy."

"I'm saying I am not sure if we did. Mary Lou called a halt to the proceedings a little early for my taste."

"And despite that, you sat there and did nothing."

"Hey wait a second. She issued an order and Naldo executed it immediately after. There was no chance to think and intervene."

Alice remained silent, ruminating on Bobby's response. She respected that he was an arch interrogator, but her mother wasn't prone to errors of judgment. She'd never seen Mama do that.

"When was the last time you can remember Mama making this kind of mistake?"

"Never. That's why we are having this conversation."

"Have you asked Naldo?"

"No way. He is loyal to both Mary Lou and I. So he'd just be hopelessly conflicted."

"He's never expressed an opinion to me."

"The man watches and waits. He follows orders. It's what he does. But he has his own mind and expresses his views when he thinks it appropriate."

"Old school."

"All the way back to the Sicilian hilltop village where he was born."

"And such a charmer."

"Yeah, he doesn't believe in getting too close to a woman in case he has to bury her in the desert."

Alice's jaw dropped.

"Joke. He's been married, but she died. Long time ago and, let's be honest, in his line of work it's hard to find the right person."

Alice laughed and they both turned their heads to the sound of the front door opening.

"Talking of which, let me introduce you to Sam."

"Hi."

Bobby put his poker face on and they shook hands.

"Hi. Pleased to meet you. I'll be back in a moment."

Sam kept the shopping bags in her hand and scooted off to the bedroom. Bobby's head followed her as she departed the living room. Once she'd gone, he allowed a smirk to take over his expression.

"What?"

"Sam?"

"Yes. That's Sam."

"Samantha."

"That's what I'm telling you. For a smart man, you can be quite dense sometimes."

"And you can be quite misleading. You never mentioned Sam was…"

"…someone I really care about? Oh, I did."

"Don't be coy. We didn't you tell us about your… lifestyle?"

"Because I didn't want to have this conversation. And it's not a lifestyle choice: this is who I am."

Sam was as good as her word and came back into the living room.

"Shall I open a bottle of wine or do you have more business to discuss?"

"Business? I'm family."

"A family business."

She wandered off into the kitchen to grab something red and Alice joined her to help with glasses. Upon their return, Bobby had moved himself from the breakfast table onto a couch.

"To the two of you."

Raised glasses all round, a clink and finally a sip of a Californian grape.

"What line of work are you in?"

"Marketing. I'm at a large agency in Boston. We handle lots of the household brands."

"And you do…?"

"I am an account director."

"Not being funny but I have no idea what that means."

Sam spent ten minutes explaining the difference between sales and marketing. Then another five describing the structure of agencies.

All the while, Alice looked on, enjoying the view as her favorite people talked to each other, nodding and laughing along the way. Sam sat next to Alice on a two-seater opposite Bobby. As their chatting continued, Bobby noticed the tension in Alice's shoulders subside and by the time the corporate lecture was over, Alice had placed a palm on Sam's lap. Sweet.

"Enough about me. Alice runs the family show. What do you do?"

"Does she? I just help if I'm needed."

"Oh gosh. I never said I was in charge, Sam."

She squeezed Alice's hand.

"No honey, but you must be fairly important to spend so much time on it."

"Alice is being modest: she's up there. We don't know what we'd do without her."

"Yeah? Did Mama say that?"

"Sure did."

Alice glowed and Sam gave her a showy kiss on the lips.

"My businesswoman of the year."

"You two hungry because I'm starved. Choose somewhere nice to eat round here. My treat."

That night in bed, Alice pondered over Bobby's reaction to Sam. He was probably out of his comfort zone hanging with a couple of lesbians, but he had handled himself well and appeared glad that she was happy. He was a cool dude.

"I'VE HEARD OF this guy in Silicon Valley."

"Great. Why don't we invite him over for dinner?"

Mary Lou and Bobby lay by the pool next to the summerhouse. He'd been back from Malibu about a week but had decided not to voice his concerns about Coby. Alice was right. They both had a good nose for trouble and he had confessed. Let that be an end to it. Wrapped up in his own thoughts as he had been these past seven days, Bobby forgot to tell Mary Lou about Sam. She knew her daughter had met someone—but was unaware of the precise details.

He had known his wife over twenty years but, even if he'd had a clear head, Bobby wouldn't have an idea how to explain Alice was a dyke. He wasn't especially prejudiced himself but Mary Lou came from the deep South and they have different rules down there. Like hanging blacks and burning crosses.

Mary Lou sighed, dragging Bobby's attention back to reality.

"This is serious. I've got an idea to make some significant money."

"Does it involve narcotics?"

"Not at all."

"Talk to me, babe."

Mary Lou outlined the scheme she had in mind. The guy she'd been introduced to, while Bobby was lying by the beach, had access to high-tech equipment—computers, circuit boards and so on. They had contracts to make precision instruments for the Pentagon. This is when the dude should have kept his mouth shut but Mary Lou used her powers of persuasion to keep him blabbing away.

Two options opened up to them. They could invest in the stock and use their inside knowledge to know when to sell or buy a bigger stake. Alternatively, they supply the instruments under George's supervision and get a direct line into the US government.

Bobby loved the vision, and making a dollar out of insider trading sounded fun, but he knew from her tone that Mary Lou was interested in fighter jet instrumentation. He was far from convinced. The idea a company controlled by a Lagotti would win and keep a defense contract was absurd, crazy even.

"Give me his details and Naldo and I can have a sniff around. See if he's legit."

"Feels good."

"Yeah, but to be honest I'm not too sure. Doesn't sit right in my gut."

"It's the future, Bobby."

GEORGE LIM APPEARED to be a stand up fella. A house out in the valley and recently married to a local girl. He was a natural born American and his parents had emigrated from Taiwan before he was even a twinkle in his father's eye.

Neither Bobby nor Naldo could unearth any vices to slow the dude down. Didn't gamble, smoke or drink. And didn't fool around with other women. From what they could tell, he lived to work and was one hundred per cent dedicated to the business. The company specialized in jet fighter kit. Details of what the place did went way over their heads, but George had told Mary Lou the truth.

"If he's got such a straight back, why is he prepared to play such a curve ball?"

"Dunno boss. At least, not yet."

They expanded their search to find his angle but there was nothing on him. Naldo focused on the wife while Bobby worked on the rest of the family. Then everything became crystal clear. Mrs. Lim was a bookkeeper and beyond reproach. She serviced several local small firms and that was all. And she wasn't pregnant even though they were trying.

Papa Lim told a different story—he created George's desire to walk on the wild side. The man was ill. His pancreas was failing him. Kidneys too. With no intervention, he'd be dead in three months, six if he was lucky. He came from the old country and hadn't invested in medical insurance and was up shit creek without a paddle—to coin a surgical phrase. So George wanted cash—and fast.

The scale of the surgery was way beyond anything a personal loan might deliver. He was smart enough to realize he needed access to dirty money. At heart, the guy was a square which was why Bobby didn't trust him.

"Once his dad is all fixed up, he will have no use for us and no desire to keep playing our game."

"Perhaps, but when he's swum with the sharks, he must meet any obligations he has to me."

"You're relying on his good nature to ensure he stays on the wrong side of the tracks."

"These kinds of opportunity come along once in a lifetime."

"Not sure about that. This gift horse relies on a straight fella. I don't think we should hang our colors to this mast."

"I disagree. There's a ton of money for very little effort. What's not to like?"

"Do me a favor. If you have to see this thing through, do everything through intermediaries. Never meet him. Never let him hear your name. I've got a bad vibe—really do."

"Promise."

"For real?"

"Cross my heart and hope to die."

THE FIRST OCCASION internal compliance checked on George, he folded faster than someone holding a pair of twos. Mary Lou hadn't even had time to release any funds to him. So there was no crime to confess apart from conspiracy and the guilt was too much for his carcass to bear. Word reached Bobby that George was discussing their plans to the local cops but because the Pentagon was indirectly involved, the whole operation was about to go sky high.

A single call to Naldo nullified their risk and George met with an auto accident that night. The boys in blue had sent him home and arranged another interview the following day when the Feds would swing by. He never made it—nor did his dad who died two months later, around the same time Mrs. Lim found out she was pregnant.

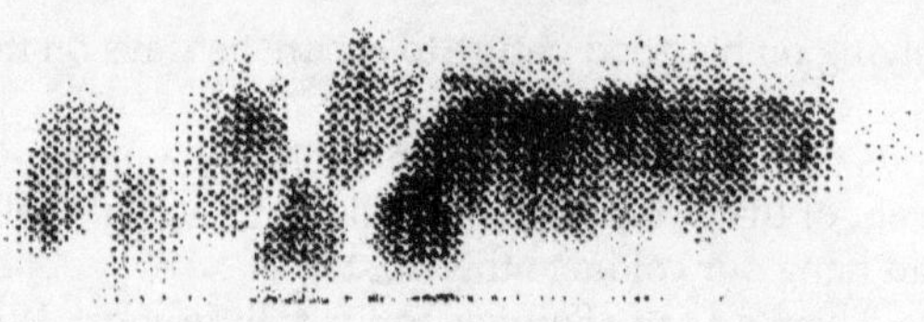

16

"WELL, IT'S A pleasure to meet you."

"And for me too. Alice has told me so much about you."

Mary Lou and Sam shook hands and everyone moved into the living room to sit down, leaving overnight bags in the hall. Drinks were offered and dispensed. Then that small awkward pause when no one quite knows which topic of conversation to kick off.

"This looks a lovely place you guys have got here."

"Thank you. Bobby: why don't you give Samantha a tour?"

He stood up, grabbed his whiskey and the two headed to the conservatory and then the pool. Alice and Mary Lou stayed where they sat. In silence.

"What have I done wrong?"

"You've disappointed me, darling. Why didn't you mention Sam was…"

"…a woman?"

"Yes, was it so hard for you to tell me you're gay?"

"I was scared of what you might think of me."

Mary Lou laughed. She was a child before the Sixties. Why would she be that prejudiced?

"Provided you are happy, that's all I care about."

"So how have I disappointed?"

"You should have just said. Passive aggressive doesn't suit you and it's not how I brought you up to be."

A tear rolled down Alice's cheek which she quickly smeared away. How could she have misjudged Mama so badly? And now she hurt inside and had the childish impulse to run over to get a hug, so everything would be okay. Only it wasn't.

"I didn't know how you'd react. It's not something we've ever talked about. I'm sorry but I could not conceive of the right words. Showing you seemed the only way."

"It must have been difficult living that lie—I get it but I am your mama and you can always rely on me. You don't hold on to my apron strings but you may still receive help from me. It's not a sign of weakness."

Bobby and Sam sauntered through the room and into the kitchen before heading upstairs.

"I just want to stand on my own two feet and be the best person I can be."

"You are a Californian, I'll give you that. Your mother is always here for you in rain or shine. You shoulda said, is all."

"I'm sorry. Forgive me?"

"Of course darling. I love you."

Sam sat back next to Alice, who kept her hands to herself and looked as though she wanted to curl into a tiny ball. Sam dangled an arm on Alice's leg as she leaned forward to grab her drink. Bobby watched Mary Lou as she saw the hand rest on her daughter's body. He noticed his wife's spine stiffen momentarily and he wondered what had been said between them to make Alice's eyes red. Sam must have spotted this too because she maintained her hand on the thigh after she returned with her vodka tonic.

THE TENSION IN the room dissipated once everybody sat down to eat. Irma had cooked up a storm and by the time she'd served coffees, everyone was full. Alice and Sam cleared the plates after each course as dutiful children do.

"How do you find Boston? My son, Frank spends a lot of his life out there."

"It's a lovely chilled town. The people are friendly unlike New York, but they've still got some drive to them."

"And it isn't a retirement village like Palm Springs."

"Mama, there are folk my age living here only they don't mix in your circles."

"The only real downside is there are far too many students."
Alice laughed.
"It wasn't so long ago that we were at college."

"Yes, but we're not there now, thank goodness."

All four chuckled at that and conversation continued for another hour. Then Mary Lou saw the clock on the mantelpiece and shuffled forward on the couch, play-slapping Bobby on the knee.

"It's way past our bedtime, but you stay up as long as you want."

"Thanks Mama."

Goodnight kisses ensued and once all permutations had been covered, Mary Lou and Bobby headed upstairs.

"WHAT DO YOU make of Sam?"

"She seems a nice girl."

"Nice enough for Alice?"

"No one will ever be good enough for my daughter. Not in my eyes at least."

"It's a mother-child thing. I get that. But ignoring the inevitable impossibility of her meeting your high expectations… what do you think of her?"

"She makes her happy. Did you see the glow in her cheeks each time Sam touched her?"

"I did. They're a good couple. But you didn't answer my question."

"Ask me again in the morning. There's something I can't quite put my finger on. Let me sleep on it."

DOWNSTAIRS ALICE AND Sam had moved onto the patio as it was such a beautiful night. The moon shone brightly and the air was calm. They shared a sun lounger and cuddled in the darkness.

"Your folks are good people. I like them."

"Yeah? I've known Bobby all my life so I don't know any different and my mother is my mother, if you see what I mean."

"Sure do."

They both were mesmerized by the moonlight on the ripples in the pool and drifted into silence. Alice stroked Sam's thigh in response to her squeezing of a breast.

"You're very forward for a girl from Boston…"

They kissed and then Alice stood up, stripped down to her underwear and removed Sam's clothing. Then she walked to the edge of the pool and jumped in, swiftly followed by her girlfriend. The two splashed about for a while until they wound up in the shallow end and Alice took off Sam's bra and then her own. More kissing and hands meandering over each other's bodies.

"Shouldn't we go upstairs? Your parents are the other side of that balcony, aren't they?"

Alice slipped her hand inside Sam's panties.

"More time here won't hurt if you're not too loud. Then you can take me to our room and fuck me there too."

MARY LOU AWOKE late next morning. Her ability to get to sleep was hampered by the sounds of her daughter frolicking in the pool with Sam. She preferred not to imagine quite what frolics occurred and kept her mind focused on the euphemism. Like every mother, she was protective of her daughter's groin and its sexual activity—gay, straight or bi.

Now she was conscious, she had another chance to replay her thoughts about that woman. Sam had said the only downside of Boston were student numbers. That did not sound right. Surely, the biggest issue was that she was thousands of miles from Alice. Perhaps Sam didn't wish to state her undying love for her daughter—because she wouldn't have meant it or it would have been too embarrassing. But she had the opportunity to make some polite statement about wanting to be together.

This made Mary Lou want to find out why Sam was holding back. Even if Alice was living in the moment and enjoying the best ride of her young life, Mary Lou needed more. That girl was hiding something from them.

Alice hadn't been forthcoming with her about her sexuality, but she'd assured her mama that she and Sam could talk openly together. For instance, Alice wanted Sam to relocate to California but she was tied to her job. Alice knew they were far too early in the relationship for her to make that kind of demand on Sam.

By the same token, Sam resented the time Alice spent working in the family business. She didn't know precisely what any of it was—Alice made sure of that—but she could tell it wasn't all on the level. A casino manager doesn't pick up sticks and leave to live above a bordello just because her Mama asked.

And if the emotions at the heart of the relationship were sound then what was Sam thinking but not saying? What was her secret? Alice was convinced Sam had genuine feelings for her, so what could she be hiding? Something about herself or what she got up to in Boston. By Alice's own account, they'd met in the most random of circumstances and it had taken Sam ages to talk about where she came from.

Perhaps, she had trust issues or her background was so shady she refused to tell a woman she was prepared to travel across country to be with —and who might be involved in criminal operations. That limited the gene pool of possibility to a handful of ideas. If Sam was a criminal then Alice's family situation would not be an issue. But if she was at the other end of the honesty spectrum, then that'd make perfect sense.

With all the problems Mary Lou'd had with people squealing, she hadn't looked closer to home. And once this idea arrived inside her head, she couldn't shake it: Sam was a stool pigeon and had finagled her way into Alice's heart to be a mole for the Feds.

MARY LOU NUDGED Bobby awake. He grunted and tried to roll back to sleep, but she shook his arm until he got the message it was time to talk. She explained what had been running through her head and waited for a response. Bobby plumped up pillows and busied himself to gain more valuable minutes to consider her words and wake up more before speaking.

"I don't see it. They're a lovely couple: the way they preen each other is adorable. When Alice speaks, Sam is captivated by her voice. It might not be love—who are we to say—but it is a mighty strong lust for sure. She cannot fake that."

"You must admit it's weird: 'the only downside is students'. Come on, that's not normal. She's hiding something and she can't be trusted."

"Alice has been careful not to let Sam eavesdrop on any business conversations. That is one of the few causes of tension between them."

"Because the woman wants to find out what we're up to."

"Because she wants more attention paid to her than Alice gives. Bit childish but not sinister."

Mary Lou crossed her arms and sulked. She didn't understand why Bobby couldn't view things as she did. He was blind sometimes. Almost like he could see no wrong in people or he had a soft spot for young beautiful women. Men were useless.

"How can you be so sure? Nothing she has done since she arrived in this house today signals you're right. All we've seen is she's a cute ass from Boston… I bumped into them in Malibu too."

"What? Why's this the first I'm hearing about it?"

"I forgot it had happened after I returned. Besides it was only a few hours. I popped by, we ate and I left. Finito."

"What the…"

"Don't give me a hard time over this. Was just after the Coby Ingham thing and as you know, it took me a while to get my head straight after that one."

"And here we are again deciding whether we have another stool pigeon."

Bobby was silent. He had no idea why he hadn't mentioned the dinner to Mary Lou. Probably because he reckoned it only right that she should meet Sam before he did. If he'd been playing his A game, he would have said. Hey, life's a bitch and then you die.

"When I met her before, she gave me chapter and verse on the marketing industry. Could have been well-researched patter, but it didn't feel like it. She cared too much for it to have been a rehearsed speech."

""Unless she's a good actress and practiced the spiel."

"True, but that doesn't change how I felt—or the time Alice has spent with her and not suspected a thing."

"How were you when you discovered muff? You reckon Alice was any different?"

"Harsh, Mary Lou."

"Perhaps. No matter what you say, I can't trust her."

"Fine. She's not getting access to anything important—apart from the hand of the fair maiden Alice."

"It's not her hand that either of us are considering right now. And that's doubly worse for you, dirty old man."

The noise from the girls' bedroom picked up again at that precise second. Mary Lou and Bobby looked at each other and laughed.

"Full of energy, those youngsters."

"Let's see if we can beat them at their own game."

They buried themselves under the covers and tried to find new ways to make the other breathe more deeply than they'd ever done before.

17

ALICE DROVE SAM around Palm Springs in her soft top sports car. She pointed out its sights—few as they were—and stopped outside Montgomery High.

"Best days of your life?"

"Nah. Loved the classes, but I was never one of the popular kids. Tried to keep myself to myself, but with Frank in the same place, it was hard to hide for very long."

"Geek girl?"

"Yep. If Frank hadn't been my brother, I'd have had on okay time."

"Did he seek the limelight and drag you along too?"

"Er no. He played the fool, got into heaps of trouble. Teachers somehow expected me to be responsible for his nefarious activities. Kids thought I was cut from the same cloth as him because we are twins. He believed every day was party time. Still does."

"Pain in the neck but fun to be around."

"That's Frank, through and through."

"Any happy memories at all?"

"Prom night. Peter Hatheway gave me a corsage and picked me up in a stretch limo. We danced and drank the fruit punch laced with hooch. He took me by the hand and we went round the back of the buildings and out onto the running track. Lost my cherry on the pole vault mattress. Biggest bounciest bed I've ever been on."

"Was the sex any good?"

"Not for me. First time anyone gave me an orgasm was you. Before that, I was flying solo."

They kissed to reinforce the special bond Alice felt for Sam.

"How about you? Any man been worth it for you?"

"One or two, but that doesn't matter because I'm with you now."

Alice squinted at her, not knowing what to make of that last comment. Against her better judgment, she let it alone. This was neither the time nor the place.

"Hungry?"

"Ravenous. Where do people go to eat in this town?"

THE WOMEN SAT down at a circular booth in the Palm Springs Country Club. By association, Alice was known there although she hadn't visited the venue for a while. The red leather seating was threadbare when her mother first came there in the Seventies and nothing much had changed—the menu had been reprinted. The restaurant and bar continued to have a mixed clientele: it was the golf course's nineteenth hole, there were ladies that lunched and a meeting room for local businessmen. Nowadays, it had gained a reputation as a cool drinking spot for the children of the wealthier members of the community.

Alice ordered linguini with clams in a white wine sauce and Sam tried the steak. Their cosmos arrived and they clinked their glasses to toast their first drink of the day. As expected, the food tasted wonderful. The decor was shabby chic, but the proprietor cared about his guests' palates.

Once their plates were empty, they ordered more cocktails. Before the waiter returned, a pair of dudes came by and introduced themselves as Brad and Martin. They chatted for a minute or two.

"Mind if we sit down?"

"By all means."

Alice and Sam glanced at each other. The way the boys behaved, they clearly were something in this town—or thought they were. Both were clean shaven and wore designer casual wear, so they had money if nothing else. Alice leaned over and whispered in Sam's ear.

"How much do you think we can scalp them for?"

"Few hundred. Whoever screws them over the most: loser buys dinner."

A nod and they switched on their smiles.

"Shouldn't you boys be out working? In a supermarket or however you earn your living."

"We have investments that do the work for us. Let the chumps toil—we prefer to play."

"What's your handicap?"

"Huh?"

Sam sighed disdainfully and pointed at the eighteenth green outside.

"Oh, golf. Not my idea of a game: chasing after a ball you're always hitting away from you. Makes no sense."

Alice laughed at Martin's comment. Bobby said the same thing, but it didn't stop him from teeing off every week.

"You enjoy games, Brad?"

"Sure do. I'm a gambling man so I prefer the odds stacked in my favor, but any card game floats my boat."

"Me too. There's nothing like the thrill of taking a leap into the unknown."

The waiter arrived with the cosmos and Brad put green on the table for payment. The attendant looked at Alice and she nodded consent, so he picked up the cash and walked away.

"Thanks for the drink, Brad."

"My pleasure."

"If you don't play golf Martin, how do you spend the hours between waking up and falling asleep?"

"I keep myself busy: hosting pool parties, hanging with beautiful people —like yourselves."

Sam and Alice smiled and fluttered their eyelids. These saps were one hundred per cent ego with no space for anything else.

"Haven't been to a pool party in years…"

Martin heard Alice's cooing and got the hint.

"Fancy coming over now? I can make some calls and get the gang over later."

ALICE AND SAM stood opposite Brad and Martin with martinis all round. Martin had made a big deal about how to concoct the perfect vodka martini, so he'd set himself up to fail. The cocktails only disappointed but the women weren't here to critique his bar tending skills. Alice had parked her soft top at the front of the house next to Martin's Italian beast of a sports car.

"Here's to partying on down."

"I'll get some music going."

Once Martin returned, electronic beats poured out of the PA pumping onto the poolside veranda. All four tapped their toes and a minute later, the boys had grabbed the girls by the hand and encouraged them to dance. Five or six tracks on—who was counting?—and slower rhythms hit the air and the couples paired off for more intimate moments.

Alice wasn't too happy with Martin's octopus hands but when she glanced over to the other couple, Sam didn't appear to be annoyed that Brad's fingers were clamped to her ass, squeezing her like a used sponge. To her surprise, Alice minded though. The point of being here was to rob the overgrown kids and her jealousy spurred her on to go for broke.

As Martin kissed her on the neck, she undid his shirt and put a hand on his belt buckle. Sam saw what Alice was up to and followed suit. Neither of the boys objected and their egos bloated a little more than was usual as the women undressed them down to their shorts.

"Your turn, but don't get fresh. I'm keeping my undies on… for now."

The warmth of Alice's whisper against Martin's earlobe was more than enough to make him follow her orders to the letter. Brad copied his friend with a similar warning from Sam, who then walked him over to the base of the diving board. She sat down, legs apart, and reeled him in toward her until she wrapped her thighs around him. Christmas was coming early for Brad it seemed.

Martin stepped forward, within an inch of Alice, who embraced him again and shoved a hand down his shorts to maintain his interest. She twisted the two of them round so she could see the diving board and monitor what was happening with her Sam. The sight of Brad's pure white ass nestling above the waistband of his bermudas told her he was at the same level of excitement as Martin.

The women winked at each other and made their move.

"Let's get naked and then we can fuck in the pool."

Martin nodded and whipped off his shorts then called over to his friend while Alice slowly undid her navy and white striped bra.

"Come on guys! Get with the program."

Brad kept a hand on Sam's breast as he looked around, assessed the situation and grinned.

"You up for some more fun?"

"The sooner you stop talking, the quicker we'll be fucking."

His smile was so broad, Sam saw his teeth. Her bra was already on the floor. She took her time, putting her hands on her hips to avoid undressing further. Five seconds later, Brad and Martin were in the water with their hard-ons. Alice and Sam reacted fast by grabbing the guys' clothes and throwing their own back on before the guys could do anything.

Alice palmed Martin's car keys he'd dropped on a patio table and turned to face the pool.

"Sorry boys, changed our minds now we've seen your equipment."

Sam laughed to emphasize the point. Then they both dashed to Alice's soft top.

"Take my keys and follow me. Don't ask questions: there's no time."

As she spoke, she looked back and saw Brad and Martin heading toward them. Neither man was in a particular hurry so they didn't know about the car. Sam appeared flustered but hopped into the driver's seat nonetheless. Alice unlocked Martin's vehicle and they sped off, leaving him to swear at them in the distance.

Alice kept a steady pace below the speed limit until they arrived at the airport parking lot. She drove to what she hoped was its furthest corner and carefully parked. Sam sidled over and let Alice take over the wheel.

"That was hot."

"They deserved it."

"I could become used to the criminal life."

"Stick to grand theft auto and you'll be fine."

"You'd better get me home fast before this buzz goes away. I don't want to use a drop of this rush on anyone but you."

"Why wait? There's an airport motel coming up just about… now."

AN HOUR LATER they left the motel and headed back to Mama's to pack. In the coolish light of the early evening, Alice reckoned not being in Palm Springs would be a good idea. Martin would be unlikely to want to tell the cops he got stiffed by two out-of-town broads, but he'd have to report his car stolen to have any hope of getting it returned. Alice had wiped her prints off every surface just to be sure. The vehicle retailed at north of a quarter of a million and Sam pointed out it might have a tracker so he had no need of police help. She was probably right.

"I stole the car so you are definitely buying dinner when we get home."

"Worth every penny."

Alice hugged Bobby and kissed her Mama goodbye while Sam stood patiently by. Handshakes and adios for her, then into the soft top and away. On the way back, Sam mused about their trip.

"I like your folks. They come across as warm and welcoming."

"Bobby is a good man. Says little, but he watches and learns."

"He's always been chatty with me."

"The man can be charming too."

"Switches it on for the ladies, does he?"

"A man with a dark past from what I see, but neither Mama nor Bobby have ever told me what he got up to before they hooked up."

"Sordid and dirty—all free love and squirming naked bodies?"

"Bobby? I don't think so. More likely to be a tragic death and unconsummated passion."

"Shame. I was hoping for a tale of bondage and a secret dungeon where he tortured leather-clad souls within an inch of their sexual deaths."

"You lost me at bondage… I need to decide where you'll take me for my prize."

"Almost forgot about that. When will we get in?"

Alice glanced at the clock on the dashboard and added numbers up in her head.

"Nine at the latest."

"Do you mind if we stay in tonight? We'll have more time to think of somewhere real special for your prize. Besides… I've got some other ideas about how we could spend the evening instead of sat in a restaurant."

Alice needed no further explanation as Sam reached over and placed a left hand on her crotch.

"Take away pizza will do just fine."

She parted her legs slightly and pressed down on the gas pedal.

18

MARY LOU AND Bobby decided they needed to find more opportunities to sidestep the heroin racket. And as much as they wanted to stay local, they knew there was money to be made outside LA. They were not turning their backs on the City of Angels as spreading their wings.

She'd had her eye in San Francisco for some time. The place had never been under mob control and as a small operation, Mary Lou thought they could make their mark quickly given the muscle they'd bring.

With November fast approaching, Bobby wanted to get lottery card production up-and-running although Alice preferred to supervise that end of things. Logistics resolved that argument in Alice's favor: it was cheaper and quicker to truck over the fake cards than build a new plant.

A fresh batch of sales representatives were hired and cash poured in, just as it had in LA. The state's finances might be in disarray but Mary Lou and Bobby were almost literally printing money in Bakersfield. The sudden influx of green made her want more out of San Francisco.

"What else would be easy to set up?"

"Girls… and boys for that matter."

"It's not a gay city—just has a gay area."

"Anyway. The answer to your question is sex. Let's ship in some girls from our LA clubs to begin with until we can recruit local bait. If we use the gentle art of firm persuasion, we could run three lap dancing bars before the weekend."

Bobby and his enforcement crew spent two days driving round town to locate suitable venues. He was searching for the rare combination of relative success and weak management. If you possess a knowing eye and are prepared to sit in enough dive bars, then you can find almost anything. His gang were under strict instructions to drop a few notes on the girls but not lose sight of the prize: to check out security arrangements and how much muscle was hiding behind closed doors. He told them he'd let them have a weekend pass with any of the floozies they wanted once the Lagottis were running the joints.

Three locations were selected and his crew split up and attacked each at the same time. Existing management was offered a cash payment to leave that night. Given the size of the offer, two accepted in an instant and walked out immediately with a brief case crammed with money. The third venue contained a more reluctant host.

His perspective was that he'd built the Booty Bar from nothing and a bunch of out-of-towners would not get him to shift just because they asked.

"I understand you have not planned to exit this establishment but I can assure you, it would be left in safe hands."

"You don't appear to be listening too well. The place is not up for sale."

"We have offered you money, which you have rejected. I heard you say that clearly. So I won't embarrass you by making the offer twice."

"Finally, you get the picture."

Bobby laughed. This small-time operator stood before him thought he'd walk away with his tail between his legs.

"The best thing I can suggest you do now is to give me the Booty Bar as a gift—man to man. And because I am a businessman at heart, I shall find other ways than cash to show my appreciation."

It was Anton Markov's turn to laugh.

"You been smoking the whacky baccy before you came in here or the sight of all that pussy outside has made you crazy. Watch my lips: I am not giving you the joint and I'll not sell it to you."

"That's a shame. Is that your final word on the matter?"

"You bet your last fucking dollar it is."

Bobby smiled and put his hands in his pants pockets as he turned to face Naldo.

"The guy thinks I'm a comedian. But if he won't sell and will not give the place a way, what can we do?"

Naldo lunged forward at Markov and thrust a knife straight into his heart. A violent deep incision and Markov hit the floor. One minute he's talking business, the next blood is pouring out of his mouth and onto the carpet.

"We kill you, motherfucker. That's what we'll do."

Naldo started cleaning up almost the instant he had rested Markov's head on the ground. Bobby watched him for five seconds and then looked at the other two fellas he'd brought with.

"Make yourselves useful, eh?"

BOBBY LIKED THE layout of the Booty Bar with private dancing rooms close to the stage and the bar at the rear of the auditorium. Whoever they installed here to run the joint would have a great line of sight over the whole proceedings. And an office behind the bar so you'd never be too far from the action.

When the last john left the building at six in the morning, Bobby locked the doors and explained to the hapless workers they had options. Stay and work for him or fuck off with no hard feelings and today's wages. Everyone stuck around, which was no surprise as two of them had seen Markov being dragged out the back and dumped in the trunk of Naldo's car. Word had got out about their erstwhile employer before Bobby had a chance to talk to them.

He gave everyone a bonus to keep them sweet and then sent everybody home so his crew could comb through the place to make sure there were no complications. They looked out for any unopened safes and ensured there weren't any others hiding in the shadows, too scared to confront the new owners.

No Markov minions but two ledgers and one safe. Bobby had low expectations about its contents as the box was small and found at the bottom of a cupboard. They dumped it all in his car and he drove off to apply his skills to crack it open. Naldo made yet another trip into the desert to offload Anton Markov, onetime owner of the Booty Bar.

MARY LOU MIGHT have harbored the belief that San Francisco was a chilled out town but no one had explained this to its more recent arrivals. When the Italian mob's control over organized crime wavered in the 1990s, other groups leaped on the opportunity to take over. Many of these people came over from the newly independent states of the former Soviet Union—and from Russia itself.

Their background in abject hardship under the yoke of Communist oppression set them up to be ruthless dictators in charge of their own gangs.

This made the Markovs no different from hundreds of families who entered the country illegally to seek their fortunes, having created seed capital from the black market back home.

If Mary Lou had known the specific history of the Markov clan, she would have advised Bobby to tread carefully around Anton instead of whacking him during their first argument. As night follows day, the Markovs moved with tremendous speed after Anton's death.

Two nights later, smoke was seen coming out from under one of the private rooms of the Booty Bar. Within a quarter of an hour, flames licked the stage and only five minutes after that, the second floor collapsed on top of the auditorium. Everyone escaped unharmed but the unflinching revenge sent a clear message to Bobby. They sure had picked on the wrong person to chisel out of a bar.

Mary Lou took the news badly while Bobby thought having control of two out of the three venues was good work. She believed the Markovs had taken a diabolical liberty by destroying her property. The fact it had been theirs forty-eight hours before was irrelevant to her. Everyone needed to see you don't mess with the Lagotti family—otherwise any upstart with a shotgun could come calling. Her reaction was simple.

"Find out who did this to me and kill them."

"We took the fight to them by shooting one of theirs."

"And we will finish this by putting more of them in the morgue."

"I'm not sure we should escalate this. Both sides could put each other's actions down as an unfortunate incident but a fair trade. If we retaliate now, then they'll come back and hit us harder. It's inevitable because that is exactly how we would respond."

"I don't give a shit how many bodies pile up, we must be seen to be stronger than them. Else we'll lose leverage everywhere."

"Sure thing babe, but we are weak over in San Francisco. Our power base is in LA not along the coast. Do you think we should divert resources away from making good money just to show a bunch of Russkies we mean business?"

"Damn straight. We can't let them come over here and walk all over us. If they do that, within three years they'll have everything and you and I will be six feet under."

Bobby sat pondering Mary Lou's words and mulled over his own concerns. She had more energy than he had. And his crew were most likely to wind up dead. He hated organizing funerals and dealing with crying, resentful widows. But taking it all into account, Mary Lou was right. Yesterday it was the Booty Bar and tomorrow it would be gaming, the rest of the girls and then the narcotics operations. They needed to destroy the parasite before it throttled its host.

THE MARKOV FAMILY occupied the Tenderloin district on McAllister and Larkin. Generations of impoverished inhabitants had lived and died on the same streets as these stocky Russian gangsters, who landed on the west coast and sustained themselves through a highly effective protection racket which blossomed into prostitution in all its guises.

Their girls were streetwalkers in the main run by a bunch of punks and a network of pimps. The Booty Bar had been a rare attempt at refinement because the senior family members understood the importance of rising out of the criminal primordial ooze. They needed ways to make more money and controlling a legal venue gave them the opportunity to hire out skanks at a much higher rate. While a cathouse would have boosted revenues, the Booty Bar delivered greater respectability too. Besides you could legally comp a cop a short private dance but lending them a hooker for half an hour was a whole different ball game.

Hence the vicious response. Anton may have been stubborn, but he was in charge of the only shred of legal activity operated by the Markovs. They could not let the affront to their reputation go unchallenged.

BOBBY AND HIS crew—Naldo and three trusted associates—began by cutting girls on the street. This was simple and sent out a clear statement: if you hit our revenues by burning down our building then we will scar your product. Only the sickest of the sick wants to fuck disfigured hookers.

The Markovs replied by attacking the other two bars under Lagotti control: the Red Stocking and the Dahlia. On this occasion, no matches were applied to the situation. Instead goons were despatched to threaten the staff —girls, bartenders, the lot. The following day, everyone was too scared to enter the premises. Mary Lou sent guys and whores in from LA but they received the same clear message.

On the night of Christmas Eve, Mary Lou ordered her fellas to slash throats and less than a week later, the body count had reached double digits on both sides.

"This madness has to stop. This war of attrition is hurting all of us with no sign of letting up. We've lost good people and for what? A stake in the ground and a chance to sell the sight of an ass a few miles further north."

"Organize a conference. We can afford to allow ourselves a graceful defeat on the prostitution because the lottery cards are going gangbusters."

Mama's Gone

19

MARY LOU REFUSED to come to the meet and insisted Bobby go instead. He knew this was a mistake but her mind was made up. A seedy hotel conference space with a view of a car lot—if you bothered to look outside. Naldo frisked the Markov attendees and one of their goons checked they weren't packing pieces. Everyone was clean.

The room had capacity for six chairs and a rectangular table which was exactly what was required. Bobby sat with Naldo to his right and Ernie Santo, a third generation American who'd worked alongside Naldo for years. Solid, reliable but occasionally prone to chatter. On the other side of the oak veneer was Nikolay Markov and two guys who were estranged from their clothes. It looked as though this was the first time either had worn a jacket. However, Bobby understood these individuals will have been the ones who torched the Booty Bar and murdered his people. They might seem like redneck hicks but he knew better than to underestimate them.

"You have encroached on our territory and performed horrific acts on our property."

"Let's be honest with each other Nikolay, both sides have deployed knives and guns causing pain and misery. Nobody is innocent here."

Bobby paused and stared at the three sitting opposite. There was no way Markov could seize the moral high ground.

"The point is, we're sat here today to put an end to the bloodshed so we can all go back to work."

"Agreed. But we must take into account you killed my nephew Anton."

"There is no need to bring out a roster for the dead but I acknowledge the death of your family member and I am sorry for your loss."

"Thank you. He was a stubborn cocksucker, but he was my sister's stubborn cocksucker. I hope you understand."

"I do. This is my proposal: we cease our efforts this year to stretch our wings in San Francisco's prostitution market. You stop attacking my people and we'll not muscle into any lap dancing clubs or hooker networks, whether owned by you or not."

"I see."

"By now, you should have done your homework and found out who we are and the reach we have in California and Nevada. We do not intend to stand still despite our… local difficulties here. You have shown yourselves to be formidable fighters and we respect that."

"You are right to give up on pussy in this town. This time next year, I shall be the only man selling ass on these streets and you won't get in my way. But you have forgotten about Anton."

"Direct compensation will be difficult because I've already just given up rights to prostitution and also because Anton had a simple choice and he picked foolishly. No disrespect to you or your sister."

"The boy was not the sharpest tool in the box. What are you suggesting?"

"A business relationship with us. To keep the girls on the streets or pumping those poles while they lap dance, I imagine you ply them with narcotics. We would like to supply them to you. This will be at a lower price than you pay now and of a higher quality, not that it matters to you. The compensation is the amount of green you save. Tell your sister whatever you want but that's the most Anton's life is worth."

The corners of Nikolay's mouth raised upward in the best imitation of a smile he could muster.

"Drugged up and fucked up—that's how we like them."

"Are we agreed?"

"Sure, why not? If it doesn't work out, I will go to a different supplier and then find and kill you for betraying our agreement."

Nikolay stared through Bobby who grit his teeth and inhaled deeply. Now was not the time to rise to this Russian's bait. They both knew the Lagottis were getting a beating. Only Nikolay wouldn't let Bobby off the hook.

"Oh, and one last thing. We shall relinquish immediate control of the Dahlia to you but keep the Red Stocking. Naturally you will supply all the girls to the club for a fee and a month ago you didn't have the Dahlia in your operation so that is a gift from us to you."

"Very well. At least I'll know where to find you. Our commission is sixty cents on the dollar—of the profit."

"Let's not get greedy so close to the end of our discussions. You can have fifty per cent of all revenues from the girls but not a penny more. Anything else we wring out the johns is our affair."

Bobby sat back in his chair and noticed Naldo place both hands on his lap. The man was ready to pounce because this was the moment when the deal all came together or fell apart into violence. Bobby had ceded ground until his final push and Nikolay might not fall for the ruse.

"This is acceptable."

Nikolay leaned across the table to shake Bobby's hand and the two smiled. He knew better than to trust the Russki but he'd stopped the bloodshed—for now. And they had a new customer for their brown sugar.

As they walked out onto the car lot, a gust of wind hit them all in the face like they'd been slapped back into reality. Far in the distance someone was playing carols. The sound of sleigh bells permeated Bobby's consciousness and he remembered what time of year it was.

"Merry Christmas to you and yours."

"Huh? Oh yes. Season's greetings."

They stood facing each other for a second until another blast of wind cut through them. Bobby nodded, slapped his hands together in a failed attempt to improve blood flow to his fingers and walked away. Naldo waited a short while to watch the Markovs depart.

"We should have killed them while we had the chance."

Bobby glared at Naldo's rare intrusion into family decision making.

"We'll make money out of them and no one has to die over the vacation. Besides, we only promised to stay out of prostitution for a year. The man has dreams but at heart he's a street fighter and they get toppled by the next guy with a bigger baseball bat."

SAM SPENT CHRISTMAS Day at Alice's, watching the sea beat against the beach although they popped over to a restaurant for a five course lunch. She enjoyed her time with Alice but the initial buzz had worn off. Separated by thousands of miles, the relationship needed a kick up its ass. Because they only saw each other one or two weekends a month, they both made sure there were no arguments or any reason to spoil the experience when they were together. That also meant all their different expectations and opinions remained unresolved.

Alice was besotted with her, but Sam could no longer tell herself she reciprocated. The sex was still good and the presents lavished on her were not to be sneezed at. All the same, she was bored but didn't have the energy to end it.

Mama's Gone

Christmas Day was a perfect example of what was wrong. Each individual moment was wonderful whether eating the most perfectly cooked turkey in the world, sitting watching the sun set over the Pacific Ocean or clinging to the headboard of Alice's four poster bed. But they added up to nothing. They would never be a normal couple and when they talked about the future, they were kidding themselves.

So Sam sowed the seeds of her departure before she even arrived, blaming a work party for her need to return to the east coast. The sadness on Alice's face almost made her cry but Sam tried her damndest to ensure Alice had the best Christmas away from her Mama she'd ever had. If not the finest then filled with the most sex.

AS SOON AS the plane landed at Logan, Sam felt a tremendous weight lift from her shoulders. She scurried back to her apartment, cracked open a bottle of wine and got merrily drunk watching TV reruns until she gurgled asleep in the late evening.

The next day, she opened her address book and investigated the party scene in her home town. With only three days before New Year the last thing she needed was to spend the upcoming nights alone. Good news: she was in luck. Every night had something to offer until the clock struck midnight on Sunday, December 31.

Thursday evening was a washout. Sam found herself cornered by a rich doofus who was more interested in his opinions than hers but that didn't stop her taking him home. His punishment for the tedium inflicted on her was to hail a cab on the street at four in the morning when she decided he wasn't going to be any more use to her in bed.

Having secured two days vacation time, Sam headed to the gym on Friday afternoon and dolled herself up. She wouldn't make the same mistake tonight. Kickass: that was her new motto.

The party venue was a penthouse overlooking State Street and, given the height of the apartment block, looked like it had a great view of the bay. Sam mingled, chatted with a few interesting people and was considering leaving to find action elsewhere when she sauntered to the makeshift bar for one last drink.

"Champagne?"

"Why the hell not?"

"I've yet to come up with a good reason myself."

"In that case, let's see what happens. What's the worst, right?"

Sam clinked glasses with the guy who was very self-assured but wasn't trying to take over the conversation.

"You local or breezing through town for the festive season?"

"Grew up in New Jersey but I've been living here since I left college."

"Study here?"

"Used to."

"Bright girl. And smart enough to stay in this beautiful city."

"And you?"

"I split my time between here and my other ventures on the east coast."

"Entrepreneur?"

"Do my best. Business is never easy…"

"…but you're doing well to afford that suit."

Sam reached out to feel the material of the jacket and the guy smiled and seemed to puff his chest as she did it. Having fingered the schmatta, Sam pressed down the lapel so it was flat again and gave herself the opportunity to lay her palm on his upper torso above his heart ever so slightly longer than was proper.

They continued to talk and she moved onto a cosmo or two, a habit she'd acquired from Alice. The guy took Sam's glass and placed it on a nearby table. He put his hand on hers and led her to the dance floor where a DJ was cranking out the tunes. He had some good moves but focused on dancing with her rather than impressing her. The same couldn't be said for most of the others hovering near her like flies buzzing around a picnic hamper.

When the beats slowed down and half the people sloped off to drink a little more, he got intimate without getting fresh. For Sam that meant she was happy for him to kiss her neck and put his hand on her ass but he didn't rearrange her panties. What a gentleman.

"Would you mind if we found somewhere quieter?"

"Good plan. Like to come back to mine for a Java?"

"Your place sounds fine. Okay if I bring some party powder to help with the… coffee?"

"Nice idea. I'm Sam Wray."

"Frank Lagotti."

SAM AWOKE FACE up from the brink of a horny dream to find her feet on the pillows and Frank's head between her thighs. She stretched her arms and arched her back. In the corner of her eye she saw two lines of white on the bedside table.

Although she needed a hit to kick-start the day, there was no way she wanted to interrupt Frank who was hard at work creating ripples of tingles throughout her body—emanating from her groin but spreading to her toes, her fingers. Even her eyelids felt more alive.

Later they snaffled up the remaining coke and spent the rest of the day naked and sweaty. The simple act of having Alice's twin in bed with her turned Sam on. The rush was immense.

"So am I better than Alice?"

"If I thought you'd compare yourself to her, I'd never have mentioned it."

"Don't lie. Must be freaking awesome to have a brother and a sister."

"Has its moments, for sure."

Sam didn't want to get bogged down by thoughts of Alice and her delectable body. She was having fun and wanted more.

"Are we going out tonight or shall we party at home?"

"No need to decide. You throw a dress on and we'll hang out with some people I've met and if everything's cool, we can invite them here—or to mine —to carry on the entertaining until the sun rises again."

Sam rolled on top of Frank, rocking forward and back until his breathing changed rhythm.

"Sure thing honey—only not just yet, eh?"

1996

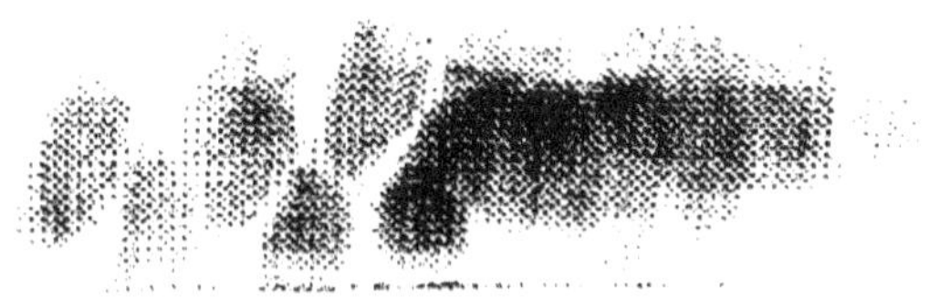

20

THE PREVIOUS YEAR ended with Indiana's decision to reintroduce a handful of riverboat casinos. One of the earliest licenses to be granted was run from Chicago, out of East Dubuque and Mary Lou saw this loosening up of gambling laws as a natural extension of their existing casino operations. All she needed to do was convince the Gaming Commission that Alice was an appropriate person to own the vessel.

"Another day, another license to be bought."

"How is Teddy Prescott?"

"Been better. He had a heartache three months ago and there's talk he'll step down soon."

"We should have a conversation before he does anything rash."

"I'm sure he will be pleased to see you. Always has been in the past."

"Send my regards."

Bobby flew out to Prescott's mansion the following day. The butler answered the door and showed him to the library. This room with its musty books felt like a home from home although Bobby had only visited Prescott a handful of times. Unlike every previous occasion Hannah Prescott appeared in the doorway in place of her husband. Bobby stood up from the insanely luxurious armchair and took the five steps forward to introduce himself and to shake her hand. Hannah kept her arms by her side and her expression reflected her disgust for him. Teddy had briefed her.

"Mr. Trevestan, I am so sorry you have had a wasted journey."

"Call me Bobby. How is Teddy?"

"Far too ill to receive visitors, I'm afraid."

"So he knows I am here then? Or have you reached that decision on his behalf?"

"Mr. Trevestan..."

"... Bobby..."

"... my husband has made me only too aware of you. He asked me to convey his apologies but you will not be seeing him today."

Bobby stared into the eyes of this shrewish woman. Chances were she was just trying to protect the senator from the myriad strangers who spend their lives lobbying politicians.

"Has Teddy told you how he and I first met?"

"No, he hasn't mentioned..."

"... then you can't possibly expect me to believe Teddy won't see me. So either you have decided for yourself or he isn't here anywhere. Which is it, Hannah?"

Bobby's expression gained the edge of a grimace and he moved a step forward to enter her personal space.

"Fellows like you do not intimidate me. You think you can walk into people's homes and order them about, but you are wrong."

"And women like you believe you can boss men like me around and we'll do what you say. You are making a very poor mistake. I could help your husband get the finest medical treatment, for example. I am able to protect him, you and your entire family from life's misfortunes."

"Don't threaten me, Trevisan."

"Lady, this is no threat. Answer my question: is Teddy in this joint?"

Hannah looked at Bobby's eyes and her cheeks flushed red.

"Yes he is, but he's too tired for visitors. He asked me to send you away as he doesn't have the energy to see anyone nowadays."

"He'll see me. Now."

Mrs. Prescott nodded and walked out of the room at such a pace that Bobby could easily follow her up the stairs, along the landing and into a large bedroom. Hannah pulled up a chair near the bed and Bobby sat down facing the tired man lying under the sheets. Without turning around, Bobby issued a clear instruction:

"Shut the door on your way out."

Hannah parted her lips as if she planned on replying but closed her mouth and left.

BOBBY RELAXED BACK in his seat and watched Teddy Prescott wheeze in front of him. The heart attack had knocked him sideways.

"Hi Teddy. Good to see you."

"Seen better days."

"That may be so, but you've got some great years ahead of you still."

"Not sure about that from what the doctors have told me."

"Ah, their job is to make money out of you being ill. They want to keep you down. You will bounce back from this. Just focus on building up your strength and you'll be in the Palace humping your way through our girls like there's no tomorrow."

"There may be no tomorrow for me. That's my point."

Bobby watched this old man's face. He had a real fear he was on his last legs.

"I hope you're wrong, Teddy - for your sake and mine."

"You always want something but this time I'm far too gone to do your bidding."

"You're still here, Teddy. And this isn't about you. It's about your darling Hannah."

"Leave her out of this."

"I can't ignore her when you sent her down to meet me instead of calling me up here to speak to you, my friend."

Prescott began to cough, caused by the tightness in his chest: the stress of seeing Bobby.

"Do you fancy a beer? I think I do. Shall I find Hannah and ask her for one?"

Beat.

"Did you ever tell her?"

Teddy's pale complexion gained a reddish hue.

"Thought not. I mean, how can a man explain to his wife he raped an underage prostitute to death with a glass bottle? Fucked if I know how to start that conversation, but that's what you'll be doing soon unless you listen carefully to what I need you to do, you shit bag."

A pause as Bobby crossed his legs and picked off a piece of white fluff from Prescott's sheets.

"It's your reputation on the line, not mine. In five minutes time I can tell Hannah what you did and then you'll be dying and divorced. Well, what's it to be?"

"What do you want me to do?"

"I brought a letter with me today and you will sign it to recommend Alice Lagotti as a fine upstanding member of the community to the Gaming Commission. The family wants to run a riverboat casino."

Bobby pulled out the typewritten sheet from his inside jacket pocket and fumbled around until he found a pen. Teddy took it and Bobby held the paper so he could write a wobbly signature.

"Thank you for your cooperation. As ever, we appreciate the assistance you've provided over the years."

"This was the last time. I can't..."

"Don't be ridiculous, Teddy. You can - and you will. We ask little but, as you know, sometimes we need an accommodation. Besides, mark my words, you'll be out of this bed soon enough. I made this offer to Hannah but I'm making a promise to you. I shall arrange for one of our doctors to pay you a visit."

"Please don't..."

Bobby stood up, put the letter in his pocket and patted Prescott on the shoulder. He might never have liked the senator but Teddy had always come good for them and he looked pitiful right now. Worth showering a few thousand dollars on the old goat if only to make Bobby feel better on the off chance he had to call again.

ALICE ENJOYED SPENDING time with Mama especially as she had been entrusted to kick off another key project for the family. East Dubuque nestled just south of the state border with Wisconsin and on the opposite side of the Mississippi to its bigger brother, Dubuque in Iowa. To describe the town as small would be an understatement but Mary Lou wasn't shacked up in the East Dubuque Regal to settle down and make a home for herself.

She and Alice only needed to spend a few days here to set up a boilerplate legal entity and to ensure Alice met the residency requirements laid out in the statutes to secure the casino license.

"We'll have to stay past the weekend, won't we?"

"Looks like it right now. Can't be helped. People don't move fast in these hick towns—and we're from California."

"I know, but this is the first place I've been where I feel bigger than it."

Mary Lou smiled: she'd raised herself a city chick.

"It'll grow if we have anything to do with it."

"Saturday, shall we visit Chicago for some shopping?"

"Spoken like a true Al Capone."

"A girl has to have fun sometimes. All work and no play..."

"...makes Jill a rich woman. I'm teasing. Chicago is a great idea—unless you'd rather meet up with Sam instead of hanging out with your old mom."

"You're not old. Anyway, I told Sam I'd be busy the next few weeks so she wouldn't think I was ignoring her. The family business comes first."

"It'll take two hours to drive over there, less if I'm behind the wheel so why don't we stay overnight?"

Alice clapped her hands with glee like a little girl and gave Mama an enormous hug.

"That'd be great. Just like we used to pop over to LA when I was a kid."

"Only one difference, darling."
"Huh?"
"This time you're paying."

SIXTY YEARS BEFORE, Chicago had been at the epicenter of mob activity thanks to its location smack in the middle of the country's waterways for transportation and to the pliability of its local law enforcement officers. That was then. Now the organized crime syndicates were no more and anyone could walk the streets safely without the grinding fear of being shot—unless you were black and poor of course.

Mary Lou and Alice checked into their hotel and sat in the bar contemplating where to eat dinner. Alice thumbed through the local newspaper while Mary Lou went to a phone to speak with Bobby. When she returned five minutes later, concern was written all over her face. Alice's back stiffened as she braced herself.

"What's happened?"
"I've got to go."
"Where?"
"Atlantic City."

With those two words, Alice's heart sank because it meant only one thing: Mama needed to bail out Frank. Mary Lou saw Alice's expression shift from excitement to misery.

"He needs me so I have to help."
"And how old does he have to be before you let him stand or fall by himself?"

"Probably never: he's my son and I love him so I must care for him. Just as I love you and want to look after you."

Alice glared and sulked, hiding her head behind her paper. This was not the weekend she'd wanted. Frank always got in the way.

"This isn't a debate. I'll book a flight now. Would be great if you'd drive me to O'Hare but I'll take a taxi if you won't."

"Don't be like that, Mama. I'll drive you for sure. I'm disappointed. That's all."

Each word was true—Alice was saddened but not at the prospect of losing a weekend's shopping because retail therapy could wait. It was her mother and her blinkered attitude to Frank. That was disappointing her because it never seemed to change. The boy snapped his fingers and Mama came running. Every single time.

FRANK FACED DISAPPOINTMENT of his own but this was business and not personal. Leonida had vanished and so had a cool half a million in cash from the Lucky Nugget safe. The two events were connected because it was too much of a coincidence and a member of the reception staff saw Leonida leave with a case in his hard. Frank might not have been Philip Marlowe, but he was no schnook.

His gut told him to track the motherfucker down and slice his skin off while his head said he should focus on the business and not let the red mist take over. In the short-term his head won and he called Palm Springs only to hear Mama was somewhere in Illinois with the golden girl, Alice.

A fresh layer of anger descended on his shoulders and he vowed to find Leonida and settle matters the old-fashioned way. Two hours later, three men burst into Leonida's hotel room. The guy hid in plain sight in AC instead of fleeing town at the earliest opportunity. All wore plastic masks but only one spoke to the prostitute sitting astride Leonida.

"Put your clothes on: the party's over."

As the whore scuttled off Leonida's body, he stretched his hand to the bedside table. Three revolvers aimed at his head.

"Don't do it. Not even to get your piece."

"I was going to pay her."

"No need to bother. My treat."

The girl just finished putting on her dress and Frank pointed at her panties lying on the floor. She nodded, put them on as quickly as she physically could and looked round the room.

"Got everything?"

A nod. She tried her best not to make eye contact.

"How much does he owe you?"

"Thirty plus tip. No offense."

"None taken. We all have to earn a living."

Frank pulled out a thick roll of bills from his pants pocket and held out a C-note.

"Now beat it. And remember you were never here."

As the girl took the bill, Frank squeezed her ass under that short dress with enough venom for her to know he wasn't fucking about. The masks and the guns were sufficient reminder however, so she knew it was a just a cheap grope. Under the circumstances, she let it ride and scurried out the room.

By the time Mary Lou arrived that evening, Leonida had three fewer fingers as Frank was no expert in torture. They were holed up on the third floor of the Nugget which Frank had never bothered to renovate. Leonida was tied to a chair in an otherwise empty room. The two windows had one shutter ajar and a bare bulb was on, hanging in the middle of the ceiling.

Frank's problem was simple: how to get Leonida to say where he'd stashed the money. While the guy was willing to talk, he reckoned he was a dead man so had no motivation to spill his guts.

Mary Lou stood in the corner watching proceedings as she did when rats were being tortured. Her son was doing his best but all he was achieving was causing the dude pain. She beckoned Frank to stop for a moment and he walked over to her with Leonida's blood dripping from his knuckles.

"Carry on like this and he'll be dead but you'll be no closer to our money. What leverage do we have?"

Frank shrugged. His plan relied on hurting the guy until he squealed, which plainly wasn't working. Mary Lou sauntered toward Leonida, circling him before stopping in front of him. She leaned forward and raised his head by gently moving his chin.

"How did it come to this? You are not looking in good shape. I hope you understand unless you tell us what we want to know, my son will continue to beat on you until you are dead. That could take a minute, an hour or a day. Or longer. If I make a phone call, I could get someone who could kill you over the course of a week… or more."

She bent down until her lips were next to his right ear.

"A week or longer: imagine that."

Leonida strained to look at Mary Lou's face but she had to stand up before he could check out her expression. When their eyes locked, he thought through the reality of her words. He swallowed hard. Mary Lou stood and waited.

"The key in my jacket opens a locker at the station. The money's in there."

"If I send someone over and the green isn't there, do you understand I'll make that phone call?"

"It's there. I promise."

One of Frank's goons rummaged through pockets until he found the key. Then with a nod to Mary Lou he left the room. Mary Lou pulled a gun from her waistband and shot Leonida in the head.

"Clean up this mess, Frank. And then find out how you missed that key. Now, take me somewhere decent to stay for tonight. Tomorrow I want to get back to your sister."

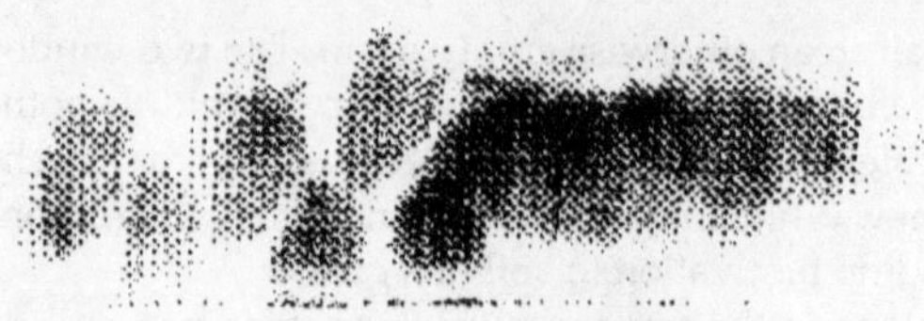

21

DESPITE HIS ILL-health, Teddy Prescott came through for Bobby yet again and soon Alice's name was added to the roster of legitimate gaming professionals. Work began in earnest. A vessel had been located, bought and renovations were in motion. The infrastructure was only half the story because a casino was successful if you used the right people and that was proving to be harder than they'd imagined.

The riverboat's route would take it on a loop between Davenport near Iowa City and Fort Madison further south. Every two-bit outfit on both sides of the Mississippi wanted to get in on the action but there simply wasn't room to fit all those beaks in the trough. Instead, Alice found hiring dealers, watchers and counters too difficult.

"Everyone we approach is in somebody's pocket—it's ridiculous. We can't trust anyone because they owe somebody else a tithe."

"And we don't have this problem with the Lady Fortune?"

"Hell no."

"That's the answer: bring in the best we have from Vegas to do a stint afloat and every outfit will see they've got no way to earn off us. They'll back off and if there's anyone worth hiring, then we can afford to pay them a premium. At least while the dust settles on the venture."

Alice understood the riverboat, which they'd christened the Queen of Sheba for no good reason Alice could fathom, would draw gamblers away from local games but their real market was tourists and high rollers. None of the penny ante hustlers nearby would lose out of the big money because neither group frequented their dive bars now.

Her other thought—and natural response which she hadn't acted on yet —was to break a few heads so the various gangs who were buzzing around their ears would receive a clear message to stay out of their way. Alice knew her Mama would want a more subtle approach. Mary Lou preferred to give everybody a chance to do the right thing. If they made a poor choice, a ton of shit would descend on them, but they had an opportunity to succeed upfront.

With the Queen of Sheba fresh out of the dry dock, they sailed the steamer up and down the mighty Mississippi as a pre-launch for the casino. A special guest list was operating where you only got on board if you were a Vegas regular or local dignitary.

Like all Lagotti venues, cameras operated in every room. Technology had moved on from the early days of the Palace and video replaced the need to pick up the film from each device. Instead surveillance was set up to catch thieves and blackmail the rich and powerful.

The launch showed the debauchery of the average joe and revealed a few minor glitches in their security. With one round trip under their belts, the rest would be a walk in the park.

THE WINDY CITY offered Mary Lou opportunities way beyond riverboat gambling and with the mob receded into the distance, there was every reason to exploit them as much as possible. In reality, the lack of any organized approach to criminal activity created a hole into which she happily jumped in.

The sheer size of Chicago as a major city meant there were millions of worker bees and the onslaught of the Reagan years had left them with fewer rights and a much quieter voice. There remained unions representing the case for labor over capital, but they had a smaller number of supporters than in the good old days. Mary Lou figured they needed an edge and she'd be happy to supply it.

Union membership was still strong among government workers like teachers and fire fighters although they weren't militant because of their sense of vocation. The same couldn't be said of the private sector and that is where Mary Lou focused her efforts.

The Roofers and Bricklayers Union represented those in the building profession and Mary Lou reckoned they'd want to ensure they had continuity of employment. With the large volume of skyscrapers still ripping through the horizon, there was a huge amount of money to be made from the inherent conflict between big business and the contractors they hired.

"So let me get this straight: you want my members to pay you out of their hard-earned wages in case the bosses turn violent. And that is something that hasn't happened in Chicago since before the Korean War."

"That is correct."

Mary Lou sat with Jerred Dudley in the headquarters of the Roofers and Bricklayers Union building. The irony was not lost on her that the joint was a decrepit mess but it was no worse than she had been expecting.

"That's not much of a proposal now is it?"

"You see Jerred. That depends on your perspective. If all you ever do is to look back over your shoulder at the lessons of the past, it doesn't come across as an interesting proposition. But if you're the man who has his eyes set on the future, that's a different matter."

"And I suppose you think I'm that sort of guy?"

"Naturally. I need not remind you of the brute economics facing your men. Big corporations spend millions to vie with each other to build the tallest, the fanciest skyscrapers in the world. They rely on hiring locals to do all the hard work. Only trouble is that union rates of pay cut into their profit and they are tempted to bring in outside agencies."

"We make our contributions so those kind of problems don't arise."

"Haven't happened in the past. Sometimes bribes are not enough."

"Listen lady, we do not get involved in bribery. We pay into an arbitration service so industrial action is minimized."

"You must consider what happens if that fails. Four major projects are about to break ground in the next six months and your members need to be on site for all of them."

"I am aware, but I don't see why you are bothering me with this."

"Because Jerred, I have it on good authority that you will face this problem very soon."

Dudley laughed and allowed himself to wallow in his perceived joke. All the while, Mary Lou sat and stared at him. Motionless.

"I suppose you want me to believe you can save us from an event that isn't likely to happen."

"Oh, it will."

"Tell you what: come back when we actually have a problem and if you fix it, we'll have another conversation. Until then, you're wasting my time."

A DROP OF blood splatted on Alice's cheek after the sharp blast of air flashed past. Nikolay slammed to the ground almost before the slug had landed in Mama's body. As though he knew it was coming. The tear that fell out of Bobby's eye and deposited itself on Mama's chin.

Total disorientation. No sooner had Alice hit the floor, she lost track of which direction she was facing. Her entire focus was on Bobby holding Mama. Her red pool growing and pouring down her body and over Bobby too.

Alice looked down at his hand and they were still listening to the sermon. The constant monotone was hard to follow. She wished the priest would shut up. A brief twist of her head revealed Frank sat on Bobby's other side.

He was bowed and his hands gripped his knees like they were about to fall off. Alice had no idea quite how he was coping—they'd hardly spoken since the day Mama died. His knuckles were white. Not going well.

Alice swallowed and blinked. Then she was back on the Queen of Sheba.

22

THAT WEEKEND, BACK in the summerhouse, Mary Lou, Bobby and Alice mulled over the week's events.

"We can nix any plans for labor racketeering. Illinois is dead to us. The lack of organized crime has turned the town soft. The unions have figured out how to get on with management so we have no leverage."

"How many did you hit?"

"Double digits: builders, carpenters, road repairers, duct repairs, refuse collectors and so on. I've tried them all and got nowhere. It's time to leave Illinois."

"Apart from the Queen of Sheba, of course."

"We need to get out—there's nothing here for us."

"Gambling. That's working really well. We might not be at full pelt yet but we're in profit and set to do even better this year and next."

"Bobby's right. And I know we can build on the work we've previously done. We should not walk away at this point."

"There's a time to stay and a moment to go. And now we should say goodbye to the Land of Lincoln."

"Why not sleep on this? The revenue from the riverboat has been good for us already. We shouldn't throw the baby out with the bath water."

Alice nodded to reinforce Bobby's concerns. Her eyes flitted from him over to Mama and back again. All her hard work was about to be poured down the drain by her mother. It made no sense but what flashed across her mind was how the decision was so irrational.

"We're leaving Illinois and there's nothing more to say."

Alice walked out the room and headed into the kitchen for more coffee. As she returned, she found Bobby sat on a lounger with a cigar in one hand.

"Did you storm out or were you thirsty?"

"BOTH. DO YOU know what happened in there?"

"Not too sure. Mary Lou hadn't talked about this. I can see why the labor racket is not for us. But the Queen of Sheba is set to rake in a lot of cash."

"Yep."

They were silent for a spell and the only sounds came from Mary Lou inside the summerhouse.

"What'll we do?"

"Keep the place running—at least for a while. Mama has had a series of knockbacks and that has clouded her judgment. Give her time for the dust to settle."

"How long is she going to need? I mean I can't sit here for a week and wait for her to see sense."

"If you go back tomorrow, I can handle the situation here."

"You intend to deal with Mama?"

Alice allowed an enormous laugh to erupt out of her mouth—so much so, her hand was forced to quickly muffle the noise. They both turned their heads to check on the summerhouse door but it remained firmly shut. Bobby smiled.

"She's a force to be reckoned with, but she has been known to listen to me."

Alice raised one eyebrow in disbelief as a response.

"No, really. But I don't have those kinds of conversation in public."

"That's your idea of pillow talk, I suppose?"

"Do not get fresh, young lady. In private, away from people, is all I meant."

ALICE AND BOBBY sat down with Mary Lou, who had been sitting at the desk making lists. Once she noticed their return, she stood up and joined them on the more comfortable seating.

"Is there anything else for us to discuss?"

"Alice will go back to the Queen of Sheba tomorrow and begin the wind down. I'm sure we can find someone to buy the license pretty quick."

"No more boat trips, you understand darling? We are quitting Illinois as of this minute."

"Yes, Mama."

A glance to Bobby. Alice was far from happy lying to her mother but they couldn't afford to stop the riverboat operation now. The payoff for all their hard work would land in their laps over the course of the next twelve months.

"Good girl. I can always rely on my Alice."

Mama hadn't spoken those words to her daughter since before she was in High School. She almost felt like a child again. This perspective repeated itself that night when Alice stayed over in her old bedroom. She was so unnerved that when she woke up in the darkness just after midnight, she crept downstairs and crashed out on one of the living room couches.

Before the rest of the house surfaced, Alice got up and headed back.

BOBBY RECKONED HE awoke first but Mary Lou was already staring at him. He rolled over and they hugged.

"I think I heard Alice's convertible roar into action a few minutes ago."

"Me too. I wonder why she's off in such a hurry. She could have waited for us to have breakfast together."

"Perhaps she wants to beat the worst of the traffic."

"Even so."

She nuzzled in and they hugged some more.

"Do you still feel the same way about Illinois this morning?"

"Yes, babe."

"Because I'm not so convinced."

"Oh? The Queen of Sheba will make us a lot of money over the next two or three years."

Bobby was puzzled because Mary Lou had made a complete turnaround since last night.

"Keep the riverboat?"

"Sure thing. Why not? You think we should ditch it? To be honest, Alice has done another fantastic job and we should let her carry on. It's right for her and good for us."

"I agree."

"I thought you just said the opposite. You really should decide what you believe and stick to it, babe."

Mama's Gone

Bobby continued the hug which turned into kissing and before long, neither were focused on the Prairie State.

ST THERESA CHURCH stood on East Ramon and South Farrell Drive. A new build from the 1940s, it didn't come across as a bastion of the Holy Roman Empire from the outside. The modern facade hid the grim reality of the Christian temple. As you walked through the entrance, you were greeted by row upon row of wooden benches facing away from you and positioned so the altar was the main attraction. Halfway along on the left was a large cupboard with two doors, one at each end.

Without giving it a moment's attention, Mary Lou headed straight for the confessional and entered on the right-hand side. The space was poorly lit and a small window slid open once she'd closed the door behind her. She kneeled down because there was a cushion on the floor and no chair.

"May God, who has enlightened every heart, help you know your sins and trust in his mercy."

"I haven't been to a church or spoken to a priest since I was fifteen years old, but I want to speak with one now."

"My child: this is a confessional. I am happy to spend time and discuss what troubles you, but unless you wish to confess your sins to me, then we must go somewhere else."

"Then what are we waiting for?"

Mary Lou followed Father Ardal Carmoody past the altar to a door on the other side of the church, which she hadn't noticed when she first arrived. The priest led her down a short corridor and into his office, indicating for her to sit down while Carmoody walked around to sit at his desk.

"So what's troubling you, my dear?"

"HOW'S THE WORLD of Mark Twain?"

Bobby and Alice sat in her South Dubuque office overlooking the harbor. It wasn't her favorite place, but it was functional. Tables, chairs, window, filing cabinets—without the luxuries she'd enjoyed at the Lady Fortune. The town lacked the charm of Las Vegas too—or rather it had none of the razzmatazz.

"Same old. We need new ways to squeeze the green out of the tourists. The high rollers seem to enjoy not being stuck inside a darkened hall."

"Nice to hear we're doing something right. But you didn't ask me to visit this backwater to give me good news."

Alice took a sip from her coffee and swallowed as though the liquid contained razor blades.

"How's Mama, would you say?"

"Fine. She is concerned we still have too much exposure in narcotics but apart from that, she's okay."

"I'm not talking about business. Is she in a good shape?"

Silence. Bobby ground his molars and stared at Alice, making no sign of answering. He glugged some of his coffee down and Alice felt as though he didn't take his eyes off her for a second.

"Why d'you ask?"

"Have you forgotten what happened with Mama just the other week?"

"Are you still thinking about that?"

"Of course, aren't you?"

"She was tired—not thinking straight."

"I'm not sure that's all it was. I mean: the next day you said she acted like the night before never happened."

"Lack of energy—no more and no less. I spend way more time with her than you do so I know what I'm talking about."

"I am concerned, Bobby. Mama never gets anything as wrong as she did then—as though she was a different person."

"Don't worry, it's all fine. Only low blood sugar."

Alice shook her head but failed to respond. She couldn't understand how Bobby wasn't able to see what she could. Mama was not the same, but she had no idea what was up.

"You don't sound certain. Think for a minute. Is there anything you can think of?"

"Tiredness is all."

"Then give her a vacation. If you're right, take her away for some R&R. Then she'll come back and be completely better."

Bobby picked at a piece of fluff on his sleeve while Alice watched and tried not to fume. Her concerns were genuine and he appeared to ignore them completely. In reality, he had noticed his Mary Lou had behaved a little strangely. She would vanish for hours at a time and not say where she'd been. More than that, she acted as though she hadn't been anywhere even though he knew she hadn't been at home.

He considered tailing her but decided against it: whatever she was doing was none of his business. Unless she had started an affair which was unlikely because he was still getting action in the bedroom. A vacation might clear the air.

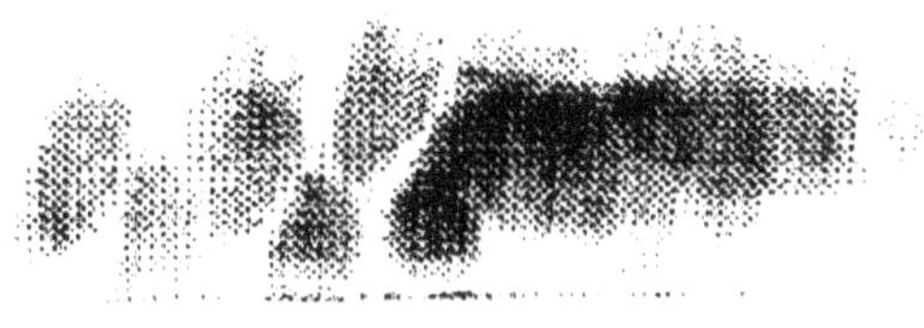

23

MIAMI SURE WAS a crazy town—the mix of people and the Latino beats conspired to produce a city teetering on the edge of excitement every day of the week. Boca Raton was where gangsters went to die and Miami was the place for those who chose to live.

Their seafront hotel was close enough to the action on Ocean Drive to be fun, but the Jackson Hotel had sufficient stars on its hoardings to ensure the hardcore party animals stayed away. Mary Lou and Bobby sat at a table in the patio restaurant watching the world walk past. They held hands all the while and pointed out to each other amusing sights: rollerbladers with neon pink thongs and their miniature pooches, bowling ball shaped men sweating into white linen suits, wrinkled hags wearing leopard-print butt-length dresses. The freak show that was Miami Beach.

"I'm glad you talked me into this."

"We both deserved a break. It's been a tough few months."

"I'd forgotten how much I love this town."

"Didn't know you'd been here before."

"A lifetime ago. Before we met."

"I see. Were you with Frank?"

"He wasn't born then."

"I meant his father."

FRANK LAGOTTI FOLLOWED Mary Lou into a boutique of Collins Avenue filled with chichi beachwear. She grabbed six or eight different bikinis of varying styles, colors and patterns. After what felt like an interminable amount of time, she reappeared from the charging rooms with a red and white striped bikini which looked the same as all the others to him. She kissed him as they left the store.

"I've never had anything as pretty as this in my life. Thank you."

"De nada."

She planted another kiss on him, only this time fully on the mouth. He tasted warm and she melted as his fingers ran down her spine, finishing with a squeeze of her ass. Her silver boutique bag in one hand and her man in the other, Mary Lou headed back to their small hotel and into their room to change into the new purchase.

They had fresh white linen on the bed—the maid had got in early—and the headboard was pastel blue to match the nautical theme of the rest of the furniture. Frank pulled out his swimming trunks from a drawer and Mary Lou unwrapped her bikini from its tissue paper and placed both items gingerly on the covers of the bed.

Without saying a word, but in perfect synchrony, they both chucked their clothes on the floor and stood, soaking in the sight of the other's body. Mary Lou walked round to give Frank a kiss while he wrapped his arms round her torso, one hand massaging her right breast. Tingles flashed along her spine and she leaned into him to feel him against her skin.

"I MEANT HIS father"

"Huh?"

Mary Lou was confused. She looked around and saw Bobby but only a minute ago she'd been with Frank, the man who'd given her the twins. She clung to her chair and hoped the world would right itself soon. Bobby sensed her distress as she dug her nails into his hand and decided to just remain calm and let her ride out the storm in her mind. She knew she was in Miami and she closed her eyes for a second…

Frank made Mary Lou stand up and she felt his groin pressing against her rose tattoo. A tingle sprung from her crotch as his fingers investigated her body. Despite the problems with the First Bank of Baltimore, they were in a wonderful place together. Like they were inseparable and perfectly attuned to each other. Bound by more than the sweat caused by the intensity of their sex and the heat of the night.

On the second day of their trip, they hung out the 'Do Not Disturb' sign on their room door and occupied the morning naked, in bed and happy. Perhaps for the first time in Mary Lou's life. Then they hit the beach before lunch and spent the early afternoon people watching in a cafe. When they packed, Mary Lou put her new bikini back in its wrapping and into its silver store bag before depositing it into her luggage. On the plane, she nestled on Frank's shoulder and fell asleep, content from the forty-eight hour sojourn.

MARY LOU OPENED her eyes with a jolt and saw Bobby sat next to her on the Jackson patio. More disorientation. A sip of coffee helped to give her focus and she recalled the reason for being in Miami.

"I'm glad you talked me into this."

"Tough few months, huh?"

"Sure have been. At least the boy is getting a grip on himself. And Alice is doing fine—a real treasure."

"One smart cookie, that girl."

"Always was. She'd let Frank run and wade through the swamp and then glide around the dirt to avoid the shit."

"Self-reliant too. Very mature head on those shoulders."

"Knows what she wants and ruthless when she needs to be."

"Have you come to terms about her… lifestyle?"

"I've never had a problem with Alice being gay—I just don't like passive-aggressive bullshit. That's a totally different ball game and I won't stand for it. Never have and I'm not gonna start now."

Bobby stroked her hand with his thumb. Mary Lou was a fabulous woman and he was a lucky man to exist in her orbit. He turned to soak in her beauty with the sunset in the background and realized he'd forgotten how much he was physically attracted to her.

"Shall we return to the room?"

"I'm good here enjoying the view."

"What if we go up and fuck until it's time to eat?"

Mary Lou released his hand and stood up.

"Should have said. Come on then."

DESPITE BOBBY'S CLAIM that all Mama needed was a week's R&R, Alice was not satisfied. So she took a plane to visit her brother in AC. This was her first trip to the Lucky Nugget and she tried her best not to be disappointed—or at least not show it.

Before the end of their teenage years, the twins learned not to spend too much time alone together because arguments always followed. There was something in their chemistry that caused explosions. As adults, their lives had separated and their different paths enabled each to avoid the other at almost every turn.

The appearance of his sister at the casino was a genuine surprise for Frank. Since Leonida's untimely departure, he had not yet hired a replacement. There had been several excellent candidates, but Bobby had gained trust issues and couldn't bring himself to let anyone inside his circle.

The impact of his indecision was simple: Frank was working harder than he'd ever done before in his life—and he was stressed. Then Alice appeared at reception seeking an appointment with Mr. Lagotti.

"Hello stranger."

"Hi, Frank."

"What brings you to this side of the country? I hope you're not here to offer me advice because I really don't have time to listen to your anecdotes about management acumen."

"Hadn't crossed my mind. You got problems? I'm here about Mama, not the family business."

"Yeah I had local difficulties. Hasn't Mama mentioned the trouble with Leonida?"

"Who?"

"Leonida Acerbi, my casino manager. We had to… let him go after we found his fingers were getting too sticky for his own good."

"And your problem is…?"

"I can't find anyone to replace him and it will send me to an early grave."

Alice chuckled at the thought of Frank pulling his finger out and grafting instead of fucking his way through life. Any sympathy in her bones for his situation ebbed away, but she tried not to show it as she was here to seek his help—for the first time since she was sixteen.

IN THE CONFINES of his office, Alice felt better able to talk to Frank without the constant desire to bait him. He might be snowed under by the responsibilities of leadership, but she saw a glint in his eyes—almost a glow—that made her think he was evolving as a human being in front of her. Maybe he enjoyed bossing people around.

"What's the matter, sis'?"

"Something's not right with Mama, but I can't put my finger on it."

"And does Bobby share your view?"

"No. He reckons she's tired and nothing more. That's why they've gone off to Florida this week. What about you?"

"Me? Nothing. She looked okay last time I saw her. In fact, she seemed more than fine under the circumstances."

"Your personnel issues."

"Uh-huh."

Alice wondered how reliable Frank's opinion was to her. In the past he'd shown himself to be one of the most inept and useless people she'd ever had the misfortune of knowing. Yet Mama had set him up to run a casino just like Alice. The woman had a deeper insight than Alice, for sure. Perhaps it was all in her head and she was worrying over nothing. To shut down the Queen of Sheba wasn't fantasy—it nearly became a reality.

"The thing is that some of Mama's decisions have been…"

She could not bring herself to say what was lingering at the back of her mind. Dare not utter those negative thoughts out loud.

"…ill-advised."

Frank tilted his head to one side, not sure of what to make of Alice and her concerns. He figured she must be serious otherwise she'd never have wasted her valuable time on him, but she had nothing specific to offer. Women's intuition didn't cut it with him.

"How so?"

"She wanted to shut down the Queen of Sheba because she hadn't been able to gouge any of the Chicago unions."

"And you'd have been left running the bathtub with no baby."

"This isn't about me: it's Mama we should focus on."

FRANK COULDN'T HELP himself and he let out a guffaw. Alice's concerns for Mama just boiled down to fear of appearing to fail. Like everything in Alice's life. He had almost believed her but luckily he caught himself in time.

"Alice, listen to yourself. It's not Mama that needs help: it is you. Can't you see Mama's doing what's best for the family? If a casino has to be abandoned, then so be it. Same for me here. She and Bobby have big plans and we have to accept they aren't showing us the entire picture. Not right now, anyway."

"Bobby agreed with me on this. He thought she was wrong too—only he let things blow over and Mama changed her mind. But that didn't stop us losing a million dollar a month profit from the riverboat operation. Just because she was snubbed."

Frank couldn't conceive of his Mama not making the right decision first time. So Alice and Bobby must have misunderstood. Or something. The grim possibility that Mama was wrong would not get a firm purchase in his head. There was no way he could survive without her being there for him. This was not the point for him to lose her.

"Mama's fine and you are losing your mind. I might have done too many lines of coke in my life but you are the one who's paranoid. You should listen to yourself. Mama says something you don't like the sound of because it hits your operation in the belly, next you're traveling round the country announcing our Mama is a psycho."

"That's not what I said."

"The only time you had a problem was when she threatened the Queen of Sheba. Admit it, sis'. You're afraid Mama's gonna take your favorite ball off you and lock it in the summerhouse cupboard."

"Fuck you."

"And the horse you rode in on."

Alice stood up and stormed out of the office, out of the Lucky Nugget and straight to the airport. Having calmed down, she thought about hopping over to Sam as Boston was so close. She wanted to spend the night in her lover's arms but when she rang, there was no reply and Alice didn't have the stomach for more disappointment today: she wasn't in the mood. On the flight back, she shut her eyes and dreamed of Sam's body and all its crevices.

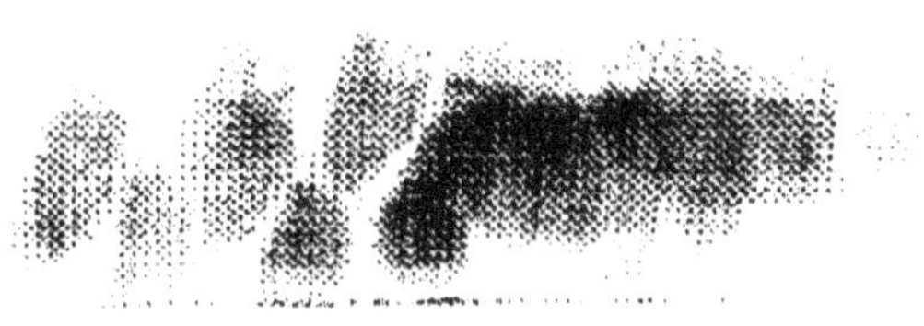

24

MARY LOU AND Bobby lay in their Jackson Hotel bed and watched the evening transform into night. Tired and a little sticky around the thighs, Mary Lou's head rested on Bobby's chest as they both watched stars appear and twinkle in the sky. Her hand stroked his kneecap while several of his fingers supported one of her breasts.

"First San Francisco and then Chicago. It's not easy anymore."

"It'll all be fine. Some you win, some you lose."

"Seems like we're losing a few in a row."

"You worry too much, Bobby. Next year we'll take San Francisco. The Russians have bought themselves a small amount of time to make hay. And as for Chicago, I never thought we'd wrap up that parcel. It was worth a trip and a few days in a hotel but we both knew we weren't serious otherwise we would have gone over there with a large crew and spilled enough blood until everyone saw sense."

"Maybe so… I spoke with Milton. The Palace didn't make money last month. First time ever. He reckoned the Hollywood johns aren't coming to the parties. There's fresh competition from gangs offering cheaper pills and underage thrills."

"That man has been blaming someone else for his own failure to run his business for twenty-five years to my certain knowledge."

"You may well be right but that doesn't mean there aren't fellas nipping at our ankles. They are real and we need to deal."

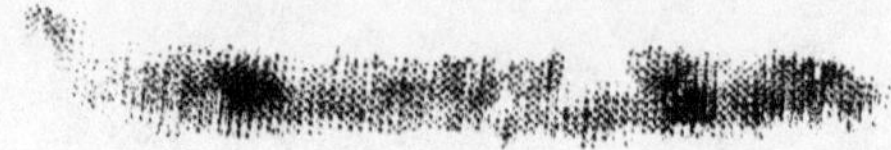

DEAL. MARY LOU'S mind flitted back to the moment she and Frank Lagotti were escaping cross-country from Baltimore and made some money in Vegas. She had no clue how to play poker but he knew it all. He held the cards in his palm like a pro and threw them down so they rotated a full circle before landing perfectly for the dealer to read them.

She admired the skills he'd built up to do it, learned in the joint during his interminable incarcerations. As they fled to California, Frank never missed a step no matter what problem they had to face. His mind raced to get past the hurdle before him. Never over—always around.

Once they got a hundred bucks together in clean bills, they hightailed it out the casino. Seconds away from being caught by the mob, the cops and the Feds. Mary Lou felt so alive: never knowing if that breath would be her last.

Like the day when she and Frank argued on the way back from a gang meet before the heist. This was at a time before they knew they could trust each other. He blamed her for sleeping with the bank rat, Carter and she accused Frank of fucking men in jail. The hate and pain in his eyes as the words left her lips. One drop of his spittle landed on her cheek and she thought he would kill her with his bare hands as soon as the jalopy screeched to a halt. They were alive in that casino though. And in love by then. What was its name?

Doesn't matter. When they walked around town and thought they were being followed by a mob guy. Frank had the brains to get them to hide in a lingerie store and the fella was too embarrassed to follow them in. She grabbed a beautiful bra-and-panties set to pretend to try on but Frank wouldn't let her keep it as they ran out the rear entrance.

"We're bank robbers, not thieves."

"Aw, but I like it, Frank."

"AW, DON'T STOP. I like it, Frank."

"Huh?"

Bobby's hand was now massaging her breast. This was in direct response to Mary Lou's hand moving up from his knee and somehow reached his groin, which she had been stroking absentmindedly for the last five minutes.

"Don't stop, Frank."

Mama's Gone

He could see Mary Lou's eyes were shut as his palm moved toward her rose, but he couldn't quite reach without moving them both. Bobby considered his options and then placed a hand under her head and replaced his body with three pillows. That freed him up to lick her torso and make his way down to her belly button, and then her tattoo. All the while, her eyes stayed shut.

"Don't stop…"

Still Mary Lou's eyes remained closed and Bobby hoped and imagined the pleasure she was experiencing. The odd judder of her thighs gave him a positive vibe. As her breathing intensified, Bobby noticed the perspiration on her stomach. Then, as he looked up her body and watched her torso heaving with the need to gather oxygen, for a moment one eye opened and cast about until it locked onto the sight of his head.

A scream and Bobby stopped in an instant, not knowing how he'd hurt her. Mary Lou kicked him in the face as she scurried to the other side of the bed, rolled off and grabbed a pistol resting in her clutch bag lying on the floor. A second later, the safety was off and she aimed her piece directly at Bobby's heart.

"Who the fuck are you?"

"I'm Bobby."

"Frank?"

"Bobby."

Calm voice. No motion to his body. Both hands visible. Staring straight into her eyes. Into her soul.

"Where's my Frank?"

"He's dead. Do you remember? He died before you met me. I am Bobby Trevisan."

She slumped onto the floor, sobbing. He walked round and removed her finger from the trigger. Then he sat next to her, holding and comforting the woman he loved until the tears subsided.

BOBBY HADN'T SPOKEN again about the incident in Miami and Mary Lou hardly noticed it had occurred by the time she'd got herself back together. The rest of the vacation passed with nothing happening of any significance. Cocktails, sun, sex and lying by the rooftop pool of the Jackson. These were the tropes of their Florida experience—and retail therapy.

When they returned, Bobby suggested he should hustle a little more and let her hang in the summerhouse and enjoy the weather. Mary Lou admitted to herself she didn't have the energy she once had and was happy to take advantage of Bobby's generosity—if only for a short while.

She spent the mornings in the conservatory and Irma made sure she ate a healthy lunch with a dose of coffee. Then a sun lounger in the afternoon. When Bobby appeared in the evening, Mary Lou had invested in a nap.

Three weeks into this new relaxed lifestyle, Mary Lou lay on a recliner around two and thought how she missed Bobby and wanted to see him. But he was out of reach. She ached for Bobby the same way she yearned for Frank each time he was in jail.

THE LAST STRETCH when he was in the Baltimore Penitentiary was the worst. Frank's Shylock step uncle kept Mary Lou in clover but that didn't help her fill up the days. Endless hours strolling around shitty areas of Baltimore waiting for the next visit. The green was enough to get by on, but not to afford any luxuries. She'd scrimp and save just to smuggle in extra smokes for Frank.

He was the only one in the gang to do any time for the previous robbery. Kid stuff: a supermarket heist gone wrong. Word on the street was that Frank's buddy, Louis had squealed to the cops who were lying in wait when the fellas exited the store. As soon as Frank was out on bail, Louis took an express descent down the outside of a building and Frank never spoke of him again.

Mary Lou never liked Louis anyway: the first night they met at one of the many parties in the neighborhood, Frank introduced her to him. Thirty minutes later, the guy had his hand on a place not even Frank's fingers ventured for several years. From that moment on, she never allowed herself to be on her own with Louis. She loved Frank dearly by the end, but his friends and family sucked elephant cocks.

Those three summers Frank was away stretched to eternity. Mary Lou was young and had needs of her own. She wasn't ready to be a gangster's moll and yearned to do more than sit at home and wait for her man's return. She dated occasionally but never someone from the neighborhood. If word got back to the Shylock that she was fucking around then she'd have been on a one-way trip to oblivion.

The sex meant nothing, but it relieved the boredom and it took her out of that tiny apartment. All she did was spend a few brief hours in someone else's cramped home with her legs apart and the tingles flowing if she was lucky. Most of the time she'd jump into the shower as soon as she returned to wash away the dried spunk and a sense of being dirty generated by the couplings. No matter who was trying to make her orgasm, she felt so painfully alone.

Mama's Gone

She spent the last six months with an S&M freak hoping the different experience might help her feel something but handcuffs and nipple clamps left her sore and just as empty as any other way of fucking she tried during those long years away from Frank.

The only solace she found was watching the late evening chat show with a bowl of cereal for company. Vodka instead of milk and the constant sound of crunching inside her skull to mask the canned laughter from the TV.

THE FIRST NIGHT Frank was out of jail, Mary Lou had tried to be as understanding as she could. It had been years since he'd been with a woman and her expectations had been low, even though she longed to be intimate with the man. After he had fallen asleep and she'd finished herself off, Mary Lou went into the bathroom to take stock. She stared at herself in the mirror, assessing every blemish of her skin and freckle on her face.

At some point, she poked at her breasts as though they were bearing the weight of her ennui. Then her attention returned to her nose and she leaned in to get the best look. The coldness of the basin dug itself in against her rose as she moved her head one way, then the other, to assess the damage done despite the paucity of her years on this planet.

Every so often, she heard Frank talk to himself as he slept and an occasional vehicle zoomed past. This was the last time she would be by herself. Her moments of solitude were over now he had returned.

Mary Lou pulled down the lower lids of her eyes and let the skin flip back into place. A childish game she repeated two more times. Then she blinked to get her sight to return to normal.

She opened her eyes and knew exactly where she was: Oakcrest Drive. The crow's feet in the corners were a clear demonstration of how much time she had allowed to pass in her life. Mary Lou knew she had to stop this malaise. She couldn't waste her days away again like she did waiting for Frank to serve his debt to society.

On vacation, Bobby had been right: there had been too many losses of late and the moment for action had arrived. They needed to bring the fight to San Francisco.

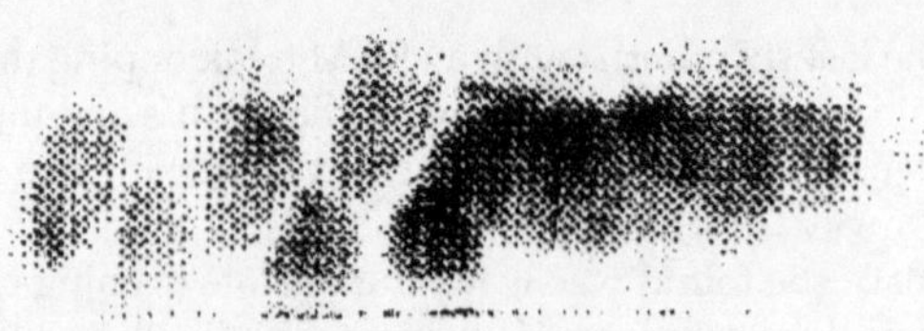

25

MARY LOU WOULD not sit around and let herself get cornered like happened with Frank when they were fleeing the heist. If she'd learned anything from the time spent in Burbank Airport, it was to watch your back and come out fighting. They were out to beat her and so were the Russians in San Francisco. She could kneel on the ground next to the lockers, pinned down by gunfire from the hoods, or she could pick up Frank's piece and shoot her way to freedom.

We must obliterate the Markov scum from this world and that is what she would do. To put this plan into practice, she needed some high class muscle, so she asked Milton for his help.

"Thanks for dropping a dime. We don't speak nearly as much as we used to."

"I need your help in a matter I wish to resolve. Can I count on you?"

"With my life, you know that. What do you need?"

She outlined her idea and Milton listened intently. When she finished, he whistled allowing his exhalation to form into a single note. He hadn't heard anything as bold for many years. Respect to the woman.

THE NEXT DAY, Mary Lou drove over to LA to speak with Milton in person. The Palace had faded over time, the paintwork was chipped, plasterwork crumbling, but Mary Lou didn't notice as she walked along the corridors to Milton's office. Like every other operation the man had ever touched, he had let it turn to shit. The only difference with the Palace's call girl racket was that it took twenty long years instead of Milton's usual six months to fuck it up.

"Thanks for the opportunity. I doubt if you realize how good it is to be working with you again. I've missed being so close to the action."

"Don't know what you're talking about. Let's get down to business, shall we?"

"Sure, I'm listening."

"You need to source at least ten reliable men."

"I'll need a short while as I am not in that line at the moment, but it can be done. Just a function of time and money."

"Once we've all met up to go through the details, then we'll take the place when it's full."

"When all the Markovs are in one building?"

"Yes, that's what I said."

"How many vehicles do you want for the hit? Everyone in their own or as few as possible for a fast getaway?"

"There's no point doing it if we can't get safely away."

"Right..."

Milton tilted his head and looked at Mary Lou. He couldn't decide if his hesitation was caused by not concentrating on what Mary Lou had just said or if there was a disconnect between her words now and what she'd told him on the phone yesterday.

"You got a problem with this?"

"Not at all. I won't lose any sleep over a few dead Russians. From what little Bobby mentioned to me, sounds like it's payback time."

"Shoot 'em in the knee and get the hell out of Dodge."

"Knee? I thought we're killing them."

"Yep."

"Murder, not maim."

"Homicide is the name of the game."

"Good. You lost me there for a second."

"We send one fella in early to stake the place out and then the rest of the crew swoops in, does the job and gets out before any law enforcement can grab us."

"Shall we use Naldo?"

"Whoever you think is best. There'll be big bonuses for everyone when we get back."

"I'd advise you and Bobby to stay at home—or rather book and go to a restaurant that night. You must have a watertight alibi."

"Bobby?"

Mary Lou looked straight at Milton, who returned the gesture. There was his confusion coming right at him again.

"You don't want him there, do you?"

"Use the best you can get."

"And Bobby?"

"You decide—I told you."

Milton's mouth went dry as a sense of anxiety welled up inside. Was this an elaborate ruse by her to put Bobby in the line of fire? More likely he was being oversensitive and needed to keep his head in the game, but his instinct to double-check with the man might place a target on his skull.

Over the years, Mary Lou handled treachery the way a surgeon dealt with a malignant tumor. She smiled at him and relaxed back into her chair as though the main order of business had been taken care of.

"How's the Palace doing?"

"So-so. The Hollywood parties are fewer: the stars prefer a more private space for their booze, narcotics and fucking nowadays. It's the control of the studios: they want their product to be wholesome and clean. But our regulars still pass through although the cops are getting harder to pay off because we look more like a cathouse than somewhere for the rich and powerful to come. And play."

"Times are tough, Milton. Every year, it gets more difficult to make money out of the things on which we could always rely: prostitution, narcotics. Even gambling."

"For real? I thought the casinos were doing great guns."

"They are today, but look what's happened in Vegas. Entertainment companies now own mob venues. Crazy. And the only reason gaming has been permitted outside Vegas is so states can get their grubby hands on hard-working people's money. So that means they'll over-regulate the fuck out of it and we'll be pushed to one side. Not today or tomorrow, but eventually."

ELEVEN MEN AND a solitary woman sat in a large disused room at the top of the Palace. Mary Lou, Milton, Naldo and nine other guys who you'd be a fool to mess with even on a bright day in the middle of summer. Each had found a chair and they'd formed a loose circle like they were attending a group therapy session.

Milton made some cursory introductions so everyone more or less knew each other. Most of the crew had worked with at least some others before but in the heat of the moment, it paid to know who your friends were.

"When we go in, we enter hard. The best we can hope is that they aren't expecting us. Once the first shot rings out then they'll draw their guns and fire back. We need to be slick, fast and ruthless. If we leave one Markov alive, they will come and destroy us."

The men murmured to each other—not because the job was too difficult but because their adrenalin was already pumping and they weren't even in the right city yet. Mary Lou ran through the family tree and took pains to make it clear she wanted them to identify each body so she could keep an accurate tally of who they still had to whack.

"Is there anything you want to add, Milton?"

"Not really. You covered the important points."

He glanced at his watch and a bead of sweat dropped onto his wrist. Then his eyes darted to the corridor and flitted back to Mary Lou. Almost on cue, the door opened and Bobby walked in and the entire room fell to an eerie hush.

"What're we doing here, people?"

"I've instigated an operation to clear up the Markov problem."

He nodded and took her off to one side so they wouldn't have to talk in front of the fellas.

"What are you doing?"

"Cutting out a tumor."

"We have a peace agreement with them. We shouldn't move on them unless they become an irritant or they break their word."

"They can't be trusted and we need to preempt their inevitable attack."

"No, it is to our advantage to get them to build on their San Francisco empire. That way, when we take over, we'll have something significant to own."

Bobby turned round to face the guys.

"Thanks for coming but there's been a change of plan. You can step down for now. Of course, we will cover your costs with a bonus for any inconvenience. Milton, will you get things organized?"

"Sure, Bobby. Always happy to help."

Mary Lou fumed where she stood. Arms folded, she said nothing and couldn't understand why Bobby was treating her this way. The betrayal of it all. In contrast, he could not wrap his head around why she believed now was the time to take out the Markovs. They didn't utter a single word to each other all the miles back to Palm Springs.

The next day Mary Lou woke up as though nothing had happened, but Bobby knew and remembered.

26

BOBBY POPPED OVER to Alice's apartment rather than spend time in her cramped and crummy office. A heap of Chinese food had just arrived and they spread all the boxes out on the dining room table.

"I think we've over ordered."

"You reckon?"

They sat down and pecked at the noodles, chicken, veg and rice until they thought they would burst. Half the meal remained untouched: Alice's prediction was right. Then she poured two more beers and they moved over to the couches to settle in for the evening.

"We nearly went to war a few days ago."

"What was the Bay of Pigs moment?"

"Don't joke. We were damn close. For reasons that escape me, she wanted to take absolute revenge on the Markovs."

"From San Francisco?"

"The same. She got Milton to put a crew together for a St Valentine's Day massacre. Good news is that even Milton, who's as craven as hell, knew it was wrong and dropped me a dime."

Alice sat and stared, mind racing, trying to process the implications of what Bobby just uttered. She had never heard of Mama be countermanded before. The idea of Milton and Bobby conspiring against Mama was shocking. The fact they felt they needed to do that was jaw-dropping.

"We walked onto their turf and tried to muscle them out, right?"

"More or less. There were poor choices on both sides which led to the bad blood. Didn't take long to resolve, which shows it wasn't that big a deal."

Alice accepted what he said but his response showed there were other situations not yet mentioned. Once he'd filled in the gaps, Alice had her head in her hands.

"This is the end."

He raised his eyebrows and sipped his beer.

"Not for a long time, but we need to make changes. Mary Lou needs more of a rear seat role—whether or not she wants it."

"You're not talking about ousting her."

"Encourage her to choose a more consultative position."

"Get her to step down, you mean."

Alice's words hung in the air and the two soaked in the idea that someone else must take over. Neither wanted to engage with what that meant or talk about what was to happen later. They sidestepped the whole topic for ten minutes as they lapsed back into general conversation.

ALICE SPENT THE next day ruminating on her chat with Bobby. They had discussed whether Bobby should run the business but he was insistent that he was not up for the job, claiming age and not wanting to tread on Mary Lou's toes. He was careful not to express an opinion who it should be even though there were only two contenders.

Did his silence on the matter imply he was in favor of Frank? Bobby rarely had any desire to stand in the center of a family squabble. He always ensured he was in a different room whenever the twins argued as kids. This left Alice with a simple thought: how could she make her mark as the leader of the new family? She didn't entertain the notion Frank should run the show for even a second.

Her analysis was quick and honest: Mama had worked out they needed to diversify and expand. The best way to grow was to form an alliance with another gang. A partnership forged out of strength would last the test of time because both parties would gain something significant from the other. The Lagotti family had large multi-state gaming and narcotics operations, and owned a string of call girl rings. They even had some stretch on the east coast and had the occasional Senator in their back pocket. These were assets other gangs would dream of having.

Alice knew the family's weaknesses too. They had insufficient hired hands to attack new territories: San Francisco showed that to be all too painfully true. And they'd been stumbling around desperate to find the Next

Big Thing they could seize for their own but nothing had appeared on the horizon.

Another issue was that their call girl operation hadn't moved with the times or expanded for as long as Alice could remember. Milton might be an old associate of Mama's but hadn't been pulling his weight. The Palace had always been a disgusting venue, but it was poorly managed too. Even Frank had worked out to split the Nugget into gambling and lap dancing.

When Milton saw the parties were going off the boil, he should have converted the first floor into something else: pole dancing for sure, but a gentleman's club, maybe, to attract a better quality of john who'd pay for a cocktail with a whore on his knee, before he walking upstairs to pop a pill and fuck her.

No matter. What they needed to do was find a partner: one who had muscle but little reach. Someone with the desire to grow but would cooperate and not just screw them over. Somebody with imagination. The interesting thing about the Markovs was that Nikolay still came to the table even though a nephew lay in the morgue. That showed he was serious about his business and believed the Lagottis could do him harm if the fighting had continued. These traits were what she was looking for although Alice was aware that many would see him as an enemy.

ALICE REACHED OUT to Nikolay Markov, who agreed to meet for a coffee. He was surprised to receive a phone call from the Lagotti girl and was intrigued to know what she had to say. Her mother and stepfather had acted like mooks a few months ago but it never hurt to talk. Nikolay might have been aggressive when negotiating with Mary Lou and Bobby, but despite appearances his ego was under control.

"Thank you for agreeing to meet up."

"I was surprised you called. Does your mother know what you are up to?"

"I'm not up to anything. The last occasion you met with members of my family, matters came to a head somewhat violently. Now the dust has settled, I thought we should at least have a conversation or two. There is an agreement operating in San Francisco."

"The truce is holding—for the moment. What makes you think there is anything to discuss?"

"Our shared operations in…"

Alice stumbled over the venue's name.

"…the Red Stocking. You should do your homework better."

"The name is less important than the fact that profits are up ever since we worked together."

"True. We have all benefitted in the short-term. Doesn't mean the place will make money in a year or two."

"But I'd like to think if revenues were to go south, we'd either figure out how to fix matters or use our brains and shut it down."

Nikolay stirred the sugar he'd dropped into his coffee. His eyes focused on his cup and then he stared at Alice without responding. He was keeping his cards close to his chest, but she expected him to play things cautiously.

"I heard your men were fierce fighters. They handled themselves very effectively against us."

"Your people are Americans. They have grown soft over the generations since they stepped off the boats from Italy. My guys are fresh arrivals with the blood of Cossacks coursing through their veins. They are tough; if they show any weakness, then I kill them."

A HOLLOW CACKLE erupted from Nikolay and Alice did her best to echo his extraordinary good humor but all she could manage was the smallest of grimaces.

"Once you've been in this country a while, you learn that sometimes it is who you know that counts and not what caliber pistol you're holding."

"There are stories that you hold politicians in your pockets and I offer the utmost respect to you if those tall tales are true."

Now it was Alice's turn to stir her cup and stare at Nikolay. That was his first positive statement about her family the man had ever uttered. Almost as if he knew the direction she was taking the conversation and wanted to hustle her to the end point.

"Work with people and you build up relationships that can last for decades."

"Your mother's achievements are well known. If we hadn't got off on such sour terms, I would have had the chance to find out more about her. These are the difficulties you face when blood is shed—not that my nephew was worth jack shit. I was concerned about the principle, not that sniveling piece of garbage. He came from my sister's loins, not mine."

Alice perceived a judder run along Nikolay's body as he mentioned his sibling. She almost felt a connection with him at that moment, but wondered if she had merely projected her own thoughts onto his actions.

"Family life isn't always a bed of roses."

"Tell me about it."

Nikolay checked the time on his watch.

"This has been a most pleasant exchange, but unless there is something specific to discuss, then I need to make a move."

"I wanted to hear your thoughts on us working more closely together. Our tribes would benefit."

"You and I?"

"Our families."

She knew he'd only asked her that to rattle her and she'd almost fallen for his ruse, but she was a smart cookie.

"If there are particular opportunities, then I am happy to consider them, but on similar terms to the Red Stocking."

"That deal was agreed to create a ceasefire. What I'm suggesting is a long-term partnership so we would split profits equally and fairly. That stops resentments building up, which lead to perceived sleights and loss of life. Successful businesses should be about making money, not killing people."

"I understand you might not want the Stocking as a basis for future considerations, but one thing is not negotiable: I would always be in charge. No woman has ever told me what to do and it ain't gonna happen now."

ALICE CONTINUED TO mull over each of Nikolay's words two days later when Sam made a rare appearance on the west coast. Despite telling herself how much she needed Sam in her life, Alice hadn't noticed her absence as she thought she would. There was only that time when Mama cracked before her eyes that Alice yearned for her lover.

In bed entwined with Sam's body, Alice wondered the extent she could trust Nikolay and whether a man—like Bobby, say—might thrash out a better deal, just to play off Nikolay's prejudices. Also, she needed to work out what he would need to be offered to give up control over any new operation.

Her musings were interrupted by Sam's fingers and tongue which were busy toying with her erogenous zones. She relaxed into the experience and spent the next hour fondling and fucking until both she and Sam were exhausted. With her head still within licking distance of Sam, Alice asked herself what other options did she have? Bobby was too old, Frank was too much and Milton was too incompetent.

"If you will hang around down there, do something useful, dear."

Sam's admonishment shook Alice back to reality. The Markov dynasty must wait at least until the morning. While Sam was in her bed, she should make best use of that succulent body. Thirty minutes later, she was asleep while Alice carried on ruminating on Nikolay Markov.

Mama's Gone

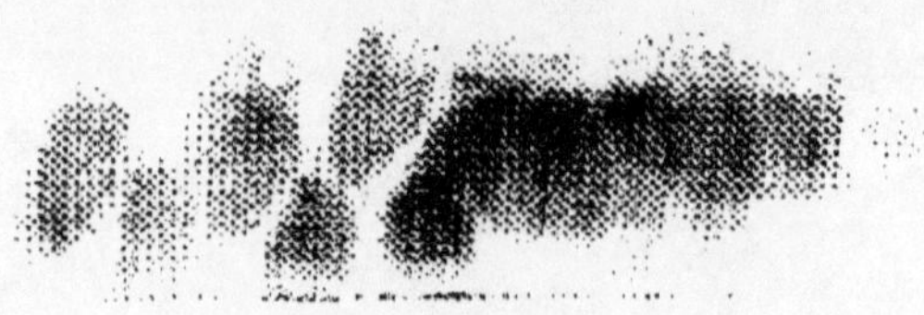

27

ALICE AWOKE WITH the shock of finding Sam between her legs and the pleasure of all that implied. Later, Alice got out of bed to make them both a coffee. Sam stepped onto the balcony and had a smoke. When Alice returned, she popped the coffees down and lingered on Sam's silhouette. That woman still turned her on and her stomach butterflies flew around in a circle while she gazed at the beauty in front of her. She soaked in that long back and visible spine, those calves and up to Sam's curvy ass.

Sam looked over her shoulder and saw Alice staring. In response, she sashayed into the bedroom like a catwalk model, hands on hips, walked up to Alice and planted a kiss on her lips. Their bodies were so close, Alice imagined she could feel every part of Sam's body against hers. Every touch. Ev-e-ry hair.

They returned to bed and fooled around until the coffees went cold. Then they fooled around some more.

"I gotta run."

"Huh? Weren't you staying until tomorrow morning?"

"No can do, honey. I've got to go into work this weekend. I'm sure I told you. There's a major client meeting on Monday and a heap of preparation to do."

"You never said…"

Alice saw zero point in hiding her disappointment because she wanted to be with Sam and when they met, she didn't get the vibe her feelings were reciprocated. Sure, Sam flew across the country to see her but she always seemed to itch to go home. This morning was a typical example.

"Do you enjoy being with me?"

"Don't start this again, honey."

"But do you, because I love the time we spend together."

"Good times, yeah."

"Only good. Nothing more?"

"I've told you repeatedly, it's great with you but the rest of my life is in Boston."

"The company is headquartered there so you need to be in the center of things. I get all that, but what if I set you up with your own practise here?"

"In Malibu?"

"Anywhere in California. San Francisco, LA. You tell me."

Sam stopped stuffing her possessions into her travel bag.

"You'd be willing to do that for me?"

"So we could be together… more."

"Are there strings attached? Sounds as though you would only support my business if I carried on sleeping with you. Makes me sound like you want to be my pimp."

"What? No. I mean that if your work is the only barrier to being together, I can sort that out. A business deal is just that: business. What you and I have outside the office would be separate. Do I wish us to get even closer now? Yes. Will living on the same side of the country help? Yes it should. Do you want to do that? I have no idea."

Sam sat on the bed and held Alice's hand.

"That's a fabulous offer, honey. Really. But I need to go away and think about it. You see, the truth is I don't know how I feel about any of this. I love our being together. The sex is amazing and you are truly great company but I have no idea what I want of my life. Until then I can't answer your questions because I just don't know any answers."

"I understand but I still must know. Take your time, but if you don't want us to carry on, be honest and say so. Do not leave me hanging."

A tear dripped out of Alice's left eye and splashed onto Sam's hand. They hugged until the redness around Alice's pupils had faded. After, they lay down and fucked again. When Alice was resting, eyelids closed, Sam kissed her again and slunk out of the apartment.

ALICE STAYED IN bed the rest of the morning. She spent the first hour replaying her conversation with Sam. By the end of that time she had no greater insight into what Sam wanted or would do than when she started analyzing the thing to death. So she moved onto Nikolay Markov.

He was open to some form of alliance but he couldn't bring himself to cut a sensible deal with a woman. Yet. Alice needed to create the opportunity for him to work with her so he could judge her based on her deeds and not his prejudices. The trick would be to find something he wanted which would be an easy give-up for him so she could get her foot in the door. One thing was certain: nothing about the Red Stocking arrangement should be on the table.

ANOTHER DAY, ANOTHER cup of coffee. Alice and Nikolay sipped and covered as much small talk they could both stomach. Alice kicked off proceedings by thanking him for meeting up again. She knew how to manipulate male egos.

"I've been thinking about our last chat and have a suggestion I'm hoping you'll find of interest."

"There had to be some proposal otherwise why meet up. Unless you wanted an excuse to see me again."

"That's right. But as we're here, I'll explain about my idea, anyway."

Nikolay half-smiled and sat forward in his seat.

"We discussed how your men are so effective and I was wondering if you'd be interested in a simple trade. Six of your fellas for either hard cash or narcotics."

"I don't need your drugs."

"Our product is cheaper and better quality, but that's your choice. How about the green?"

"My men aren't cattle to be bought and sold."

"Nope. They provide a useful service and I am proposing to pay you for them to render that to me. With one addition: I provide you with an extra amount upfront so that if things work out, after twelve months they move over to my wage bill. If it doesn't pan out, no harm, no foul and you pocket the money I've already given you. The end."

"I underestimated you, young lady."

"You're not the first."

Mama's Gone

ALICE STAYED OVERNIGHT in Fog City as she'd agreed to continue the discussion with Nikolay the following evening over dinner. He picked an ordinary looking pasta joint in the Tenderloin district, near to the Red Stocking. She arrived in the neighborhood sixty minutes early because the venue was in the heart of his territory and she wanted check the area out. She had no desire to let herself get kidnapped—or worse.

There was nothing out of the ordinary about the restaurant, the surrounding buildings or any of the people who came and left in the thirty minutes before their scheduled appointment. Nikolay arrived a little over fifteen minutes early while Alice made him wait until the allotted hour.

As she headed for their table, Nikolay stood up and Alice offered her hand which he took and leaned in to kiss her on both cheeks, European style. The Old Country remained inside him despite being so many miles away. He pulled the chair out for her to sit down—ever the gentleman and quite the reversal of his gruff exterior the previous day.

They ordered food and light conversation ensued. Nikolay came across as an earnest figure surrounded by hordes who wanted to knock him off his perch. His situation wasn't that much different from the Lagottis. Only he had a Russian accent and Mama had a Southern drawl, even after all these years away from the Confederacy.

DESSERT WAS SERVED and all she had achieved was to massage Nikolay's ego and in return he'd paid her several compliments about her dress, her hair and other aspects of her appearance. Business hadn't been mentioned and Alice was getting impatient.

"Have you considered my proposal?"

"Yes I have. While the terms are well structured, I wonder why you have need of Russian muscle. What ruse are you planning that you wish to exclude me from?"

"Good question, Nikolay. It's thinking like that which makes you an attractive business partner."

"And?"

"You want me to lift my skirt before you've said whether you're in the game. That's not how I operate. Show me you choose to work with me and we can share in the profit together. If you don't pay into the ante, you have no right to look at my cards."

"You can have six of my men for a year. That is not a problem. Give them fifty per cent more than I do and you buy their loyalty for every minute the money lasts. An upfront consideration of twenty thousand will be sufficient."

"Even though I am saving you much more than that in wages alone, I accept those terms as a sign of good faith."

"Agreed. Now tell me your plans."

"I am looking for some enforcers because it is time to break new ground. Our gambling operations stretch across California, Illinois, Nevada, New Jersey and Massachusetts. I want to use these locations to move into neighborhood prostitution and labor racketeering if possible. We would need to seize opportunities on a case-by-case basis and have fellas who can handle themselves for that. Ours are great but it never hurts to hold more baseball bats than the other guy."

"I would love to have a piece of that action."

"For a price. Your strength lies in your ability to find tough men, but my understanding is that your reach doesn't stretch much beyond the Tenderloin. A statement of fact and not a criticism."

"No offense taken—yet."

"Seems to me if we are a good fit together, success will follow for both of us."

DESPITE HER PROTESTATIONS, Nikolay insisted on driving Alice back to her hotel—or rather his driver took them both. When the limo pulled in, they carried on talking until Alice thought it only polite to suggest they continued the conversation over a an aperitif. Nikolay agreed in an instant.

"What would you like?"

"I insist. Let me buy you a drink."

"Very kind. A cosmo is always welcome."

Nikolay ordered the cocktail and a vodka tonic for himself. Once the drinks arrived, they moved to a table which had more comfortable seating and gave Alice a view of the bar area leading to the hotel lobby.

"You reckon we can pull this off?"

"With my brains and your brawn, we'll rule the world."

"Your beauty and my experience, you mean."

Nikolay squeezed Alice's knee under the table but removed it back onto his lap. A momentary invasion of her personal space, which raised a red flag in her head. For the rest of their time in the bar he did nothing else inappropriate and Alice relaxed again.

"It's been a great evening. And I reckon we've made a lot of progress."

"Certainly. Looks like we are a good fit as you were saying earlier."

They were in the lobby by now so Alice halted. Nikolay stopped too but gave no sign he was ready to leave the hotel. She tried to think how to call it a night.

"Let's call it a night."

Sometimes go with the obvious.

"The least I can do is to walk you to your door."

"There is no need."

"I insist."

Alice shook her head, shrugged and headed to the elevator, accompanied by Nikolay. At her door, she unlocked it and turned round. Nikolay pushed past her and strolled in. She sighed and followed.

"Now you've seen me in, it's time for you to go."

Nikolay walked up to her and picked off a piece of fluff from the front of her dress, just above her breast. She swallowed hard, grasped his hand and put it by his side.

"Don't be like that. I thought we were getting on fine."

"We have been: so far, but you're overstepping the mark."

"No I haven't."

With those words, Nikolay grabbed the front of Alice's dress and ripped it apart so the material above her waist fell away. Standing semi-naked, her knee instinctively traveled straight up to smash against his groin. Nikolay hit the ground clutching himself as Alice towered over him.

"If you think I'd want your dick anywhere near me, you are delusional. Now get the fuck out of my room, little man, before I cut it off."

January 1997

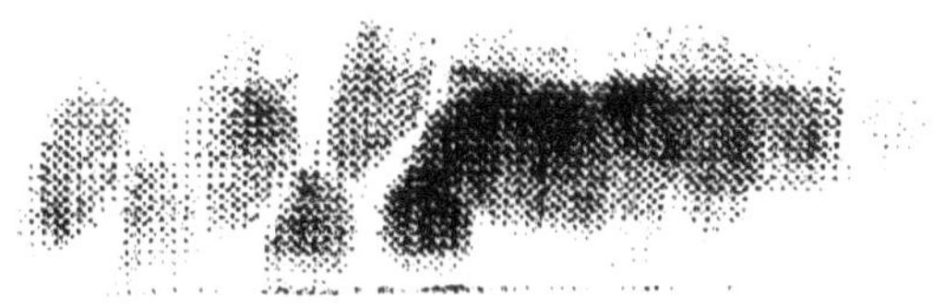

28

NIKOLAY'S RESPONSE WAS more subtle than Alice could ever have imagined. Instead of coming back that night and slicing her open with a bolo knife, he put the squeeze on the Red Stocking and anyone associated with it. Bobby then instructed Naldo to pay a visit to the Bay City to find out why the Markov clan was getting fresh. He returned with bupkis so Bobby told him to take a bite out of their territory.

The next day, Naldo visited the B-Bang, a lap dancing club on the edge of the Tenderloin. There was nothing to distinguish it from any of the other clubs on the same drag once you got inside. The exterior comprised an ordinary facade with a ten feet high neon sign perched on the roof of the low-rise building. The lights depicted an animation showing blue panties lowering to reveal a red pubic triangle. No one could claim they didn't know what to expect when they walked through the door.

Naldo scooted round the rear of the club and found a yard filled with garbage and three girls, coats over their shoulders, sat having a smoke before returning to the drudge of their work. In the meantime, they gossiped and laughed, ignoring the slight chill of the night. Naldo opened the metal gate and stepped inside. One girl, wearing yellow and black, noticed his arrival.

"Beat it, bud. This is for staff only."

He ignored her instruction and ambled toward her.

"Go round the front if you want to watch. This area ain't for the likes of you."

Naldo nodded but continued his journey to the girl, both hands in his jacket pockets. The other two stood up and formed an approximate line either side of Yellow-and-Black. He stopped when he was four feet away from the nearest skirt. None of them were over sixteen and Naldo closed his eyes for half a second.

"If you don't get out, I'm gonna call the manager."

As he opened his eyes, his right hand whipped out of his pocket to reveal a three-inch blade and he swiped at Yellow-and-Black's face. A line of red appeared below her left eye and she screamed, clutching the side of her head. Naldo stepped a pace forward and swung at the other two. By the time his arm returned to rest by his hip, all three were cut and screaming. One headed to the backdoor and Naldo turned round, out the yard and vanished into the night. Although they didn't realize it, they were lucky. Under any other circumstances, Naldo would have slit their throats, but he was following strict instructions: give Markov a warning not an all-out assault.

The moment Bobby ordered the attack on the B-Bang, he knew his people in the Red Stocking were at risk. Sure enough, an hour after Naldo left the yard, a firebomb hit the front of the building. Then things got nasty and the field of battle spread way beyond the confines of the San Francisco city line.

Within a week, blood was spilled on both sides and operations halted or destroyed. What nobody in the Lagotti family factored into consideration was that Nikolay Markov was Russian. That meant he had connections far beyond his immediate reach in the Tenderloin in SF. And the fellas he knew had almost unlimited resources and not one inch of sentiment in their bodies.

MILTON SPENT ANOTHER night sleeping in a fuck-room in the Palace. Ever since the Markov trouble had spilled outside SF, his time had been occupied inside the Lagotti fortress, protected by extra armed guards, to keep him safe. Six men in three shifts were stationed at his family's home in Palm Springs and that made him feel better. He had been around the block long enough to remember the twins' kidnapping.

The one thing he missed was Elsie, with whom he'd been having regular encounters for the past two years. He spotted her the day she started at the Palace: he was down in the reception area when she walked in and lit up the room for him. Before she got the chance to earn any money, he put her on his personal payroll and bought her clothes, trinkets and her own apartment.

A week without Elsie felt like a lifetime and that was too long for Milton. At first, he hadn't wanted her anywhere near the Palace because it might be too dangerous, but seven days later and his opinion had shifted.

"Baby. Pack yourself a bag and get your tail over to the Palace. Papa wants to have fun and he's been missing your loving."

"I'll be right over. See you in thirty."

Forty-five minutes later Elsie had yet to appear, but Milton accepted that LA traffic was shit any time of the day or night. After an hour, he started pacing and tried to take his mind off the wait by watching footage from the peephole cameras. When ninety minutes had passed, he began to fret and two hours since the phone call, Milton flipped his lid, hopped in his car and headed over to Elsie's apartment.

When he got there, the entrance was an inch ajar. He pulled out his pistol and pushed the door open and walked inside, eyes darting left and right. Something was wrong. Intruders maybe. Through the hall and into the living room. The answer lay in a large pool of red on the rug by the couch: Elsie was naked and knife wounds punctured her torso, her legs, her groin.

Milton squatted and threw up. Once he'd pulled himself back together, he thought he heard a creak from the master bedroom. He took two deep breaths, crept to the door and listened. Definitely a noise. He kicked the door open and pointed his gun forwards. A flash and a bang and everything turned black.

ALICE, BOBBY AND May Lou were in the summerhouse and ten men surrounded the perimeter, some with sniper rifles hidden in crow's nests in the trees. Irma popped her head round the door after knocking and said there was someone on the phone. She thought it might be Naldo, but as ever she hadn't asked. What she didn't know couldn't kill her. Bobby walked back to the house to take the call. When he returned two minutes later, he was ashen.

"They've killed Milton. Put a bullet in his brains and dumped his body on the sidewalk outside the Palace."

Alice's jaw dropped and Mary Lou looked on, stone-faced.

"IT'S TIME FOR you to come home, son."

"I'm fine, Mama. Why d'you need me on the other side of the country?"

"We have issues and I require you by my side."

Frank lay in bed with one hand on his girlfriend's stomach and toyed with her belly button as he spoke. For Mama to place the call meant some heavy shit was going down. And the lack of information she was offering showed him she was concerned about ears on the line.

"I'll get over as soon as I can."

Frank put the phone down and sent his fingers below the belly button.

"Come on, you and I are off on a little trip."

"I don't think that's a good idea."

"Nah, it'll be fine. My family is very accommodating of strangers. And you're not that strange at all."

"Even so, I should stay here."

"Nope. If what might have gone down has happened, you won't be safe. I won't be able to protect you."

"Just remember I told you I shouldn't come along."

"Duly noted. Now put your panties on so we can get going."

She giggled then wriggled into her skirt, ignoring Frank's underwear instruction. He smiled and licked his lips.

"Dirty minx."

FRANK AND HIS girlfriend arrived in Palm Springs and headed straight to Oakcrest Drive. Into the house and up to his old room, which was now a spare bedroom after all this time. They unpacked and lay on the bed for half an hour.

Eventually Frank had enough and went downstairs.

"I've got a headache. I'll be down later."

Frank shrugged and made his way downstairs. Empty. So he walked through the conservatory, out past the pool and into the summerhouse. Bobby and Mama sat talking and they both smiled at his arrival. She ran over, gave him a hug and tiptoed to kiss him on the forehead.

He suffered in silence—a grown man treated like a child—but when she messed with his hair, he brushed her away. Mary Lou laughed at him and sat back down. Frank slumped down on his own in an armchair to prevent further maternal attacks on his dignity.

"Where's Alice? I thought all ships were coming into the harbor."

"She'll be along later. Right now she's under Naldo's protection in a safe house."

"Why does she get special treatment? Can't she look after herself?"

"More than you'll ever know. We thought it best for her not to stay in her apartment as it's difficult to defend from attack."

"Are we on some kind of lockdown?"

Bobby glanced at Mary Lou who stared at Frank. Neither of them felt the need to respond to him and he waited to find the answers to his questions.

"Was the flight okay?"

"Yeah, we had a smooth run and thanks for sending a car to pick us up."

"De nada. We?"

"Yes, I brought someone with me. If lives are going to be threatened, I want to know she was safe too."

"Who?"

"My girlfriend. She's taking a rest right now but you'll meet her later."

"Does she have a name?"

"Sammy. I think I might be serious about her, but before you get too excited, it is still early days, so don't freak her out."

"Bravo, boy. And well done to Sammy: the first woman ever to tame our little boy."

"Leave me alone. All I ask is that you're nice to her and try not to make fools of yourselves around her."

"We know how to behave. The question is whether you can keep it in your pants until you guys are in the privacy of your room."

"Are you ever going to let that go? I was eighteen and you weren't supposed to be back until the following day. Jeez."

"Both of you: stand down. We are facing a dangerous situation and the last thing we need is to lose focus and fight among ourselves. Please, people."

AS IF ON cue, in came Alice with Naldo in tow. When he saw the whole clan was here, he nodded to Bobby and shut the summerhouse door behind him as he left. The man knew not to intrude on family business.

Hugs for her Mama and Bobby, then Alice sat down next to Mama, a single glance at Frank, only acknowledgement of his existence she could muster.

"Is someone going to tell me what this is all about?"

"The Markov clan has attacked a number of our west coast operations. Meth labs, heroin labs, prostitution. They've hit the casinos, but so far they haven't damaged the Queen of Sheba or Bakersfield Printing. We have to assume it is only a matter of time though."

"And we've just sat back and taken this insult?"

"Not at all. Under Naldo's stewardship, we have brought their call girl operation to its knees and cut their supply lines for cocaine, ecstasy, opium and meths. Blood has been shed: us and them."

"So why am I hearing about this only now?"

"This may have been a disturbance to business, but we thought it was relatively contained. Until last night. They shot Milton in the face and cut off his dick. Stuffed it in his mouth and dumped his body on Sunset Boulevard."

Frank fumed and Bobby was certain he saw steam seeping out of his ears. Alice inhaled deeply on her cigarette as she tried to keep it together, despite Milton's loss.

"What are we waiting for? Let's get all our men over to San Francisco and kill the motherfuckers."

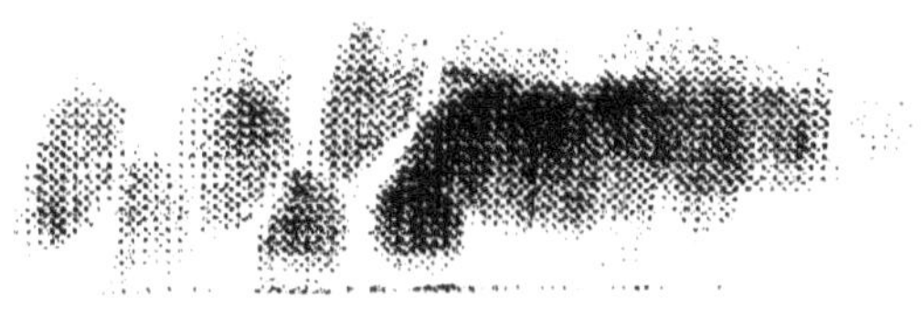

29

"BEFORE WE RUSH over to San Francisco, we need to have a plan—and know it'll succeed."

"Kill them. Kill them all."

"Not helpful, Frank. We've tried direct violence and harassment and it hasn't worked. We have to find a different solution to this problem."

He sat back in his chair and sulked. No one was listening to what he had to say. Nothing in this family ever changed. Here he was skulking around his Mama's house when he was making real money out east and nobody seemed able to recognize he'd done it alone.

"Is there anyone who might intercede on our behalf?"

"Pasquale has been out of the game too long. He's the only made man I've ever known and trusted. Beyond him, we are on our own."

"There's only one Nikolay Markov and three of us."

"Four," chimed in Mary Lou.

"Sorry, four of us. Let's call a peace conference and kill the fucker."

"Let it go. We need a solution the whole Markov family will stand behind and mass murder is not the answer."

If Frank had bothered to listen, he would have detected a definite edge to Bobby's voice. The man was tired of Frank's unhelpful repetitions. As for Alice's scowls, Frank always discounted her disapproving expressions.

The only person whose opinion mattered to him was Mama and she remained perfectly calm. Totally still—like these discussions didn't matter in the grand scheme of things. That response gave Frank the strength to believe she was on his side. Why else had she dragged him across the country? His methods were direct and blood-soaked. She'd have nixed his idea if she really wanted to silence him.

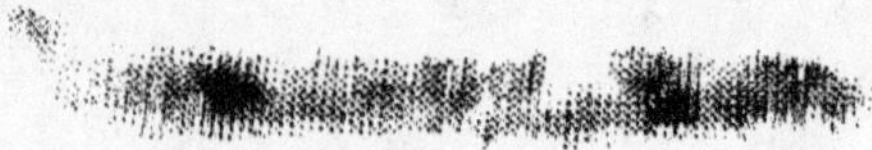

ONE LONG HOUR with everyone circling round the same problem and offering no useful fix, Irma popped in to warn them food was to be served in a handful of minutes. Frank left the summerhouse and inhaled fresh air. His family was doing his head in—how much more he could take? Sammy was still asleep when he got back into the room, so he blew in her ear to rouse her. First she flicked at her earlobe as though a fly was annoying her but persistence paid off and a minute later, she opened an eye.

"Time to eat."

She tried to generate a half-smile but failed and only transformed her expression into a grimace. A sinking feeling hit the pit of her stomach. This meal would be painful, but she'd known this day would come and had done nothing to prepare herself or Frank for its arrival.

"I need to change first."

"Well, get a move on then," he said as he placed his hands in her panties."

She squirmed as Frank fooled around and gasped when matters got more serious.

"Now we can eat, right?"

She nodded and slipped into a blue dress while he did up his pants. Sammy held his hand as they left the bedroom, which he mistook for affection. Fear of meeting Alice was the real cause.

FRANK AND SAM walked into the living room and Alice's jaw opened wide. Bobby's eyes darted between Sam and Alice, while Mary Lou watched benignly.

"Good to meet you, dear."

Sam's mouth twitched a smile as she had no idea what to do next. His mom hadn't remembered her but Alice sure as hell had.

"Hi all. How are you doing?"

Frank appeared to not notice the confusion and embarrassment on everybody else's faces. Then he blinked and realized he'd stepped into the middle of a Noel Coward play. Mumbled responses to Sam's question ensued as Bobby, at least, tried to salvage the moment and steer everyone well enough to sit down to eat.

The silence was broken by Irma who took them into the dining room to serve their meal. Bobby and Mary Lou at each end of the table with Alice sat opposite Sam and Frank. A pleasant family meal. The knives were needed more to cut the tension than the veal which was tender and flavorsome.

Alice trawled the food around her plate. When Sam first walked into the room, as Alice exhaled, a wave of anger overtook her body and she wanted to grab a gun and shoot Sam through the head. Then she inhaled and withdrew from the world, wanting to curl into a little ball and vanish into nothing.

Now she glared at Sam, occasionally scooping a mouthful of veal or potato. Mary Lou ate her meal in silence, focused on her delightful food and not experiencing the same emotional fallout as the rest of the table. Bobby knew better than to stand in the way of the twins, their lover and their mother.

Almost the minute Irma cleared the plates away, Sam declared she was going up to bed. Frank shrugged and, given the lack of joy in the room, followed soon after. Alice listened as his footsteps announced his arrival on the second floor.

"Why didn't you tell me?"

"He called her Sammy and she hid in their bedroom until just before dinner. I found out the same instant as you."

"Fucking whore."

Neither disagreed but Mary Lou remained resolutely silent. Bobby opened his arms and Alice walked towards him and accepted the hug. All three sat down in the living room and attacked a bottle of Scotch. Two hours later, Alice crashed out on the couch: she couldn't face being only a wall's width from the rutting couple.

"We still a need plan."

"Kill the bitch."

"Not what I meant…"

FRANK TUCKED INTO his pancakes with gusto while the rest of the family was subdued. He and Sam had a long conversation the night before when she explained to him what he was too emotionally illiterate to comprehend for himself and now he understood why everyone was acting so strange. The man remained untouched by everybody else's emotional fallout, but Sam made him promise not to lay into Alice—for her sake and a quiet life.

His response was to fill his face with food because he couldn't be sure anything apart from barbs would come out of his mouth if he spoke. Sam pecked at her maple syrup soaked circles but could only meet Alice's gaze once or twice.

Alice's sense of loss stayed with her from the moment she woke up but she recognized nothing and nobody would make her feel better—in the short term. She wasn't hungry but despite this, she made sure she ate some of Irma's cooking and instigated a tiny amount of small talk. The silence was too oppressive and centered on her.

"These are so good."

"Irma's done a fabulous job."

"Yep."

"Anyone had fresh thoughts about the Markov problem?"

"You won't hear me say this again in my lifetime, but Frank might be correct."

"Thanks sis'."

"Hold back the hugs: you didn't let me finish."

"You could be right that direct intervention is the answer. But you're probably thinking about rushing in with a crew and committing merry mayhem."

"Pretty much. Go in, kill 'em, escape."

"That is the opposite of what's to be done. We need to cut off the head of the snake and leave the body alone."

All silverware was placed on plates as Alice grabbed everybody's attention.

"What are you thinking?"

"One person—not a crew—go to the Markovs and once they are facing Nikolay, a bullet to the head solves all our difficulties. The rest of his family and fellas will fold immediately."

"And who should get this assignment?"

"Nothing personal Sam, but perhaps we should carry on this conversation in the summerhouse."

"It's okay, sis'. Sam knows about my business."

"And about ours too?"

"No, Alice. Just Frank's world. He let me in."

A glare for a response and Alice stood up.

"You coming? We've already said too much in front of her."

The ease with which they'd moved from breakfast to assassination showed how Sam had entered their circle of trust by stealth. Now she had enough to run to the Feds and pocket herself a healthy reward. Bobby thought for half a second and stood up, which encouraged Mary Lou and Frank to follow.

ENSCONCED IN THE safety of the poolside building, Alice was more relaxed.

"So who should go on the mission? Can't be me because Markov won't believe I have any interest in him or his family. Mama and Bobby aren't believable either."

They all did the Math and that left only one person.

"You looking at me?"

"I don't see anyone else here."

"Got to be kidding. I want Nikolay Markov dead but only if I am still alive. I'm not volunteering for a suicide mission."

Alice's eyebrows raised themselves up on their haunches and she smiled.

"I thought you wanted to kill them all."

"Not at any cost."

"Good to come home to a warm bed, huh?"

"Does my sleeping with Sammy bother you?"

"Children!"

Mary Lou bellowed across the room at the squabbling twins. The effect was instant silence and sheepish looks.

"Sorry, Mama."

"If you're not willing to go, who should we use instead?"

"Someone from out of town."

"We could get Naldo to recommend a shooter. He's seen some action in his day."

"Sure has. They need to be beyond reliable. That's the trouble with strangers: how can we trust them? With all due respect to any suggestion from Naldo."

"Is there any chance of finding Markov alone long enough to hit him and get away?"

"Naldo already checked that out. He's always with somebody by day or has armed guards surround him at night. There's too much firepower near him."

"Sniper?"

"That's a possibility. A rifle trained on his bedroom window might work but he keeps the blinds shut at all times so basic aiming would be tricky."

"We're getting nowhere with is. All we've figured out for sure is we want Nikolay Markov dead."

"A BOMB? INSTEAD of a focused strike, perhaps we should blast the fuck out of an entire building."

"Family home?"

"It is one thing to hit Nikolay with an incendiary device. It's another to murder his wife and children."

"Okay. His kids don't go with him to work, right?"

"True but he doesn't even have an office. He travels round, visiting his venues collecting his tribute. The guy is shrewd: can't fault him for that."

"Sniper in a helicopter?"

"This isn't the movies. Let's not clutch at straws."

"Feels like that's all we've got."

The three continued to chew the fat until lunch but were no nearer to any useful conclusion. Sam joined them to eat and in the afternoon, she and Frank left the compound. Alice stayed with Mama and Bobby, which was enjoyable but delivered no plan.

"Maybe killing him isn't the answer."

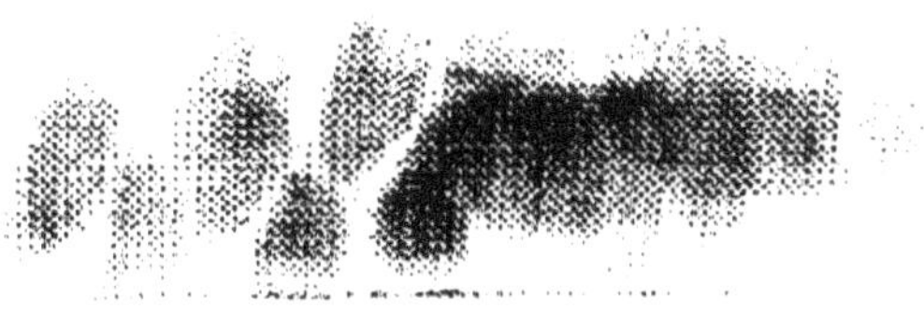

30

ALICE AND BOBBY sat in the summerhouse. It was the wrong half of the year to sit outside although the temperature wasn't that cold. Another Californian Winter's day. Mostly, they were silent in their own worlds but now and then, they'd glance at each other or mumble a few words. Bobby hid behind a newspaper and Alice didn't pretend: she was plain sitting doing nothing in particular.

Or rather, she was using the time to focus on Nikolay Markov. Until the moment when his dick took over from his brain, Nikolay appeared to be open to working together—unless the entire evening was a ruse to get inside her panties. If she set aside the fear and humiliation he'd reaped upon her, the Markov clan was a great fit. Alice did her level best to compartmentalize business from her personal experience of the man. Each family had different but complementary strengths which would support the other's weaknesses. A marriage made not so much in heaven but a lap dancing club in the Tenderloin.

Perhaps the trick was to appeal to his wallet or his ego. Puff him up and take the sting out of his tail. Once everyone and everything had calmed down, either he'd see the sense in the deal or she'd slice him open from throat to groin at some later date.

"We should make a peace instead of killing Markov."

"Do you not think we're beyond that now?"

"Not necessarily. Whether we want to admit it, we need them—or some outfit like them."

"You might be right but that's not what I meant."

"Huh?"

"We have killed his family. He's murdered Milton and we've both lost fellas too. I'd suggest relationships are founded on trust and we're living through a fundamental breakdown in that ingredient."

"Only if we let go of hope."

"You can take the girl out of California…"

"…but you can't take California out of me."

"Your optimism is astounding."

"You need faith that change is possible if you're to succeed. And sometimes that involves finding the good in people. Even someone like Nikolay, who is a cockroach. If I could stamp on him and destroy him then I would, but we can't see how to rid ourselves of the Markov infestation. That means we have to accept they'll be around and learn to live with them."

"Was that a long speech to say: if you can't beat them, join them?"

"Pretty much, yeah."

"BOBBY SAID YOU'VE come up with an idea."

"Yes, but I'm not sure how you'll respond."

"Won't know until you tell me."

Bobby sat still and let the women continue their conversation without interruption.

"If we can't assassinate Nikolay Markov then we need to join forces with him. There's no other way a neutralize him as a threat."

"Sounds the exact opposite of what we should do. How can we trust a man like that?"

"I'm not saying we do. Just that it'll be the easiest route to stop the war. If the killing reduces, we have a better chance of making money and surviving until Easter."

"Sure would be great to find some calm. All this hostility isn't good for the soul."

"Right. The man is too difficult to destroy at the moment, but that will change once we get him to lower his guard. To do that, we must build a peace with him. Create a joint operation to work on together and then make a move."

"That's fine but I would need to be top dog. He would report to me on this project."

"I can't guarantee that'd happen Mama. Besides, the endgame is his removal. If he rules the roost, that would just put him in the place we require for him even faster."

"I couldn't take orders from that man. Milton's in his grave because of him."

"It wouldn't matter. Within a month, he'd have called off his hounds and then we deal with him."

Bobby stood up and headed for the door. With a hand on the handle, he turned around.

"Alice is right. To get Markov into the morgue requires us to put him on ice first. Until that point, we suck in any discomfort."

He didn't wait for any reply and walked out.

MARY LOU STARED at the closed door and Alice wondered if she was in a trance. Then she blinked and mentally returned to the room. Mama smiled quietly to herself and turned her attention to Alice.

"You met up with him."

"What?"

"Nikolay. You had a meal with Markov. What happened that meant you wouldn't tell me you'd even seen him?"

"Don't want to talk about it. I made a mistake."

"One that's cost us several good men. From what I've been told, all this maelstrom of blood letting started shortly after you broke bread with him."

"I am all too aware."

"And the fact you kept it from me means either you're about to turn traitor, he did something wrong or you behaved inappropriately. Which was it?"

"I'm no traitor, Mama."

"Sure, dear. You wouldn't be the first woman in this family to have had to fend off sexual advances from a man."

Tears ran down Alice's cheeks and they hugged, but Alice refused to go into any details about what went down in her hotel bedroom and Mama didn't elaborate on what had happened to her when she visited Uncle Frankie and he laid his hands on her.

FRANK HAD NEVER been to San Francisco. When he arrived, he was not disappointed and he was not alone: Isaak Vasilev sat next to him on the plane. When he realized a firm hand was required and a violent disposition, Isaak was the first person who popped into his head.

They had met when Frank had got into a spot of bother in Morocco shortly after leaving school. The local dealers weren't impressed with Frank's attempts to introduce a little healthy American-style competition to their country. Isaak appreciated Frank's entrepreneurial efforts and applied a knife and a gun to the problem. They had kept in touch ever since and when Isaak moved to the States, Frank ensured he found the man work that suited his talents for murder and mayhem.

Over the course of a week, Frank and Isaak made inroads into the Markov empire. First, they unearthed a meth lab which supplied Nikolay and sent Molotov cocktails into the building. The next day on the other side of the bay, they did the same to a crack house.

Isaak paid a visit to the Red Stocking and sliced himself some whore faces so they hit the Markov cash flow very rapidly and without getting spotted. By the third sunrise, the Markovs noticed Frank's antics. The good news was that they were like a needle in a haystack to find. Two men in a city of millions gave them the best odds to survive.

BY FLYING UNDER the radar, Frank was having a low-level impact but his activities were far from a game changer. His family would learn to trust him if he showed them he knew what he was doing. So the next logical thing to do was to build an operation in SF, something no Lagotti had achieved.

A narcotics play would take too much time to prepare, but a brothel would do the trick and only required rent to be paid upfront and girls would earn that night. Twenty-four hours later and Frank held the keys in his hand to an undesirable residence on the edge of the Tenderloin as far away from any Markov establishment they knew about.

While Isaak set about organizing rudimentary furniture for each bedroom, Frank hit the bus station to grab fresh tail among the new arrivals to the city. A rental car took the hapless ladies to the house and Frank gave his employees a full staff induction. He showed them the bathroom and explained how they kept their tips but the first thirty dollars from each john belonged to him. Any trouble, they screamed and Isaak would sort the dude out.

The next day, Isaak added partitioning in the larger upstairs rooms and Frank returned to the bus station for more ass. Without Nikolay noticing, Frank had kicked off a San Francisco operation by slowly boiling the frog. Slamming into an existing deal would never work, Frank reckoned.

He stayed in the area to get to know the locals and to hire a timekeeper and troubleshooter. As fabulous as the cathouse was, Frank had other plans for his time which didn't involve fucking. He smiled at that idea: he never imagined such a statement might ever be true. Besides, when he got home, he'd have Sammy in his bed and what she could do with her body was worth waiting for.

31

PASQUALE BASSANI WAS an old man, who enjoyed nothing more than sipping coffee at a cafe, a casual round of golf when he had the energy and quiet conversation with his family and friends. Florida was the perfect state to retire in because its weather was fine and the stresses of his former life were far away. There had been a long tradition of gangsters staying in Miami-Dade dating back to Al Capone so Pasquale was in good company.

When he retired to the Sunshine State, Pasquale sold up all his investments in the various illicit assets which he owned and ensured everyone knew it. He'd heard too many stories of revenge being taken on the older generation because they were sitting ducks.

Visitors were welcome but Pasquale had no desire to be dragged into the problems of today. The mob world was behind him and he lived with the riches that life had generated for him. So when Bobby called to ask his advice, Pasquale was cautious. Not out of any distrust of Bobby: he and Mary Lou had been doing business together since the early '70s.

He didn't want his words to cause someone to be killed and a misguided relative take retaliatory action against him. Pasquale had survived way too much to be whacked by a teenager with a gun and a point to prove. No one would make their bones by sending him to the morgue.

Bobby and Pasquale sat on his patio and sipped a glass of red wine each.

"Thank you for allowing me to come here to speak with you."

"Most welcome. How is Mary Lou?"

"Fine. She sends her regards."

"Strange that she is not here in person. Matters are so difficult you need to see an old wizened fool like myself, yet Mary Lou stays at home. Talk to me, Bobby Trevisan."

"We are in a dangerous situation and I am seeking your advice. We have no idea what to do."

"Go on."

Bobby explained the Markov war and outlined the issues with Mary Lou's decision making. Once he had finished, the old boss took small sips from his wine glass and contemplated the problem in silence. Bobby knew his job was to not speak and give Pasquale the time to think things through. Five long minutes later, the man cleared his throat and had another sip to moisten his tonsils.

"Forgive me. My medication gives me a dry cough. It's for my blood pressure, so the doc says, but I'm the most relaxed I've been since the day I was born."

Pasquale slipped into silence and pondered more. And Bobby waited—politely and with the utmost respect for this once-powerful old man.

BOBBY DID HIS best not to hold his breath or tap his fingers with impatience. Pasquale had been the firm hand supporting their efforts through thick and thin. He had been there in the early days and gave Mary Lou her big break when she first drifted into town. Five years earlier, the fella had been the only person to try to save his children. He was solid as a rock and deserved the time to think. No matter how long that took.

"You have exhausted your options through violence, you say."

"The Markov men are real tough and whenever we cut one down, another appears in his place. It's like they're lining up in Russia waiting to join the fight over here."

"They probably are. The break up of the Soviet Union strengthened the Russian mob. Khrushchev never allowed crime families to get too strong. With freedom comes chaos."

"Khrushchev?"

"Whoever. My point is the same and I hope well taken."

"Yes, Pasquale."

"As far as I can see, you have two options. First, find reinforcements and destroy these foreigners. Second, make your peace with them and merge your activities. Half of a large pizza is better than all of a child's portion."

"Where would these extra men come from?"

"Is there anyone else who has a beef with these guys?"

"I don't know."

"Worth finding out then, wouldn't you say?"

A nod. Bobby was embarrassed that none of them had thought of that. They were too close to the trees to see straight through the forest.

"And is a merger the only other option you can see for us?"

"On what you've told me: yes. From what I hear, it's the way of the world. We have always had to adapt to survive. Shed your old skin to let your new one come alive."

"Doesn't that make us a bunch of snakes?"

"And what of it? When the mammals are long gone from this stinking planet, we'll be left with the reptiles and the insects. Serpents and cockroaches will rule the Earth, my friend. Rejoice that you are a snake and not a disgusting roach."

Pasquale knocked back the dregs from his glass and got Bobby to refill it. After he put the bottle down, he mulled over Pasquale's words, sifting through his prejudices to find out if he could deal with the consequences of working with Nikolay. The options: do that or die. Not much of a choice.

He spent another thirty minutes with Pasquale talking about the good old days with both catching up on who had died in the other's circle—Fabio was one of the many names. Then he thanked the great man and took his leave. Pasquale occupied the rest of the afternoon reminding himself of happier times when the Feds didn't have wiretaps and could barely match fingerprints.

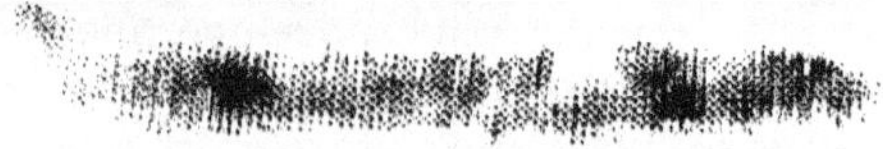

WHEN BOBBY ARRIVED home, Mary Lou was already asleep, so he waited until morning to tell her what Pasquale had recommended. As ever, they sat in the summerhouse to talk business, having used breakfast for couples conversation.

"First the good news: Pasquale is doing fine, living out his days in the Miami burbs. The rest is less positive."

"Spill."

"He says we should stop the war before it gets out of hand. Either we find a group with aligned interest in the destruction of Nikolay Markov or we reconcile our differences and learn how to work together."

"Peace is not an option."

"Only if we ignore it and Pasquale was very clear. We need to give peace a chance."

Mary Lou sat and thought. Then she shook her head.

"I can't do that. What Markov has done is not forgivable and needs to be punished. Milton is dead because of him. The guy might not have been the brightest spark in the fire, but he was decent to his wife and to his mistresses. And that should count for something."

"It does, but some things you have to suck in and that's one of them. I'm not saying we ignore what he did to Milton, just that we don't have to act now. His revenge can be served cold—later this year or the next: whichever is more convenient for us. Today we need to make money and spill less blood."

BOBBY COULDN'T TELL if Mary Lou was thinking, sulking or both. He could not read the taciturn puffing of her cigarette. All he knew was her silence. When she stubbed out the remains, he received her response.

"We can win the fight if we carry on and don't give up hope. Look what Frank has achieved in only a handful of days. He and his sidekick have thrown sand in Nikolay's face and set up a cathouse under his nose. That proves we should attack Markov and grow our business interests without the need to sit down and talk. Let alone share the profit from our hard work."

"Short-term gains. Two guys on their own? Of course, they can make early inroads. Will the story be the same in a month? Nah. The whorehouse'll be shut down and the girls'll have their throats cut. And we shouldn't wait four weeks just for me to be proved right. Me, Alice and Pasquale. We've all reached the same conclusion. It is time for a peace conference."

"Frank is leading the way. If we each set up a small group and chip away at their businesses, in a few weeks we'll be in a very different situation. We will starve them of money. Without that, they are nothing."

"Aren't you forgetting their connections?"

"Huh?"

"In Russia."

"Russia ain't America. Fuck his Russki paymasters."

"They have deep pockets and an army waiting to ship overseas. We mustn't underestimate them simply because they don't speak our language."

"A bunch of chimpanzees in suits. I'm not underestimating them: merely discounting them instead. They are thugs and no more. If we want, we can hire our own ape army, but the better approach is to destroy them slowly while generating cash. That's more than they are able to do. Frank has cut off narcotics supply lines already. Every day they lose money, the weaker they become. In less than a month they'll have nothing. Nada. And then we move on Nikolay Markov."

MARY LOU COULD be stubborn, but Bobby felt there was something more at work here. Yes, she was digging in her heels, but her argument was based on Frank's minor success and ignored what had gone on before. As though it had never happened. As if she couldn't remember that it had occurred. He shook his head. His desire to remain loyal to her pulled him in one direction and his mind tugged him in another.

He could not deal with the thought he needed to countermand her plan —again. Perhaps he wasn't strong enough, grown weak after years of easy street. Also, this was the first instance in over a year that he could remember when Mary Lou had passion, fire in her belly. That had to count for something. She was so sure of herself—in a way he hadn't seen for a very long time. Like these dark times were bringing out the best in her.

The last thing he should do is rain on her parade. Now was the moment for the whole family to come together as one, including him. For richer or poorer, better or worse. His job was to stick by Mary Lou and support her. This was her show and, despite his misgivings, she gave the orders and her position was clear.

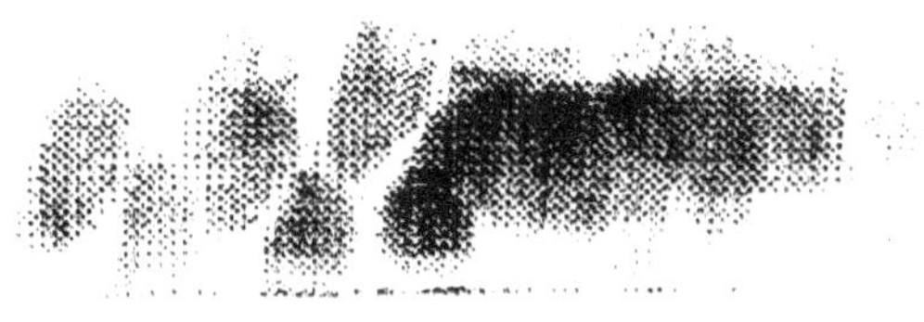

32

CRIMINAL ACTIVITY IS cyclical like so many businesses which is why Frank worked his girls hard during the weekend and came home to visit Mama on Tuesday. Sammy had returned to Boston but his mind was not focused on her ass despite what she might hope. Unlike Alice, his desire for her was entirely physical and he was too tired to fool around.

He rested in the conservatory after a hearty Irma-fueled breakfast and waited for his Mama to appear. Bobby had left the house at the crack of dawn and the place was silent, apart from Irma's hustle and bustle, which Frank plain ignored. When Mary Lou appeared, she still looked tired and he gave her the time to revive before talking shop.

"How's it been back here?"

"Difficult. The Markovs continue to hit us hard: attacking our labs and they once tried to take our trucks coming out of Bakersfield."

"But we stopped them?"

"Yes, for the past two weeks, armed guards rode in the cabins so the Markov goons were met with a hail of bullets. Didn't come back the following day—the ones who survived."

"There's nothing like a steel toecap in your face to focus your mind."

"Amen to that."

"Huh?"

"What?"

They looked quizzically at each other, neither understanding the other's response. Frank shook himself out of the conundrum first.

"I have applied the same strategy in SF and set up two whorehouses along the way using fresh girls. If we work to the side of their operation, we can eat away at their territory and fight them at the same time."

"That's what I've been telling Bobby and Alice but they won't listen."

"I hear you loud and clear, Mama. The business is safe with me."

"I know, dear and I won't forget what you've done. Never you mind."

Frank glowed inside. So much of his life had been spent being bailed out or disappointing his mom, he'd forgotten how warm positive words could feel.

"And now we must step up our campaign and you've shown me you are the one I can rely on."

"What do you want me to do, Mama?"

"It is time to chew through the heart of their operations: prostitution. You have started well but we need to knock out their lap dancing venues and cathouses. If we succeed, all that'll be left of any substance will be narcotics and you've already started to nix those supply lines."

"Hit them hard."

"Without restraint. Either destroy the buildings or take out the resources."

"You mean kill the fellas running the joints."

"The goons. The girls. If we leave the johns alone, then the cops won't touch us: we'll be doing their job for them."

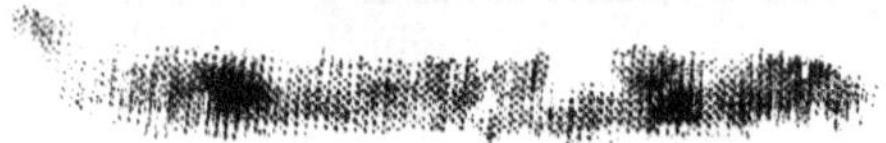

FRANK RETURNED TO the Bay City and followed Mama's orders. Isaak continued to lay waste to the Markov whores. While Naldo had used a knife, Isaak waded in with automatic weapons and a total disregard for human life, but he always attacked the staff rooms or hit the place after hours. Mama had been clear about that and it made perfect sense.

The San Francisco Police Department didn't know what to do with itself. Local precincts were reporting mass murder one day followed by a total lack of low-level crime the next. The only people who were disappointed were the men hoping for an easy fuck on the way home from work or after sinking a beer or two. They were forced to put more effort into their illicit carnal desires.

Isaak continued his reign of terror until the Tenderloin was free of brothels. Even the independent operators got the message and went on unexpected vacations. What's the point of running a joint, if at the end of the night you're face down in a pool of your own blood and excrement?

Mama's Gone

THE MARKOV RESPONSE was predictable—much as Bobby and Alice had said. Nikolay put his best fellas on to track down Frank and Isaak. In the absence of any success, all the people found in a Lagotti venue were shot. The two guys went into hiding outside the Tenderloin but soon Frank realized the jig was up.

Not enough guns to finish Markov and insufficient men to maintain control of the new territory they'd won. Their early gains had turned into a series of losses and the splatter of human remains lay all over the streets. Isaak waited until after dusk, stole a car and the pair got the fuck out of Dodge.

OVER THE WEEKEND, Mary Lou flew down to Miami for a break. Bobby stayed at home because he didn't want a vacation while chaos loomed all around. He sent Naldo with her to watch her back.

On Saturday morning, word reached Bobby that two meth labs in the depths of LA had gone up in smoke overnight. That afternoon, the Markovs attacked their main narcotics processing lab. Fifteen pounds of uncut heroin and ten pounds of cocaine had been stolen and everyone in the building had been whacked.

Bobby tried to contact Mary Lou, but she wasn't in her room to answer the phone. Nor was Naldo. Under ordinary circumstances, Bobby wouldn't have been concerned, but this hit was the kind of incident he had feared would happen and there was no way to protect Mary Lou. In the early evening, he got through to Naldo.

"There's been action. Check out of the hotel and find somewhere quiet to stay tonight. Tell her to come home tomorrow. Let her know supply lines have been hit and that I am insisting. She should understand what that means."

While the tentacles of the Feds had yet to reach their corner of Palm Springs, Bobby used caution when on a public line. He and Mary Lou had agreed to insist on something only if it was a matter of life or death. No questions asked. And for Bobby, this was one of those times.

He briefed the guards in the house to expect trouble and he told Alice what had happened.

"Do you think we'll get through this?"

"For sure. Your mom and I have dealt with worse in our time. If we remain sensible and do nothing stupid then we will nail Nikolay Markov."

"Has anyone explained that plan to Frank?"

"I'm having a Scotch. You want something?"

"Too early for me."

Bobby poured two fingers into a tumbler and added four cubes of ice. Then he raised his glass like he was giving a toast.

"Here's looking at you, kid."

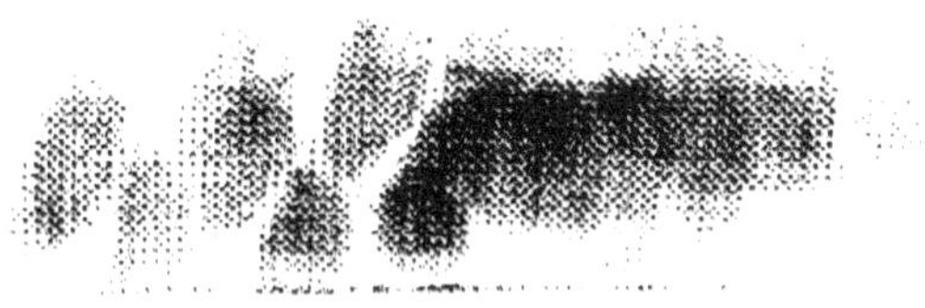

33

BOBBY AND MARY Lou sat on the summerhouse couch with Alice and Frank in separate armchairs. The events of the past week had permeated through all of them. The stress caused by being at war had taken its toll. Everyone looked fraught even Mary Lou, fresh from her weekend in the sun.

"Let's get started. What's the latest?"

"Same as the whole of the month: we've been hit hard in Los Angeles and surrounding areas. Narcotics, prostitution. There has been some disruption to our gambling operations too. Revenue is down and so are the number of live bodies on the payroll."

"In return, we have disrupted or decimated Markov whorehouses in San Francisco. We've hit their heroin supply and destroyed their pussy product."

"Nicely put, Frank."

"Get over yourself, sis'. We are hurting them. Causing them grief."

"In summary then, they're bleeding us dry on the west coast but there's been zero impact on Las Vegas, Chicago, Boston or Atlantic City."

"'Yet' is the key word here. The longer this goes on, the greater the chance they will expand their horizons. Once Nikolay escalates his actions, it'll be a matter of days before the casinos fall. He can call on an enormous number of men and we won't be able to defend ourselves."

"The good thing about the Lucky Lady is that it is in the middle of the city and local police will not be happy with anyone who disrupts the tourist trade."

"Same for AC."

"The Queen of Sheba is vulnerable: it's a boat on a river."

"Can we find reinforcements to last this month?"

"I'd love to say yes, but I have no idea where to get the right guys. Our best are six feet under and the rest heard what happens when you work for us."

Bobby's hand made a fast swooping gesture across his throat to emphasize his statement. Mary Lou stared, an impassive rock. Frank and Alice nodded or shook their heads depending on the point being expressed. They both sat on the edge of their seats—fresh to the experience of a war cabinet.

"And what are we to do?"

MARY LOU SPOKE for the first time since opening the meeting.

"We must assassinate the Russian. With him gone, all our problems dissolve like sugar in a hot cup of coffee."

"That is not an option: we have been through this before."

"No, we need to cut off the head of the snake. His men will fall in line when he's lying bleeding in the dirt."

"There are no opportunities for this tp happen, Mary Lou. We've ruled out a sniper, a bomb and a good old-fashioned drive-by shooting. No one can get close enough to Nikolay to slit his throat or plant a slug in his heart."

"We need to reach an accommodation, Mama, to take us to a new normal."

Frank snorted, his derision visible on his expression.

"Death is the end of all things. We just carry on what we're doing—only more so. We have casino money rolling in to support us but he does not. Another week, maybe a month. The longer we can last, the sooner his power will be lost. He might enjoy contacts back in Russia, but he is living in the US of A. And that is where he must die."

"Brave words little brother, but saying it doesn't make it so. Yes, we have the money to keep going but not the men. That's what we repeatedly say and no one seems to disagree. Our best are dead and what remains: they are scared and they should be. I know I'm scared. Everyone in this room should be—we are living in fucking dangerous times."

"DARLING, IS YOUR primary objection our lack of fellas?"

"It's up there, Mama. I can't see how to win in a fight when the ring is empty."

"Bobby, that's your issue too?"

"To carry on we need solid guys we can rely on when we turn up the heat."

"So why don't I get us some gold plate muchachos?"

"How're you going to do that?"

"Do you agree if I succeed that we continue with my plan?"

"I guess so. I mean, with enough guns we could pull him apart, I suppose."

Bobby shrugged. He wasn't happy because there was more to killing Nikolay than having a posse of lethal weapons. But it would help. His biggest problem right now was that he couldn't think of a good reason to disagree. If they hit Nikolay all guns blazing, he'd be dead before morning. Fog City would be theirs.

"So that's settled then. I'll go first thing tomorrow and by the end of the week, Nikolay Markov will lie in a body bag.

MARY LOU'S TRIP to New York passed smoothly enough, although her impatience to arrive nearly got the better of her. On the plane, she thought back to the day she took the same flight and assassinated Charlie Pentangelo, capo to the Baninno Family. Their empire had crumbled now and there were few left alive to remember Charlie or recall what he looked like—let alone ponder on what he achieved.

She had spent her time in Manhattan in a perpetual state of fear, afraid of every guy in a three-piece suit who glanced in her general direction. Even the ticket purchase at Palm Springs had felt like agony. Mary Lou recalled fleeing the scene of her crime and being chased across town by Charlie's goons. Such relief at finding a yellow vehicle. That moment when she got in the taxi and they drove to LaGuardia.

And here she stood in the same airport waiting in line to go into the city. This time there was no plan to hide a piece by her crotch and no need to carry any heat. Mary Lou was here to talk—and nothing else.

Just as the Bannino clan's power had waned, so too with most of the five Families that controlled New York since the days of the Big Bankroll. Organized crime in the east coast had followed a similar path to the mobs out west. As the Feds were given a mandate to attack the mob, guys ratted out their compadres and people lost their grip on the rackets under their control.

The operations didn't die on the vine. Instead other gangs took them over with an ancestry that couldn't be traced to anywhere even close to Sicily: the Latinos, Chinese, Russians, Ukrainians and many other nationalities too. A great big racial melting pot of extortion, gun running, drug supply, labor racketeering—and the list went on.

Despite all these changes to the criminal fabric of the Five Boroughs, one group had survived and still dipped their beak into several troughs: the Gagliardi family, with Fiorino at its helm. The man had survived assassination attempts and the encroachment on his territory of just about every gang the country had to offer. He continued to rule his piece of Manhattan and New Jersey with an iron fist.

Decades ago, the seat of his power would have been a swanky five-star hotel overlooking Central Park. That was then and this was now. Mary Lou and Fiorino sat at the back of a restaurant on Mulberry. He had agreed to see her out of respect for Pasquale, but her reputation did her no harm, although the most famous of her exploits deserving the great man's attention was twenty years old.

THEY ATE LINGUINI with clams and drank a glass of red wine each. By the time Fiorino mopped up his sauce with a piece of bread, Mary Lou had tired of small talk and wanted to get down to the reason for her visit.

"I'm glad to hear business is good for you."

"It's not like how it was, nothing is nowadays, but we survive."

"And how is recruitment?"

"That is never easy. The youngsters want fast money and no graft. Something for zip. This is the problem in the world we live in. No one is prepared to wait for success. Everything must happen now."

"We face similar difficulties, but on a much smaller scale."

"Don't do yourself down. I understand you maintain controlling interests in at least two casinos. That's no small boast for a woman to make."

"Thank you. Sometimes it's who you know that counts."

"Influence is a marvelous thing. How we get things done—with a little help from our friends."

"Pasquale recommended I speak with you on a delicate matter where friends on the west coast are proving hard to find."

"I'm listening. As lovely as it is to break bread with you, I assumed Pasquale was not introducing me to a tourist."

"No, I've been here before."

Mary Lou's eyes glanced toward the front of the restaurant and onwards where she sat, all those years ago, to stalk Pentangelo before whacking him.

Fiorino's eyelids closed and Mary Lou noticed him clench his jaw. While he admired her guts, perhaps he hadn't approved of her taking out a capo back when time had roman numerals.

"I am very aware of that."

"THE BOTTOM LINE is that we are experiencing some local difficulty in California and need access to some solid fellas for a week or two. Maybe three."

"And how many are we discussing here?"

"Ten would be good, twenty better and thirty would be best. The more we have, the sooner we can get matters settled and your people returned to you."

"How very gracious. What difficulties are you facing?"

Mary Lou outlined the situation in San Francisco and how it was now spilling over into LA. She described their efforts to date and how they were falling short due to the lack of competent bodies.

"I understand your problem, but thirty men is a small army and I don't want them killed or arrested. What guarantees can you offer me?"

"Fiorino, if this was a walk in the park, I wouldn't fly across the country to meet with you. We both know that some of those guys will not survive. What I wish to do is to reach an arrangement with you so that your loss is mitigated and I can show my appreciation for your support."

"This isn't about the money. It's about the people. We already agreed that good youngsters are hard to find and you are asking me to hand over thirty and expect to lose some in less than a week. In a war not of my making and in which I have no vested interest for the success of your venture."

"If you help me now, I could offer you a piece of a casino, for example. Your kind indulgence in this matter need not be paid back with a case of bills. If you are willing, I am flexible in how I show my appreciation."

"I know, but I still don't like the thought of losing good men and I wouldn't insult you by sending you greenhorns. Go back to California and let me think on this some more."

"I could stay in the city and we could speak further, if you liked."

"I'd like you to return to Palm Springs and leave me to consider my position."

Mary Lou nodded, stood up and kissed his proffered hand. Old school mafia. Then she left the restaurant and grabbed a cab to LaGuardia and home.

34

TWO DAYS AFTER Mary Lou got back, there was a knock on the door and Irma led the gentleman into the living room. Then she popped into the summerhouse to let Bobby and Mary Lou know they had a visitor.

"Would you like a coffee?"

"No, thank you. I'm not expecting to be here long enough to drink it."

"Then let's not detain you any longer than you need."

Bobby saw Mary Lou bristling and hoped she would remember who had sent Vito to their door.

"Mr. Gagliardi sends his regards and asked me to speak with you directly. He didn't want me to leave a message or note. He believes people he respects should hear news firsthand."

"Do thank him for his courteous behavior."

"Actually, I have changed my mind: a coffee would be most welcome."

Bobby and Mary Lou glanced at each other and summoned Irma to issue instructions. A quick conversation meant bad news, but if the guy was settling in for a drink, perhaps things were looking up. Vito said nothing until Irma reappeared with his mug.

"Mr. Gagliardi thanks you for making the journey to see him in person. This impressed him greatly as a mark of respect, dear lady."

Mary Lou smiled and waited. Bobby sat back in his seat, letting the experience wash over him until he knew whether to be happy or sad.

"He also was touched with your honest assessment of your situation and the way you conveyed that to him. Without gilding the lily, so to speak."

More smiling. More waiting. If you removed the yada-yada, you were left with nada so far. Why the build up? Can't he get to the punchline?

"You requested the loan of up to thirty men and Mr. Gagliardi is forced to decline."

Mary Lou stopped listening. Nothing Vito was going to say would improve her situation, so there was no point. Bobby was concerned to understand why because Mary Lou seemed optimistic when she came back.

"There are two issues he wishes to draw to your attention. First, your predicament is a problem of your own making. As he understands the situation, your bellicose approach infuriated the other party and after you reached a very reasonable settlement, you chiseled away at their territory."

Bobby felt a sickness in the pit of his stomach. Frank's exploits had been visible from New York and they were paying for the consequences of his actions.

"We could put aside the cause of your problems under the right circumstances. But second, the interests of the Gagliardi and Lagotti families are not aligned. Certain business activities have been hindered by your ongoing disagreement with Markov and we need this interference in our revenue generation to end."

Vito consumed some coffee. It felt as though he hadn't taken a breath since he told them how Gagliardi wasn't going to help. The feeling in Bobby's stomach got worse and his gastric wall tightened.

MARY LOU STARED out of the window as she saw no reason to hide her disinterest in what this olive-skinned excuse for a man had to say.

"Mrs. Lagotti: you have been given one week to resolve your local difficulties with Nikolay Markov. If you do not do so, your husband'll have need of an undertaker or a search party. Either way, you will be dead."

She tried to control her breathing as the air filled with the threat to her life.

"My apologies for being blunt but I want to be certain you understand your situation. Mr. Gagliardi is more than happy to forge a relationship with you should you vanquish your foe. What concerns him most is that no business is being conducted while you two slug it out. There is no personal animosity in anything I have said and I hope you appreciate that."

Vito stood up: clearly this was not a debate. He'd conveyed what Gagliardi had instructed and now he needed to leave.

"Can we call you a taxi?"

"Most kind."

Bobby popped his head into the kitchen to speak with Irma and by the time he got back, Vito was standing on his own. The clang of the patio door told him Mary Lou had given up on social niceties with this prick. He had just threatened her life, but he represented one of the most powerful gang bosses in America.

"Forgive my wife. She doesn't like hearing bad news, but obviously we recognize Mr. Gagliardi's respect to send you all this distance for such a short but clear message."

"It's what I do. Pass on decisions whichever way the coin lands."

"I understand. I used to be in the outfit."

"Fine. When she calms down, let her know the clock is ticking. We need this resolved in seven days or less, one way or another. Between you and me, I think Gagliardi would rather work with you but the Russian has the network and we have the product. It's a marriage of convenience and no more, but it needs peace to thrive. Capiche?"

"Got it."

BOBBY WALKED THROUGH the conservatory and out onto the patio to find Mary Lou in the summerhouse. He sat down and explained all that Vito had said and threatened.

"The mob will put a hit out on you in a week if we don't get matters sorted with Nikolay Markov."

Her jaw sunk to the floor and the blood drained from her cheeks.

"Is there no leeway?"

"None. We must end this nonsense now."

Mary Lou rummaged around for a cigarette but her hands were shaking and she couldn't get her lighter to work. Bobby bent over and lit one for her.

"A hit on me."

He nodded as she inhaled on her smoke, letting a plume of exhalation form a cloud in front of her face.

"Good news is that if we succeed against Markov, we have a guaranteed deal with Gagliardi."

"For what?"

"Vito was willfully vague, but they way he talked made it sound like narcotics. Don't know for sure."

"Perhaps they have a new pipeline into the east or from Colombia."

"...A hit."

Mary Lou's attention drifted in and out of focus until Bobby was no longer certain she was taking in anything he was saying.

Mama's Gone

THE DEATH OF Charlie Pentangelo was a pivotal moment after Mary Lou's twins were kidnapped and then rescued. But the speed with which his body was discovered and she was chased across the city startled her. It had always been a dangerous mission but her single-minded desire to kill the man, who'd caused her so much pain, had kept her focused on the act of assassination. The minute his corpse hit the ground, Mary Lou woke from her death-trance and smelled the coffee.

The thought of the mob giving her seven days before a hit sent her into a flat-spin panic. There was only one intelligent action for her to take: flee. She went into the conservatory and Bobby wasn't there. Into the living room and she heard a clattering in the kitchen. Without making a sound, Mary Lou grabbed her bag, hopped into her car and sped away, acknowledging her protective detail at the entrance to the property before bursting onto the road —and out of town.

Ten minutes later, Bobby came downstairs and tried to locate Mary Lou. Irma hadn't seen her for a while either. A quick conversation with the fellas outside revealed what had happened. Alice returned from the Country Club with Naldo in tow after an hour and Bobby filled her in on the day's events.

"We need to find Mama."

"She's in the wind for now."

They sent word out to their guys in Palm Springs to report back if they saw her. After a further hour there were no reports and Alice was worried.

"Where do you think she has gone?"

"No idea. She didn't pack: she just ran away. Could be anywhere, but we'll find her. We might have hit the mattresses but we've eyes and ears all over town and across the state. She'll be okay."

"I hope you're right."

TWENTY-FOUR HOURS later and they still hadn't found Mama. If she was holed up somewhere in Palm Springs, Bobby reckoned she'd have turned up by now. This meant she was further afield gone therefore going to be harder to find: where would be the first place she'd go? No one was too sure.

With Naldo watching their backs, Bobby and Alice began a road trip while Frank carried on his San Francisco exploits oblivious to the misery in his family. They kept him out of the loop because he had enough to worry about on the front line against Markov. Truth was, telling him didn't even flash across either of their minds. Frank had spent so many years apart from the rest, they forgot he was a member of the family.

As Alice had set up a crib in Bakersfield, they tried the printers first but Mary Lou hadn't surfaced there at all. Then off to Malibu in case she'd visit Alice's home but again they drew a blank.

"The Palace has a suite. We should try there next."

THREE HOURS LATER, they pulled into the Palace and headed inside. It was quiet. Four hookers hung near the reception in the hope of a john while the second floor was devoid of human life. Up to the penthouse in search of Mama. The living room was empty but there were crockery and utensils out. The manager said no one had been up there since Milton was killed, apart from the cleaning service.

Alice and Bobby checked the bedrooms and Naldo stayed near the entrance, always alert to external danger. Bobby heard Alice scream and rushed in to see what she had found, passing Naldo who had already drawn his weapon.

"Wait here."

Bobby feared the worst and steeled himself to find her corpse. When he ran through the doorway, Mary Lou was huddled on the bed, naked, and mumbling to herself. He couldn't tell how long she had been there, but the chances were she'd come straight here, judging by the acrid stench in the room and the mess on the floor.

Alice backed away unable to deal with the state of her mother. This once great strong woman reduced to a ball of humanity on a bed. Bobby felt the pain of seeing his lover, friend and confidante at an all-time low. And it was his job to look after her: in sickness and in health.

He held Mary Lou in his arms until her mutterings ceased and she looked at him and smiled.

"I'm glad you're here. I got lost and didn't know where you were. I was scared."

"Sure but we're here now."

"We?"

"Alice is with me."

"Alice?"

"Yes, see?"

Mary Lou peered over Bobby's shoulder at her daughter and Alice raised a smile from beneath her tears. Mama smiled back.

"We don't live here. I'll help you get yourself sorted out and then we'll take a ride home."

"That'd be nice. I'd like to eat first though."

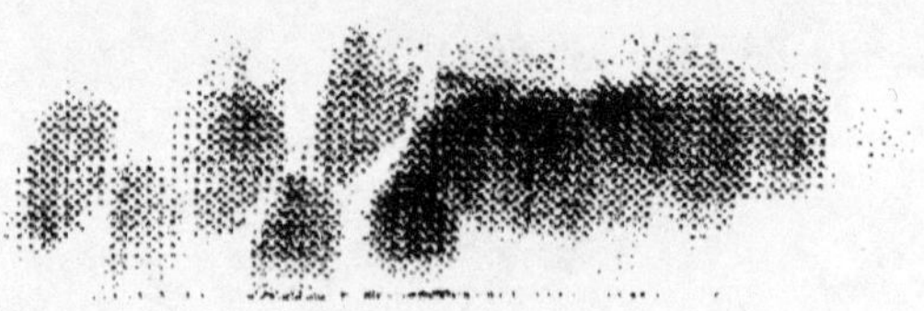

35

THE JOURNEY FROM the Palace was filled with silence in between awkward pauses. Alice was beside herself, unsure how to respond to her mother who appeared unaware anything unusual might have happened. Naldo drove with Bobby in the front passenger seat, leaving the women in the back.

"Would you like us to stop at a diner so you can have a break?"

"Not at all, dear. There's no need to fuss—I'm fine."

"Do you remember why you went to the Palace?"

"Did I? Don't think I did, dear. You might be mistaken about that."

"Leave it, Alice. We won't get very far asking her those sort of questions."

She stared out the window and held Mama's hand. It felt feeble like a child's and Alice wondered how she had become an adult. Didn't seem right. Not at all. The view from the freeway was pure tedium, but it gave her the opportunity to run through what had happened to Mama.

The woman was confused—far more so than Alice had ever imagined possible. To not know of your whereabouts or how you got there… A stream of tears left her eyes as the impact of the meaning of that hit home. But Mama wasn't old. That kind of senile confusion was reserved for much older people. Try telling that to Mama's addled mind.

Forty minutes later, Naldo pulled off the road and stopped at a diner. Despite her protestations, Mary Lou chowed down on a burger and fries while the other three had coffee and cake.

"My Frank and I spent one summer eating in diners. Lots of burgers, gallons of soda. They were good times."

Bobby eyed Alice who looked back at him and glanced at her mother.

"Weren't you fleeing the scene?"

"I guess so, yes. But they were happy days before the darkness set in."

"Darkness?"

"When I was on my own and you kids were born. Canada was a lonely time for me."

"We were babies, right?"

"Little ones. Babes in arms. Cute."

Alice smiled at the idea of being small and cuddled by Mama. Comfort from invented memories. Then the reality of the current situation slammed into her head and another tear rolled down her cheek.

WHEN THEY ARRIVED back at Oakcrest Drive, the family sat down in the living room and Naldo remained on duty outside, the Markov threat ever present. He was as constant as the Northern Star. Inside, Mary Lou announced she was going upstairs for a rest, maybe to take a nap. This left Alice alone with Bobby and the unspoken problem of her mother's mental health. Until Bobby punctured the silence.

"We can't leave her by herself anymore. She's run off once which means she could do it again."

"You're talking about keeping her prisoner."

"No. Just that we need to get a companion for her otherwise you or I will have to stay with her the whole time. And that's not practical."

"A companion? You make her sound like an old maid."

"Someone with medical training who can keep an eye on her and help tend to her needs, health-wise."

"You mean if she loses her mind again."

"She got confused and forgot where she was, but most of the time she is lucid and functions brilliantly. Be careful to remember she is still your mom and deserves your respect."

"Don't talk like that. I am aware exactly who she is. This isn't easy for me. I know I questioned her decision-making because I disagreed with her conclusions. The idea that was the start of something else plain hurts right now because we've done nothing to help her. We focused on ourselves. Never considered that she might have been hurting."

Bobby fumbled around with a cigar and lighter to take his mind off Alice's insights. He poked three holes in one end but the flint wouldn't spark even after six attempts. Alice walked over, sat beside him and used hers instead.

"We have to work with each other on this. We are both in pain now, but we have to acknowledge we will be stronger together than if we lash out at the other."

"This is a shit sandwich, for sure."

"And you're right. We need a nurse so if she goes off the rails, there's someone there to catch her who is experienced in these things."

"In the meantime, I'll get Naldo to call in one of his most trusted guys, who can be a bodyguard until we find someone better qualified. As much as I'd like Naldo to do the job, we need his talents elsewhere at the minute. We are at war with Nikolay Markov and must put that to bed."

"And soon, otherwise Mama's forgetfulness will be the least of our problems."

Bobby puffed on his stogie and let himself vanish in the moment. Alice watched him and tried to find solace in that they'd reached a decision and from now on, at least, Mama would remain safe.

The other reason Bobby stayed with his cigar was that the next thing he would have to do would be to go upstairs and explain to Mary Lou she needed a bodyguard and had to give up her car keys. This was not a conversation he wanted to have, but he understood Alice should be left out of it so there was only one bad cop in town. Even though he didn't want it to be him.

"SHE'S ASLEEP AGAIN."

"Did you tell her about the companion?"

"Yeah. She is not happy because she can't see it's necessary. To her, there are blanks in her life: she is unaware of what is going on."

"That's a blessing. Knowing you were losing your memory would be far worse."

"Devastating for Mary Lou, for sure, but easier for us because we could talk to her about it and she might see the sense in what we say. As it is, she believes we're crazy and over-obsessed."

"She won't like the next thing we have to do, will she?"

"What's that?"

"She can't be head of the family any more."

Bobby looked at his lap and his shoulders drooped. Alice was right, but he didn't want to deal. This was the woman he'd spent twenty-five years living with, loving and who had turned his dismal life around. Now he needed to be her rock as she had been for him. And it hurt.

"I suppose so."

"S'pose? We have seen the choices she's made and the consequences of her actions. We cannot allow her to keep control. Mama must pass the responsibility over to someone else—or more than one of us. I don't want you to see this is some kind of power grab by me. All I'm asking is to make sensible decisions that'll mean we survive this week and have sound leadership after that. Who does it is less important right now than the fact it needs to be done."

"AND HOW DO you propose we get Mary Lou to step down?"

Alice sighed, the air in her lungs escaping from the truths she was about to utter.

"She won't volunteer because she isn't sufficiently aware of what is going on. So we need to agree which of us heads up the organization and let her think what she likes in her more lucid moments. In reality, she is the best consigliere this family could have—no disrespect, Bobby."

"So we sideline her."

"We have little choice that I can see. Mama wants to lead us into a bloody suicide mission against Markov and the mob will kill her in a matter of days if she fails. Now is the time for action. We leave our regrets for another day."

"But I still don't like to hear you say those things. You're braver than me."

Bobby glanced up at Alice who was wiping a tear away from her left eye. No one was in a good place right now. To confront the reality of Mary Lou's difficulties took every fiber of strength and resilience in his body. Alice needed him to be stronger than he felt because she was correct. They had to be there for each other if they were to survive.

"WE CAN'T DO this alone."

"What do you mean?"

"We must include Frank. If we don't get him involved, he won't understand what's going on with Mary Lou. We'd look like we were plotting a coup against your mom instead of saving her life."

"Agreed."

"Also, if you mean what you say, we could end up deciding he is the best person to lead the family."

"That is possible. But I'm telling you I wouldn't be happy about it."

"That's a discussion for another time. First, we need to get him here and away from his jaunt in San Francisco. Next, we agree on what to do to save Mary Lou's life. Succession can wait until the weekend."

Bobby winked because of the absurdity of what he'd just said. The idea such momentous events were occurring right here, right now and not in several decades time seemed ridiculous to him. This was never meant to happen. Bobby always banked on him being long dead before anything happened to his Mary Lou.

Alice's stomach was constricted to the point of agony. The dull ache in the rest of her body had conspired to a position in her belly that made a pure pinpoint of pain. She wanted to cry and never stop but she needed to hold it together. The tears wouldn't help Bobby, who must hurt too, and she didn't want to show him weakness because she was damn sure she should be the head of the family.

Now was not the time to throw her name into the ring but the idea lingered just as the emotional impact of Mama's situation rattled around her ribcage. The funny thing was it was easier to think about that than focus on Mama's mental state, even though it was the task at hand. Was she so wrapped up in herself or was it a displacement activity to avoid the awful truth she could barely bring herself to say in her head, let alone out loud?

"Let's send word to Frank it's time for a family conference."

"Tonight. We can't afford to wait. He needs to haul ass."

"I'll put Naldo on it. Worst case, he drives over to SF and brings him back."

"Might need a conversation with you—not from me."

"We'll see what happens. Either way, we need to get matters settled before we go to sleep tonight. The clock is ticking on Mary Lou's life."

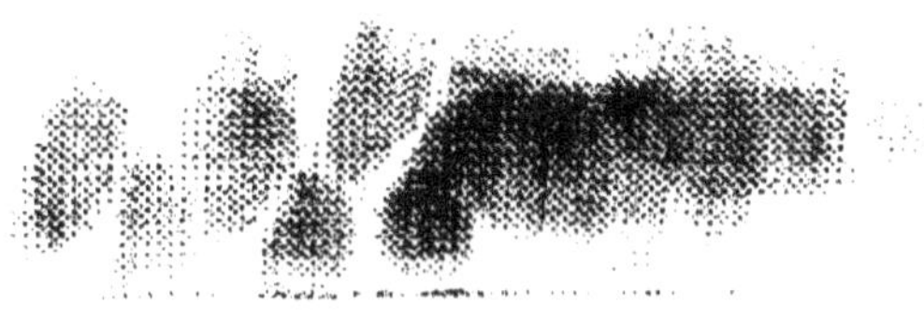

36

NALDO RETURNED FROM San Francisco with Frank in the passenger seat, not impressed with being instructed to come to Palm Springs. Again. To be dragged back by Friscetti was the icing on the cake. He was not in a good humor by the time he arrived and wanted everyone to know about it.

With Mary Lou resting, the other two were in the conservatory waiting for his arrival. The edges of Alice's eyes were red and Bobby sniffed more than usual. There had been raw emotions in the house earlier and even Frank could sense the stress oozing out of the others.

"I'm here. Where's Mama?"

"Upstairs. She's asleep."

"So we must wait for her before this urgent meeting can take place."

"Not really. We three need to talk—thanks for coming back so quickly."

"Naldo was quite insistent for a goon."

"He's more than a hired hand to us as you know, but that's not important right now. We must stay focused."

"On what?"

"Mama got lost yesterday. Plain vanished and wound up in the Palace, not able to explain or remember how she arrived there."

Frank listened but his expression implied he didn't believe what he heard.

"But you found her and all's good. I still don't see what I'm doing here and why you are in a blind panic."

Bobby told Frank about Mary Lou's visit to Little Italy and the clear and present danger provided by Vito. Two minutes later and Frank understood why he'd been driven back to Oakcrest Drive. Alice remained silent because of how incendiary their conversations could be.

"So we must finish our business with Markov in the next couple of days."

"Yes, in such a way that we're alive at the end."

"I return to Bay City and execute the fucker."

"That is still not viable. We need to agree a plan that'll work—guaranteed."

"Nikolay's death resolves the problem."

"It would if we could kill him, but there is no meaningful way to be sure he will die."

"As much as you want to assassinate him, now is not the time. Once we get over this hump, we can pick our moment and skin him alive if we choose. The war must end for certain in the next couple of days or Mama dies."

Frank stared at Alice and tried to process the notion they were going to allow Markov to breathe longer than he wanted.

"And that is the second item on the agenda. The first thing we have to deal with is the best way to get Mary Lou to step down as head of the family."

"You have to be fucking joking."

"If only. She is not in a fit state to do the job anymore. We need to be strong for her and help her move on to be our consigliere."

Alice and Bobby said nothing more as Frank's eyes flitted left and right as he tried to make sense of what he was hearing. His first instinct was to strike out and punch the wall, hit Bobby or slap Alice, but he was aware enough to know that none of these options would get him anywhere. Denial seemed an excellent choice but an hour later Frank continued to receive the same message and it wasn't shifting. His views would need to change instead.

"HOW ARE WE doing this?"

"With respect to your Mama and as smooth a transition as possible."

"Sure. I meant who will take over?"

"Doesn't have to be one person."

"Yes it does, sis'. No organization can be run by a committee. Nothing'll get agreed."

"If all three of us had a vote, then that would work fine."

"Apart from the fact that you two would always vote against me."

"Not necessarily, Frank. But we're getting ahead of ourselves. The question isn't about who should take over leading the family. I'll say it again: how can we get Mary Lou to step down, because I don't want to force her out—unless we have no other option."

"I WILL NOT be the one to push her off her perch. That's plain wrong. Our Mama deserves better than that."

"She does but we don't have the time to wait for her to agree. She doesn't think there is a problem—though we three know there is. We owe her—and all she's built up over these years—to do what's best for the family even if it's not in her short-term interests."

"Fine words sis', but it doesn't wash. I won't usurp our mother."

"If you don't, then I will. You kids might feel yourselves conflicted but I must do the right thing. I might not like it but there's more at stake than my feelings or your Mama's ego—as much as that pains me to say it."

Frank stood up, cheeks all red, and Bobby got out of his chair to square off against him.

"Cool it, guys. Stop acting like a pair of silver-backed gorillas."

The two men were ten feet apart, separated by potted plants and occasional tables.

"No one's pushing my Mama off the mercy seat."

Frank pulled out a revolver from behind his back and within an instant, Bobby aimed his piece directly at Frank's heart. Alice watched the two for a second and grabbed her snub nose out of her bag. She stepped backwards one pace, both hands gripping her gun first pointing at Frank then switching to Bobby, repeatedly.

"We all need to put our weapons down or someone will get hurt."

That was when a bullet blazed through the conservatory followed by a shower of other slugs coursing into every surface in the room.

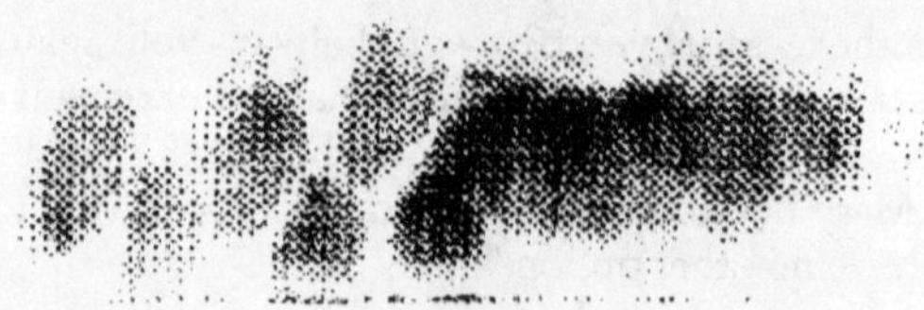

37

ALL THREE SLAMMED to the floor and elbowed their way near to some furniture.

"Where's it coming from?"

"Outside somewhere. I've got no fix on it. Have you?"

"Nope. No idea. How the fuck did they get close enough to make the hit?"

"What about our men?"

The answer arrived as soon as the question left Frank's lips. The sound of a separate wave of bullets from a different distance punctured the drone of the original onslaught. And still they were pinned to the floor with no way to fight back.

The glass in all the windows had all but shattered and bullet holes littered the walls. A woman screamed. Alice couldn't tell if it was Irma in the kitchen or Mama upstairs. The sheer volume of the gunfire made any analysis impossible. Bobby turned his face to look outside and, with a trained professional's eye, he reached a simple conclusion.

"Far end of the backyard at the tree line. Three maybe four shooters. Automatic rifles. Don't waste your bullets even if you've got a clean shot: they are not nearly close enough to take out."

Alice blinked and watched Frank grip his pistol more tightly as though paralyzed with anger at not being able to deliver immediate and bloody revenge.

"Just stay down for now. Either they leave of their own accord or our fellas will deal with them."

"How much armory did they bring with them?"

"Enough to piss me off. If this is an assassination attempt, they fired way too early. Means somebody only wants to scare us."

"Well it's fucking working."

And still the slugs landed inside the conservatory. Bobby had maneuvered himself by a piece of solid wall either side of two broken windows. From there he'd occasionally pop his head far enough out to get a glimpse of the world beyond the summerhouse. But he only gave himself half a second otherwise it would have been his last.

The twins sucked the tiled floor as though there was no tomorrow. Even Frank, despite his bravado, had the smarts not to raise his head too high, let alone try to fire back. He might be an arrogant son of a bitch but he wasn't stupid and understood that Bobby knew his way around situations like this. Frank, on the other hand, was a novice.

ANOTHER MINUTE AND everything fell silent inside but there was still the noise of shots in the backyard.

"Stay down. Nobody moves until I give the word."

Alice intended to spend the rest of her life on the floor and had no intention of being the first up. Frank considered sitting up and firing two rounds but heeded Bobby's advice.

Thirty seconds later and no more shots or sounds until sirens appeared in the distance.

"The local cops took their time. Isn't the captain on our payroll."

"He was."

"Not any more it would seem."

A shout came from the gloom. Naldo informed them that three of the four assailants were dead and a fourth was in the wind.

"How many of ours?"

"Two deceased, one injured. The cops will be here any minute and we've got weapons we need to hide."

"Keep doing what you are doing. You're a life saver."

"Prego."

Bobby indicated it was okay to breathe again. Frank went to see if Irma had been hit and Alice ran upstairs to check on Mama. She was hiding under the bed, sobbing.

"It's all over, Mama. We're all safe."

"The mob's come to kill me."

"We've no idea who's responsible right now. Could be New York but I am not sure that makes sense. Why warn you and then go back on their word?"

"They have done much worse, dear."

"I'm certain."

Alice helped Mary Lou scurry out from her hiding place and brushed her clothes with her hand to make her look less bedraggled.

"We need to get you a bodyguard."

"Definitely. They've failed once and they're sure to try again."

THE COPS CAME into the house and spent the rest of the night bagging and tagging corpses, taking statements and following procedures that made them a general nuisance. The lieutenant in charge of the investigation knew the score: complete the paperwork fast and get out of the residence quick. As he was leaving, Bobby shook his hand and planted five C-notes in the guy's palm. They'd wait until Bobby gave the go-ahead before they identified bodies or poking their noses into Lagotti family business.

Once the uniforms and detectives had departed, Bobby put Mary Lou back to bed. Then he locked the door between the conservatory and living room. Naldo had already doubled the guard on the perimeter as soon as the police had finished interviewing him. For a man in the middle of all that gunfire, he sure saw and heard nothing.

"Who did it? Anyone got any ideas?"

"Mama said it was New York but why would they?"

"Perhaps Markov. Or somebody else trying to move in on us. There's been heat in Chicago, Las Vegas and Boston recently. Some bright spark might have thought to attack the family while our attention was on Markov."

"True. Does Markov have the balls to lay on tonight's treat?"

"Yes. That man's ego is limitless and he has the resources to pull it off."

"Doesn't answer how the hell they got so close. Like one of ours turned rat."

"If we have a traitor in our midst, Naldo will find them, extract all the information we need from them and dispose of the body afterwards."

THE CRACK OF the gun sent Alice spinning, just as the speck of Mama's blood landed on her cheek.

Mama's Gone

Ten minutes later after the initial Sturm und Drang was over, Alice's stomach felt heavy like a a burden had been added to her body. And she experienced that weight as a dull ache masquerading as an unvoiced roar. As though a fractured yell was about to erupt from deep inside her. Only she knew that she would not—or could not—release that primal scream. It was bound, coiled inside. A cobra that would never leap on its prey. An agony that would never fade.

Ten hours later and the initial shock had abated and that first pang of hurt was less intense. Still noticeably there inside her, but now Alice could walk around without experiencing the jagged edges of her sorrow. She sat in the church listening to the priest eulogizing over her Mama. The ground glass of her sadness eked into every pore and the abject misery of her world permeated all her being.

FEBRUARY 1997

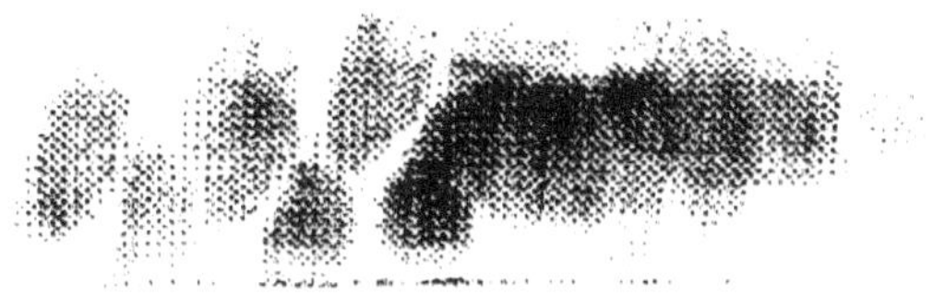

38

NEXT MORNING, MARY Lou padded downstairs with one thought rattling in her head.

"Whoever attacked us last night must die."

Bobby, Alice and Frank all nodded agreement at the sentiment but knew there was no action to be taken at present because they still had no clue who'd done it. Naldo said the hit men were from out of town and he'd never seen than before. That almost ruled out New York because Naldo remained connected to the fellas back east.

"When we find out who it is, then they'll get theirs."

"Must be the Russian. Let's kill the Russian."

"We've been over this, Mama. The guy can't be whacked that easily. Frank's spent a week in the same city as that mook and the fella still breathes. Do you think your son would have let him live if he'd had the opportunity of killing him?"

"I see. Why didn't you kill him, Frank?"

"Too closely guarded and by fierce dudes too. Mean fuckers and professional: knew what they were doing."

"If Frank can't take him out, who are we going to get to do the job?"

Alice and Bobby glanced at each other like they were living through their own Groundhog Day. Frank witnessed for himself Mama's grasp of the complex situation they found themselves in. Mary Lou could not see what all the fuss was about. It was as plain as the nose on her face that the what's-his-name Russian must die.

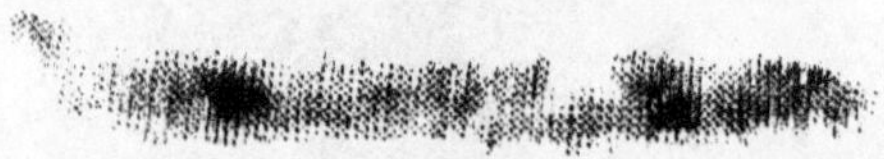

"WE MUST END the war, Mama. So that means we need to make a truce instead."

"Peace? I thought you said we finish the war. And you do that by fighting harder than the other side."

"Not always. We will win against Nikolay Markov by beating him to the punch. If we negotiate the peace well, we get better access to his territories."

"And lull him into a false security so we can whack him at our leisure later on."

"That's my boy. Let's snare us a Russki."

"But first sit down and agree a deal. That'll get the outfit off your back and we all breathe safer then."

"The mob: I've tangled with them before."

After an hour, the family got Mary Lou to focus more on a peace accord and less on whacking Nikolay.

"Let's send Naldo over with a message we want the violence to end and to sit down and talk terms—again."

"Good idea, Mama."

NALDO HAD GROWN tired of the constant trips to Fog City: too many hills and no one knew how to cook a bowl of pasta properly. Always soggy, never al dente. The first order of business was to speak with Isaak Vasilev and keep him in the loop. If Vasilev was as good as Frank claimed, he would know Naldo was in dialog with Markov and might draw the wrong conclusion.

Isaak was a shrewd one and, while the conversation was cold, he offered Naldo only professional courtesy and respect. Naldo didn't trust the fella's heritage, but they were both key participants in the lives of the rival twins. For him that meant they should follow the hierarchy but could still work well together for the greater good. Isaak appeared to treat his allegiance to Frank as all-encompassing. Perhaps Naldo took the same attitude when he was Isaak's age. Now, even Naldo had gained a sense of realpolitik and understood it was better to get along with people than create unnecessary enemies when all he wanted to do was kill for a living and protect those under his care.

With Isaak onside, they figured out the best way to send a message to Markov was to have a quiet word with Lara Mikhailov, one of Nikolay's associates who had performed her fair share of murder and mayhem these past weeks. Naldo visited her that lunchtime while Isaak lay outside on the opposite roof training a rifle sight at her head.

"FORGIVE THE INTRUSION on your meal, but I need to speak with you on a most urgent matter."

Mikhailov looked up from her newspaper, eyes flitting sideways seeking potential danger.

"Do not be concerned. I am here for a conversation with you and nothing more. If you think about it, were I to want you dead then you'd be slumped over your brisket by now. May I sit down?"

"For sure. And what's to stop me shooting you? I don't like strangers coming up and disturbing my lunch."

"Apart from the fact we are surrounded by witnesses and a sniper's aiming at your head as we speak? Nothing, but you wouldn't hear the message I wish to impart to you from Mary Lou Lagotti."

The name got Mikhailov's attention more than any of Naldo's other words and she put her silverware down to listen.

"We want to arrange a meet-up. We are all losing money and burying good people. Neither is great for business, so it should stop. The fighting must end and we need to agree the peace."

"How do I know I can trust you?"

"You don't, but a single hand gesture on my part or any outward sign of menace on yours and you will be dead. The fact I haven't instigated your killing should show our good faith. If I wanted to carry on with our war, then I should kill you. Right here, right now."

Naldo stared into her beady blue eyes and Mikhailov glared back. Four intimate seconds later and she blinked and relaxed her upper body.

"Suppose I take you at your word, what are you proposing?"

"ALL WE NEED is to agree a neutral venue and that the aim of the talks is to find an acceptable peace. A hotel in the tourist district or on the edge of town would suit us fine. Just not in the Tenderloin."

"And would reparations for past conduct be on the table?"

"As much as it needed to be to agree a peace. Remember, there has been loss on both sides so we shouldn't fixate on monetizing our corpses."

"You have the blood of my friends on your hands."

"I am sure we do and your fingers reek of the guts of our fallen. But we still want a truce and to get back to earning money."

A waiter arrived and Naldo ordered an espresso. Mikhailov continued her chewing, occasionally taking a sip from her glass of water—although Naldo couldn't be sure it wasn't vodka.

"And why now do you come here with your white flag and a promise of a bright tomorrow? What has changed since last week?"

"We have lost enough money and want the pipe to flow again."

"Nothing to do with any trouble in Palm Springs you had? We heard about the attack on the Lagotti house. Sorry business, hitting a person's home. Did anyone get hurt?"

"The housekeeper needed stitches and the morgue received three visitors. Was your hand in that?"

"No. If I had then the four Lagotti family members would be dead and not seeking peace."

Naldo scratched his chin and Mikhailov raised her eyebrows and widened her eyes as if to prepare for her imminent assassination at the hands of Isaak's sniper rifle. Naldo smiled.

"Don't be alarmed. Sometimes an itch is all that irritates me… Let's be clear: you and I are cut from the same cloth. We are professional people who can sniff bullshit a mile away because our lives usually depend on it. You could have killed me the minute I walked up to your table with the piece resting on your lap. My sniper could have taken you out any second after that, but we haven't because we understand there is time for action and a moment to listen. Make no mistake: tell Nikolay Markov to agree to sit down and thrash out a mutually agreeable truce. Both sides must earn money."

Naldo stood up and placed enough green to cover the cost of his espresso and her meal, including tip. Then he headed for the door and walked down the street. Isaak maintained position with Mikhailov in his sights for more than a minute as she continued eating her lunch.

He considered squeezing the trigger but thought better of it: Frank would not have been happy. Isaak dismantled the rifle and returned it to its case. Then he hopped over the top of two roofs and scuttled down a fire escape.

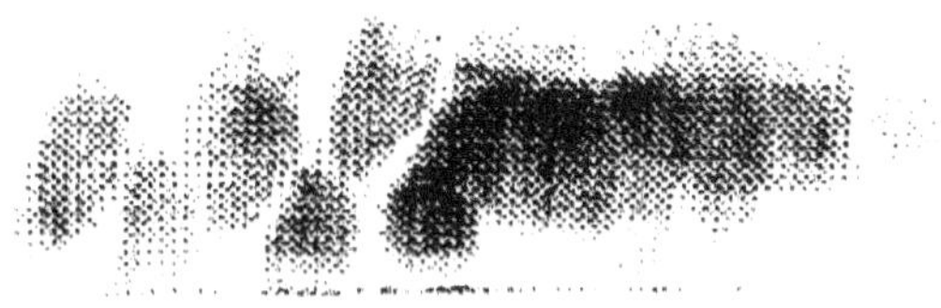

39

MARY LOU SAT on a sun lounger staring out at the pool. The rest of the family were in the summerhouse planning the strategy for the peace conference. They didn't want her there: every time she made any suggestion, someone would shoot her down. What was the point? Besides, the fastest solution to their war with Markov was a single bullet. That much was clear.

Her only problem was to find a person who'd be willing to act as Markov's executioner. The fear behind her daughter's eyes when Alice came back from secretly meeting him was sufficient justification for his death in Mary Lou's mind. Add in the current difficulties and she saw no reason to sit down and talk with that mook.

Naldo and Isaak stood outside the summerhouse door, guarding the occupants while keeping a surreptitious eye on Mary Lou, who would glance up at them now and again. She was still getting used to the permanent bodyguard assigned to her. At the height of her power, she'd protected herself and not relied on anybody else. She didn't see herself as old, but she recognized she wasn't as fast as twenty years before.

The back of her throat was dry, so she got up, but instead of heading to the kitchen, she wandered over to Isaak.

"I need some help indoors. Can you come with me please?"

Isaak looked to Naldo who returned the glance but had nothing to say for himself. So Isaak followed Mary Lou through the conservatory, up the stairs and into her bedroom. He still had no idea what he was doing there.

MARY LOU SAT on the edge of the bed after Isaak closed the door. He stiffened, uncertain of where this situation was heading. She smiled a warm curl of lips and beckoned for him to sit on the stool by the vanity mirror. Isaak relaxed and slumped down.

"There is something I would like you to do for me."

"Tell me and it is done."

"Thank you, but wait until I say what I want before you agree: go back to San Francisco tonight and kill Nikolay Markov. A knife in the chest, a bullet through his brains or a bomb under his car. It doesn't matter how you do it but that fucker must not be breathing in the morning."

Isaak shuffled on his seat, knowing this was the exact opposite of what the rest of her family wanted. But she was the head of the outfit. He couldn't think straight and played it cool to figure things out later.

"Can I enlist any help?"

"No one who's connected to the Lagottis, but if you need a local hand, knock yourself out. The important thing is that Markov must die and the only two people to know who did it are sat in this room right now."

Mary Lou glared at Isaak to impress on him the severity of her requirements and the significance of their secrecy. He shuffled again and averted his gaze from Mary Lou's stare. Fucked if he did. Fucked if he didn't. At this rate, Isaak wouldn't be alive after St Valentine's day.

"AND THIS CAN'T wait until the peace conference, with respect?"

"You mean, it'd be easier to hit a few at the same time?"

"It would make a bigger statement if it happened in public, so to speak."

"Interesting…"

Mary Lou brooded on Isaak's idea, giving it the full focus of her mind, even though he'd only said it to buy himself some much needed space to think. He was surprised she'd given it the time of day.

"You'll be in the protection detail at the meet-up, won't you?"

"I'd expect so. I mean, nothing's been decided yet, but…"

"That settles it. Once the meeting is over, you attack Markov before he leaves the room. He mustn't get out alive. And this has the added advantage that I watch him die with my own eyes."

"We'll all be frisked so I won't be carrying a rod."

"You will know the venue in good time and can make the arrangements. I'll leave you to figure out the details."

Mary Lou got off the bed and held open the door. Isaak took three or four seconds to get the hint, then he sprang up and walked out to resume his position outside the summerhouse door.

"What she want?"

"To find out if I thought a sniper could have a line of sight into her bedroom window."

"And?"

"I told her the answer was no."

"Took you long enough."

"I know you don't need or want to hear this but my grandfather said something to me on his deathbed and I'd like to share it with you."

"What was that, then?"

"Don't fuck your boss's mom."

"Wise guy, your grandfather."

"He was in an outfit."

They both smiled, wallowing in their own wit, but Isaak didn't know which way to turn. Somehow he was being set up by Mary Lou, the butt of someone's lethal joke, and there was no way out of it.

TWO HOURS LATER as the sun set, Bobby, Alice and Frank came out of the summerhouse to grab some fresh air and to clear their heads. Planning was a tiring business. Bobby sauntered into the main house and Alice plonked herself down onto a sun lounger, then lit a cigarette.

Frank paced up and down beside the pool, taking quick puffs from his smoke. Naldo and Isaak remained tethered to their posts, but when Frank stormed inside, Isaak followed him in. Naldo stood impervious to the goings on around him—or so it appeared.

In reality, little happened within his sight that wasn't noted and logged for later use. And because he stayed calm, foolish people would forget he was even there. So when Isaak popped into the building behind Frank, Naldo noticed and recorded that fact in his brain. He had no idea if it was a significant action, but if it was, then he had witnessed it and would inform somebody.

Alice continued on the sun lounger and smiled as she caught Naldo's eye. Both she and Bobby acknowledged his presence whereas almost everybody else acted like he wasn't there. Denied his sheer humanity—even Mary Lou treated him as though he was chopped liver. And they had known each other for a lifetime. Naldo had always given her the excuse that she was too important for him to expect her to treat him kindly, but after this many years, that had worn thin.

BY THE TIME Isaak caught up with Frank, he was four paces away from the bathroom. Frank looked askance at Isaak who indicated nothing was as urgent as Frank's immediate biological needs. When he came out a few minutes later, Isaak was still there, waiting and delivering his words in a hushed tone.

"I need to speak to you as a matter of supreme urgency."

Frank dried his hands on the back of his pants and ushered Isaak into his room. With the door shut, Isaak spoke his mind.

"Mary Lou intends to have Nikolay Markov killed at the end of the peace conference."

Frank eyed him suspiciously as though Isaak had spoken in Classical Armenian. He lit another in a chain of cigarettes and continued to stare at Isaak.

"How do you know?"

"Because Mary Lou asked me to do the killing. And now I'm telling you because I understand that is not the course of action that has been agreed by you and the others in your family. I am in an impossible state. If I don't follow Mary Lou's instructions, she will have me killed. If I carry out what she asks, you, Alice or Bobby will kill me for breaking the peace agreement. On that basis, I am letting you know of my situation and seek your advice how you want me to proceed."

Frank let out a slow whistle and considered matters for a moment.

"SHE WANTED ME to go to San Francisco tonight and whack him but I got her to delay the timing of the hit because if I had not then Markov would be dead by now and your plans would have been in tatters."

"But at the peace conference?"

"It was the first thing I thought of that she might have agreed to. But it won't happen, right?"

"Correct: you are not to hit Nikolay Markov—or any other member of his family without my personal authorization."

"Understood. Will you tell Mary Lou the hit is off because it's not my place?"

"Okay, Isaak. Leave that part to me. You go back to your business and everything will be fine. I'm glad you came and told me: you did the right thing even if you feel as though you've ratted out Mama. You have not at all."

"Thank you for saying so, but it doesn't sit well with me. She is the boss after all."

"You follow the orders you are given, but you are no fool and have shown you have commonsense. That is nothing to apologize for. Go back downstairs and I'll pop down shortly."

Isaak nodded and departed Frank's room relieved to have unburdened himself. He tried not to think what would happen now he'd told Frank, but Isaak was all the better for having shared the load he was carrying. By the pool, Naldo appeared not to have moved a single muscle since Isaak left, but he must have shifted by an inch, surely.

True to his word, Frank sauntered poolside and then the three Lagotti members returned to the summerhouse. A light flicked on inside and drapes were pulled shut, leaving Isaak and Naldo to stand and stare into the half-dark of the evening.

"How long do you think they'll be?"

"No idea but even if they don't want to eat, I sure as hell do. Mind if you cover me for a short while and I grab a sandwich?"

"Not if you make me one and bring it back out with you."

"Deal. Pastrami on rye for two coming right up."

FRANK'S FOCUS WAS only half on the planning taking place. The rest of his mind pondered over what Isaak had said. While he almost admired Mama's desire for violent and bloody resolution to the Markov problem, even he understood that whacking the guy was not practical—at least not now.

This meant Mama's ability to make rational decisions was flawed and so she needed to step down as head of the family. It was too dangerous to let her carry on as she was: the others were right. He dipped back into the conversation, unwilling to consider the implications of his own plan.

"Even if this pact only lasts a few months, we need a piece of their narcotics operation, especially if they have a New York side-deal already in place..."

But Mama wouldn't go voluntarily: she had no idea she had become unhinged. So there was no appealing to reason. And just pretend that somehow she was gone, who would take over?

Frank could imagine Alice wanting the job—her self-belief and arrogance would propel her into trying to run things, but that was not acceptable to him. He could see Bobby leading the outfit well, although Frank reckoned Alice would always have Bobby's ear over him.

Deep down Frank knew the only person who should be boss of the Lagotti family was him. So how to achieve that outcome? Alice wouldn't step aside—she'd need to be pushed. Same with Mama…

"We can't allow them free rein over prostitution either."

"To sweeten matters, we could offer a percentage point or two from our lottery scam."

Frank experienced a cold shiver down his spine just as he noticed a solitary drop of sweat trickle off his forehead. Pushing Mama aside only meant one thing: he was going to kill his mom. And maybe his sister too.

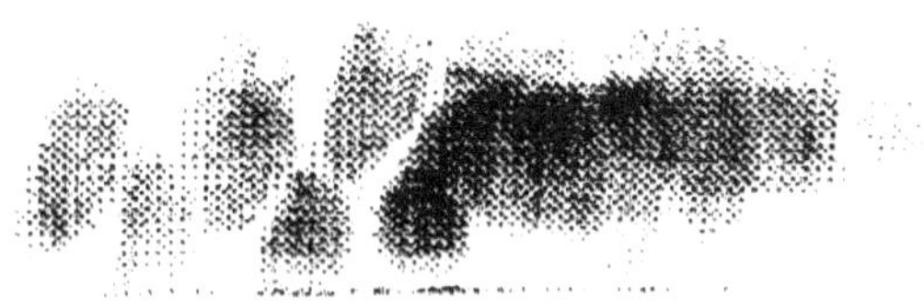

40

FRANK MENTALLY WITHDREW from the room, unable to believe what he'd just thought. That even the idea had flashed across his mind. And, despite his own horror, he was still prepared to countenance her murder. He recoiled and focused on the conversation.

"They already have points on the Lucky Lady and they're not getting another red cent—not after the effort we've put in building it up."

"Could the Queen of Sheba be offered, if only as leverage?"

"Points on it, you mean?"

"I'm not suggesting we give away the family silver. The aim is to offer him enough treats, so he doesn't notice when he's getting screwed. Within twelve months he'll be buried in the desert anyway, but in case we find a use for keeping him alive, we must negotiate in good faith and carve out a solid deal."

"Is there anything we could easily give up?"

"Our east coast interests."

"You're only saying that to goad Frank. Ignore her, will you?"

Frank nodded but did not respond as he was still consumed by the idea of killing his Mama. "Alice would do it if she had the chance," he thought.

MIDNIGHT AND THE planning was over. Bobby and Alice had figured out most of the major details although Frank had chipped in now and again. Alice walked straight up to her room and Bobby stayed in the summerhouse. Frank sat by the pool in the dark while Isaak remained nearby.

Frank lit a second cigarette off his first and stared at the stars. They looked pretty, twinkling away. Those miniature balls of light represented a tranquility he hadn't experienced on this planet, but he knew soon he would get the reward for his years of hard work and persistence.

"Isaak, come over here."

"Sure thing."

"On the day of the peace conference, I have a job for you to do. This is a special mission and is a secret that nobody else must ever know about."

"Okay…"

"You won't be in the meeting but will be located in a nearby building with a sniper rifle. Your target is Mary Lou Lagotti."

Frank wanted Isaak to soak in the news before uttering another word. When he saw Isaak blink, he knew the guy was processing his mission.

"If my sister gets hit too, that's a bonus, but the primary objective is the most important. Any questions?"

"And I'm doing this under your protection?"

"Yes. Once the deed is done, then I'll show my gratitude. Until then, you speak of this to no one. Understand?"

"I do. What about Bobby?"

"There is no need to take him out, but I will not be upset if he died in the crossfire."

"Who will protect you in the room?"

"Don't worry about me. I can look after myself."

Frank chuckled and then checked himself because Isaak was staring at him stone-faced. He was seeing the enormity of the task he'd been given and had nothing to laugh about. They had conspired to murder the boss of the entire family and this was set to happen in a handful of days, not in some theoretical future but before the weekend. Frank dismissed Isaak, lay back and stared at the stars once more. He was on the cusp of victory.

AT ONE IN the morning, Frank realized he hadn't moved and was cold, especially his fingers and toes. He hauled himself upright and slinked indoors, hands in his pockets. Through the conservatory and into the main body of the house. The living room sure was warmer but something was missing. There was a fire in his belly and he wanted companionship: either to share his hopes for the next few days or someone to fuck and he wasn't certain which he needed more. The answer was simple: Sammy.

Frank found Isaak and got him to drive to the west side of town and an unremarkable condo which was one of the many real-estate assets owned by the Lagottis for use as safe houses and crash pads. As she wasn't part of the family, neither Bobby nor Mama were happy for Sammy to spend all her time at home, but Frank had insisted they protect her and that she was nearby for him.

He'd had the presence of mind to call before he drove over—it was the middle of the night—so when he popped the key in the lock, Sammy stood waiting for him in the hallway. She had a bottle of French champagne in one hand and two glasses in the other, wearing only a dirty smile and a red G-string.

"Hi, baby. Figured you might fancy something with a bit of fizz."

"Sure do. Put those things down and we can get started."

SAMMY WOKE UP at four and wondered what the hell had happened. Her nose was next to someone's hairy shins and her crotch hurt and was bruised. She looked around, saw Frank and the recent past came rushing back into view. She'd sashayed into the kitchen to put the champagne in the fridge and when she turned round, Frank stood there as naked as the day he was born.

They licked, sucked and squeezed their way around each other's bodies until she sat on the counter and he forced himself inside her. Even though something didn't feel right to her, he only stopped when he'd come.

Sammy pushed him off and limped to the bathroom to be apart from him for a short while. When she returned, he was sat in bed with two glasses of champagne poured, waiting.

"You hurt me."

"Fuck-a-doodle-do. Sorry babe, I got carried away. Get under the sheets and I'll make it up to you."

IN THE MORNING, Sammy woke first and felt much better about herself. Frank lay sprawled out like a starfish and Sammy reflected how cute he appeared when he was sleeping. He built up a gruff exterior for most people, but she enjoyed being alone with him because he didn't bother pretending with her.

The sheets were on the floor. With goosebumps on her arms, she realized that was why she'd woken up—and she cast an eye over his arms, torso and legs.

"Good morning."

"Sure is."

"I've missed you."

"That's why I came a-visiting. I wanted you."

"Glad you did. You able to stay long?"

"Not really. Things still aren't safe but in a few days' time it will be different."

Frank let the idea hang in the air. He yearned to show off in front of his woman, but knew this was a mighty dangerous plan.

"How so?"

"We'll sort out all the family business. And when that's done, I'll be on top of the world."

Sammy giggled and snuggled into Frank, the thought of wallowing in the shadow of his glory a major aphrodisiac. She ran a hand over his chest and dug her nails into his skin enough to feel him but not to cause him discomfort. She wriggled until her lips were touching an ear and whispered.

"And I'll be on top of you as long as you want."

"It will be a great ride."

"You sure are."

They fooled around more until Frank got hungry and wanted to stop. Sammy hopped out of bed and prepared breakfast for both. Once he'd emptied his plate and glugged back his coffee, Frank made an announcement.

"Gotta go. Keep yourself hot and I'll be back as soon as I can."

He whipped out from under the sheets, threw on his clothes and hustled out the door and into Isaak's waiting car. Sammy lay there for fifteen minutes, then she showered, cleaned up the chaotic mess they'd created and carried on with her day.

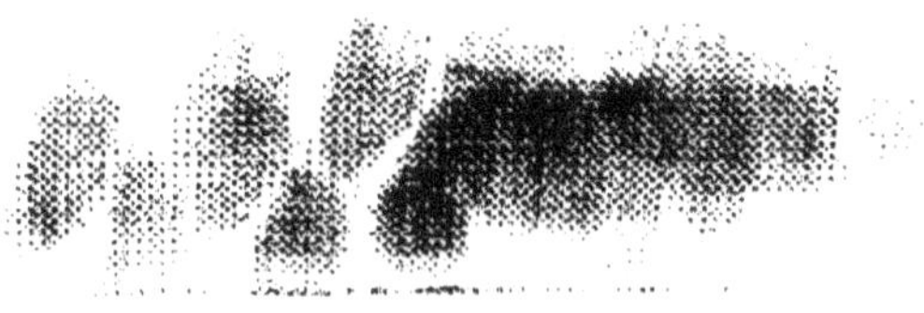

41

ALICE WOKE UP and had breakfast in the kitchen, pleased Frank was nowhere to be seen. They were getting on better these last few days than ever before in their lives, but Alice thought they were just on their best behavior due to the Markov trouble rushing toward them at high speed. Once that moment passed—if it did—chances are they'd revert to past patterns. It's what people did.

She crunched her wheat toast and sipped her orange juice in silence, the sounds of her munching echoing around her skull. Irma breezed through and offered to make her a coffee, but Alice declined: she'd wait a little today.

Breakfast downed and OJ slurped, Alice noticed a dragging sound from outside: a terrible screeching of plastic or metal. She popped out to investigate although she knew it was nothing serious: the sentries would have taken care of any external threat.

Mama was hauling a sun lounger from one side of the pool to the other —for no real reason Alice could surmise.

"Let me help you with that."

"Thank you."

"Where do you want it?"

Mary Lou pointed to a shady spot that already had a recliner only ten feet away. Alice smiled but felt ill at ease with the illogical decision Mama had made. She picked up the lounger—none of them were heavy—and brought it past the diving board and over to the other side of the pool.

"There you go."

"Thank you."

Mary Lou shuffled over and placed her towel on the new seating, then she sat down and Alice watched as her body relaxed in the shade created by the summerhouse. Alice took advantage of the calm and rested next to her Mama using the lounger she'd recently spotted. The two women remained silent for a spell until Alice broke the moment.

"I'm worried."

"What about?"

"The Markov situation, of course."

"You don't need to be concerned, Cindy. Everything will be fine."

Alice froze and gripped the armrests of the sun lounger as she heard the name of the long-dead housekeeper: Mama had no idea who she was.

ALICE UNCLAMPED HER hands after three deep breaths and turned her head to face her Mama. Mary Lou was scratching at her elbow, idling the morning away. Her skin was red with the attention it was receiving.

"Don't scratch: it'll only make things worse."

Mary Lou acknowledged with a nod, but carried on gouging her nails into her flesh. Alice did her best to ignore it.

"Do you think we'll be able to get a deal with Markov?"

"Who?"

"Nikolay Markov."

"Oh, you don't need to worry about him. He will be dead soon. You can be sure of that."

"We're not killing him, we are negotiating a peace with him."

"If you say so, dear. But he'll be in the morgue within a week."

Alice ignored this outburst because it made no sense. Even Frank had come round to the idea that they diffuse the Markov clan now and only attack when all the heat from New York was off. Wasn't ideal by a wide margin, but it was the most pragmatic solution and was the surest way to save Mama's life.

Bobby walked past to get to the summerhouse and Alice looked up at him as he journeyed by. When she glanced back at Mama, a red river was trickling down her arm and she kept on scratching, regardless. Alice sprung up and rushed over, pushing Mama's hand out of the wound and holding the elbow up.

"Oh, Mama. I told you not to keep doing that."

There was anger in her voice, partly aimed at her mom and some at herself for not taking care of her better. Of allowing Mary Lou to harm herself right in front of Alice's eyes. She ran to the kitchen to get a towel and instructed Irma to bring a plaster. Five minutes later and everything was calm again—on the surface at least.

ALICE LEFT MAMA with Irma and returned to the house to find the number for the twenty-four-hour nurse. The time for talk was over. Her Mama needed to be cared for and watched over at all times. Since her reappearance at the Palace, all had seemed to settle down and they had become complacent. But no more.

Even though they needed someone over immediately, Alice accepted they'd have to wait three days before anyone reliable could be sent. This was not what she wanted to hear, but she knew she had to accept their fate. In the meantime, Naldo would stand guard around the clock. When he slept, one of the other fellas would take over. Alice would ensure Mama had the best care available and would stay safe.

A quick walk along the outskirts of the grounds and Alice found Naldo to issue him his instructions as a trusted compatriot. Then she went back to the pool to check on Mama: all was good, so she spoke with Bobby in the summerhouse.

BOBBY SAT AT the desk scribbling on a piece of paper and didn't appear to notice Alice was with him. Quarter of a page later, he looked up and nodded, then carried on writing.

"Sorry, I'll be with you in a minute. If I don't write this down now, I will forget it all."

"De nada."

Alice sprawled onto one of the armchairs, trying to remain as cool as ice, knowing she had terrible news to impart and had no idea what to say. Her lips were dry and her tongue stuck to the roof of her mouth. Bobby stopped, put his pen down and sauntered over to the couch, opposite Alice with a low table in between them. He picked up half a cigar from the ashtray in front of him and lit it for the millionth time that day. It had been a busy morning.

"You look like you want to talk."

"Yep… How d'you say Mama's been since we got back from the Palace?"

Bobby sunk into the couch a few inches more, his positive disposition floated out under the crack in the door. He sighed and sat forward in his seat.

"Between the Markovs and New York, I haven't given it too much of my attention."

"Me neither—until just now."

"And?"

"She didn't recognize me and gouged a hole in her arm."

Words floated around, but each one stuck in Alice's throat for an eternity.

"Mama has dementia and we're not helping her by pretending it's not happening. I'm talking about both of us: I am not blaming you for any of this."

Silence.

"I called the nursing agency we found but they can't send anyone over for a couple of days, so Naldo will mind her until then."

Bobby cast his eyes downward and squeezed himself into the smallest space he could fit in. Alice moved over and sat next to him, placing a hand on a shoulder. Tears rolled down his cheeks and he rocked forward and back. A man in pain.

ALICE WASN'T TOO sure what to do. She wanted to offer Bobby solace, but she was experiencing the same agony as him. Where was his comforting hand on her shoulder? He was meant to be the adult and she was the child in their relationship. That had broken down with Mama, but it didn't have to be that way with Bobby. She let him cry his heart out from the mental loss of his wife of over twenty-five years.

"It wasn't supposed to be like this."

"No, but she's alive and physically healthy. Our job is to make sure she survives past the weekend and lives a comfortable life. Some days she'll be with us and others… she will have left the room."

Now Alice couldn't contain herself any longer—all the anguish flooded out in salty tears and Bobby held her in his arms until her crying subsided. Then she kissed him on the cheek and they sat back to collect themselves together.

"You're a good man, Bobby Trevisan."

"That's what your mother used to say to me."

"Still true today."

"Kind of you, but I'm not sure you're right."

"Take the compliments when they land."

"Thank you, then."

"WHEN YOU AND Frank were little, we used to go on picnics and you guys would be content to play with a ball. Your mom and I would lie around watching you two and simply enjoy being in each other's company."

"Happy days. I don't remember that. Earliest memory I have is of a trip Frank and I took to a factory. Some bad guys locked us in a cupboard and Mama rescued us. I didn't know if it was real or a nightmare."

"Real. I'd been out of the business two years and met your mom three or four months before your cupboard ordeal, I think. Feels like it was a lifetime ago."

"For me it was."

Bobby laughed because Alice was right. She and Frank had only just learned to walk when they were kidnapped. All over a pound of heroin and a drug deal gone south. After that the Lagotti family made its mark once Mary Lou whacked Charlie Pentangelo. She had been one hell of a woman.

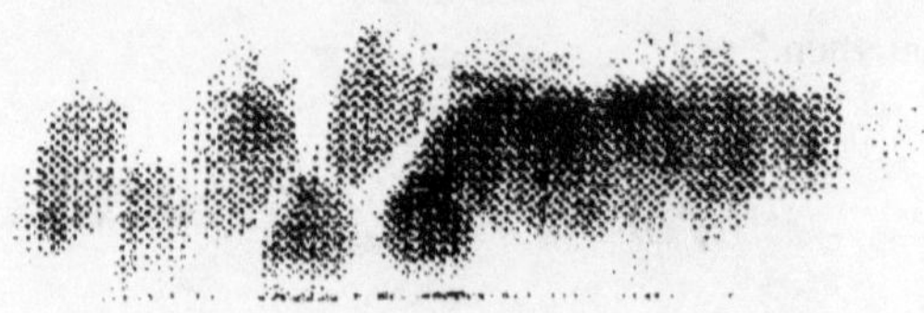

42

"ONCE WE'VE MADE peace with Markov, we will need someone to lead this family."

"Do you have anyone in mind?"

Bobby laughed.

"You, me or Frank. Or a combination."

"Makes sense. If we work together, we make better decisions."

"Yeah. Can the three of us operate as a team?"

Now it was Alice's turn to laugh. Bobby was asking leading questions, just so he wasn't the first one to nix Frank's name on the letterhead.

"I really can't answer. What d'you reckon?"

"It's not my place to stand between you two. Never has, but you guys have unresolved issues, so to speak."

"Been a long time since we agreed on anything. And he's too quick to temper: always looking for a fight. I mean, one minute we agree to negotiate a truce and before the words have left our lips, he runs off to San Francisco maiming, killing and setting up brothels. Those are not the actions of a team player."

"I hear you, but he gets shit done. He flew over to Boston then Atlantic City and created a quality revenue stream from nothing. Neither of us have achieved that."

"And what are the lottery cards? Chopped fucking liver?"

"Sorry, that's something I haven't achieved—not for decades, anyway."

"Better. Sometimes I wonder if anything I accomplish gets noticed. The effort to get the Queen of Sheba up-and-running nearly killed me. Mama was more interested in bailing out her precious Frank. Again."

"We knew how hard you were working and how difficult it was. As you're so reliable, we got into the habit of leaving you alone because you don't generally need hand-holding. Frank has been tied to his mom's apron strings for far too long. It's only since Boston that he's stood on his own two feet."

"So you're saying Frank should run the show?"

"DON'T PUT WORDS in my mouth. I'm just pointing out he's a lot more capable now than he used to be."

"So do you want him or not?"

Bobby sat back and inhaled on his cigar. He enjoyed having the prop in his hand because it was perfect excuse to give himself time to ponder. The end of the stogie glowed orange-red as he took the smoke into his mouth, rolled it around his palate and exhaled.

"He shouldn't run the family. Can't talk about the future, but he's not ready now."

"And what about me?"

"Do you want to? I mean, without me by your side?"

"Dunno. I like the idea of it, but I'm not sure if I am strong enough. Losing Sam hurt me more than I realized and I don't know if I'm weak at heart."

"Mary Lou and I have been an effective double-act for years. You and I could try the same thing—if you were up for it."

"At least until I regained my confidence. I used to say I was going to rule the world. Now I'm not certain I am cut out for global domination."

"You'll get there. The way you've handled yourself over Sam has been amazing. You have shown dignity and class when most people would have either hidden in their rooms or bitch-slapped her into the seventh circle of hell. You did neither and that takes guts. More than you give yourself credit for."

"HOW WILL FRANK react if we carve him out?"

"Not positively. He'd have to go."

For emphasis, Bobby stubbed out the remaining inch of his cigar in the ashtray, grinding it into oblivion. He flicked a piece of tobacco off his hand and it fluttered to the floor. They both watched the brown speck until it was motionless and looked at each other square in the eye.

"Let him keep his east coast businesses and cut commercial ties with him, right?"

"Don't know that'd work, Alice. We might need a more robust response."

That euphemism hung in the air, but Alice didn't want to deal with its implications: that they'd have to kill Frank to stop him from murdering them.

"I couldn't be a part of that. He's my flesh and blood. We are twins…"

Bobby stared at her with a bemused expression. The pair of them had been sparring all their adult lives and now Alice wanted to convince herself she could not deliver the final blow. So be it. If she wouldn't—or couldn't—take care of business then he'd step in and sort matters out to give the family the best chance of a sustainable future.

"Don't worry about it. We send Frank back to AC to empire build and everyone can leave each other in peace."

"Good. And Mama is our consiglieri on her better days."

"Yeah. We need to be careful not to show any weakness tomorrow in front of Markov so, if Mary Lou is able, she should appear to head up the negotiations."

"Cut a deal with Markov and then a smooth transition of power."

"Sounds like a plan."

FRANK HAD GOT himself a taste for Sammy and was spending time with her. While Alice and Bobby were discussing his future, Frank was penetrating Sammy from behind in the shower. Once he was done, they washed themselves and returned to bed to continue their gallivanting.

She didn't enjoy being held prisoner and had been feeling lonely and ignored. There was no point hooking up with a gangster if she was never given the opportunity to show off his fabulous wealth or to live in extremely comfortable circumstances. At least Alice had an amazing place in Malibu—Frank had dumped her in a crummy apartment and not been back for days.

So when Frank came over, her eyes lit up and she wrapped her limbs around his torso until she absorbed all his energy: he was a monster in the sack. For all Alice's intimate understanding of her body, she was a mild lay compared to Frank. Both had their plus points, but being with Frank was exciting and dangerous. Alice wanted to settle down and Frank just wanted fun.

That was the biggest difference between the twins. Sammy was aware of the irony because to the outside world, the greatest contrast was that one was male and the other female. Those details were uppermost in her mind as she went down on Frank again. His sheer physicality literally filled her head and the judders up and down her spine echoed how much he turned her on after she was finished with him and he had returned the oral favor.

MARY LOU SAT by the pool and stared into nowhere. She enjoyed the time by herself: she used it to reminisce about happier or clearer times. And to contemplate her conversations with Father Carmoody. That man sure had changed how she thought about the world. How fleeting was her life on the planet and how you risked an eternity of damnation if you made the wrong choices.

If it would save her soul, Mary Lou would hand the organization over to her children but she felt their own time in hell's fire would be affected. Perhaps they should wind down all their operations. That idea crossed her mind more than once, although she hadn't acted on it yet. A bad deal with Nikolay Markov could be precisely the excuse necessary to pass over the business to him and save her family from the Devil's clutches.

Then the memory of walking past all the cars in the lot, blood dripping off her skirt and her fingers, after her Frank was gunned down at Burbank Airport. Mary Lou recalled each vehicle: color, mark, which direction it was facing in its parking space.

Every little detail like it was yesterday. How she drove five miles below the speed limit all the way back to the hotel. What was its name again? The aroma of his dried blood on her hands. That acrid flavor of rust on her tongue.

Her entire world condensed into a journey across a lot to escape from the FBI and hang on to the takings from the Lansdowne branch of the First Bank of Baltimore. A personal fortune to start the family business which she'd turned into a small empire. Mary Lou and… what's-his-name. They'd done it together.

IN THE EVENING, Frank lay on the bed, head resting on Sammy's thighs. She made a good pillow and he inhaled the scent of sex which was smeared over both their bodies like a high-class perfume. He considered his plan for the peace conference, running through each element in his mind: rehearsing every moment. For him to succeed, he needed to execute a subtle play in the room and Isaak had to deliver the best marksmanship.

Sammy wriggled out from under him and propped him up with pillows. Then she nipped to the bathroom. When she came back into the bedroom, she sashayed off to mix them two cocktails, offering him one, which he gladly took—his mouth seemed parched.

He sank the curious green liquid in a single swig, smacked his lips together and announced his desire for a refill. Sammy shrugged and handed over her own glass as she couldn't be bothered to go off and mess about with the cocktail shaker and all that ice. Too cold and too much hassle.

She stopped right by the bed to reach Frank's hand with the drink. He knocked back the second cocktail, throwing the receptacle onto the carpeted floor causing it to bounce once and roll to a halt on the other side of the room. Sammy giggled as Frank turned around to face her. His head was inches from her groin and he placed a palm round her ass to draw her in nearer until she collapsed on top of him. As soon as he was done, Frank pushed her off and stood up to put his clothes on. Then his shoes.

"Been a blast. I'll be back tomorrow evening. Wear your red G-string for when I come over."

He closed the front door before Sammy had time to say a word. She dialed for a pizza and rummaged around to find a dressing gown before the boy with her food appeared wanting his tip.

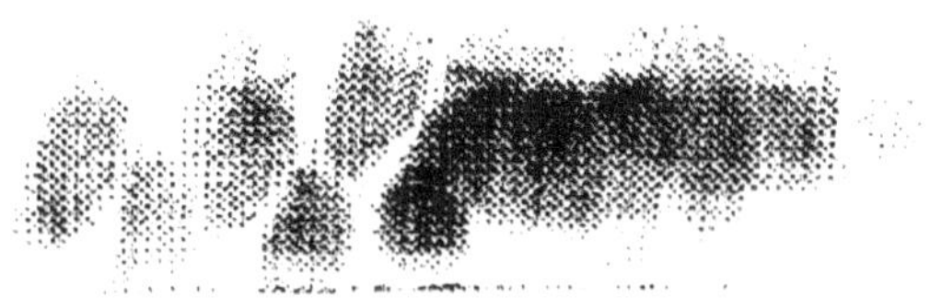

43

THE PALLADIUM HOTEL used to be a go-to venue in San Francisco, but its heyday had long since receded. Nowadays, families occupied it in high season as a cheap alternative to one of the plush hotels in town. The rest of the year, sales reps and conference delegates took advantage of its competitive rates.

Half the rooms boasted a balcony view of the bay and a well-stocked minibar, comprising an array of liquor, bandages and prophylactics. Nobody assumed all three would be used at the same time, but this was San Francisco so no one judged.

The reason the Palladium survived despite its tawdry exterior was its location—and its competitive rates. This combination was the precise set of reasons Naldo selected the hotel for the peace conference. It was cheap, in the middle of town and there were loads of civilians milling all around in case anyone planned any funny business.

Both sides had scoped the meeting room on the second floor together. Each item of furniture subjected to a rigorous check: there was nothing hidden underneath, inside or elsewhere. Either Naldo or Lara Mikhailov slid a hand behind the mirror and the various paintings on the walls to ensure no blades were available for use if tensions arose. Once they were both satisfied, Naldo and Mikhailov stayed guard outside the only door into the place.

Bobby, Alice, Frank and Mary Lou arrived around ten and Nikolay appeared two minutes later. Everyone acknowledged each other, but no one shook hands. Coffee and water was served and everybody sat down, apart from Naldo and Mikhailov who continued to stand behind their respective leaders.

"If I had known so many of you were coming, I'd have brought my entire family this morning too."

Nikolay smirked and sipped his coffee. Alice ground her molars and held back the disgust she felt for this man. Mary Lou smiled benignly, because she didn't care about Nikolay's childish comment or because she had no idea who he was or what she was doing there.

"Shall we get on? We are here to broker a truce, not engage in idle chat."

"YOURS IS A large outfit with resources stretching from coast to coast. We are a small family with control over the Tenderloin and not much more."

"Nikolay, you do yourself an injustice. Your friends stretch all the way to Russia, so let's not pretend you have no reach. If you were just a cockroach, we'd have crushed you like a bug by now."

"Thank you for recognizing I am someone to be reckoned with. We all work hard in this pitiful country."

"The land of opportunity is big enough for all of us to carve out successful lives. We must agree how to slice up San Francisco."

"The way I see things, you came to my city, stole from me and killed my own. We agreed an accommodation and then you returned, took some more and attacked me again. You owe me and all we need to decide is how you shall pay for the harm you caused me."

Before Alice responded, Frank slammed his fist on the table, causing everyone to jump perceptibly and to rattle every cup of coffee in the room.

"Listen to me, little man: there has been damage done to both sides. What you need to consider more is how to make restitution for the killings with your name on it. If you think I'll bend over and take it up the ass from you, you're smoking more opium than you can sell."

Frank glared at Nikolay, who responded with a casual stare and gritted teeth. People didn't talk to him with such scant respect usually and survive. Mary Lou smiled benignly at the argument unfolding before her and Alice maintained her composure. Her primary aim was to prevent Mama from saying too much, so Frank's outburst aligned with her interests. As agreed, Bobby intended to remain silent for as long as possible, so there was one calm voice if tempers frayed.

"THE WAY I see things: we've got you by the balls because we have cut off your heroin supply and that musta hurt business. Without the brown sugar, how could you keep your skanks sedated enough to fuck the degenerates you get in your whorehouses? And your operations rely on the cash you generate from selling those bags too. So talk less about reparations and more about what you will do to convince us to open your franchises again."

"I am sure we are here to discuss, negotiate and agree, boy. If you want me to not make demands of you then you must stop laying down the law to me."

Frank stared through Nikolay and Mikhailov adjusted position to his right to get a better take on Frank's state of mind. Alice looked to Frank, then to Nikolay and finally on Mikhailov—in case she tried a move against Frank. No one needed to resort to violence given they were sat around a table talking.

"LET US BE clear. You admit you are blocking our supply lines, so the first thing you must do is to open our access to our own narcotics."

"Of course, we can do that but you get nothing for nothing in this life. What will you offer in return?"

Nikolay smiled again and glanced out the window as a boat motored across the view. Then his attention floated back inside the room and he focused on Frank and his challenge.

"What could I possibly give you that you don't already possess?"

"Someone in your position should have the imagination to make an offer and, even if you can't, you should be aware enough of your gang's actions to name something within your largesse. If you are the man, you think you are."

"Do not goad me, boy."

"Stop acting like the cheerleader who got fucked by the jock at the end of the prom and didn't expect anything to happen. You are here to negotiate and all you've done so far is to piss and moan."

Nikolay remained silent and drummed his fingers on the table. The annoyance seeped out of his fingertips until he regained his composure. Hard to tell if it was because Frank had called him on his behavior or because Markov would be forced to give something up. Frank remembered never to put out any number first in a negotiation, so was desperate to force Nikolay's hand, but the Russian didn't want to play ball. Maybe he'd received the same advice.

"PROSTITUTION. I CAN offer you a percentage of that San Francisco racket, if it was of interest."

"Always into making money out of fucking. We could open the supply lines for fifty per cent of your prostitution revenues and leave you to run San Francisco. Or we could accept only twenty cents on the dollar, but you would cease interfering with any of our whorehouses in town."

"A fifth for doing nothing. That's quite an offer."

"The revenue keeps your skanks alive and the smack flowing. Don't make yourself seem foolish: you understand the value of what I'm offering—and it's insulting for you to pretend otherwise."

"You forget why you are here, boy. Our biting at your heels so much has impacted your operations. Not just in this city, but your lottery racket is within our reach. So don't talk to me like a pimp to one of your whores. I am at least your equal and achieved more than you as I started with nothing while you were gifted your success by your mother."

Now it was Frank's turn to fall into silence and suck in the air until his pulse stopped racing. So far, all the two men had succeeded in doing was to goad each other, and they were no closer to any agreement than when they arrived. Alice was not impressed. If Frank wanted to preen his feathers, so be it, but they needed to bring Nikolay's plane safely in to land: no bumps, no bruises and no crashes.

"WHAT MY BROTHER is trying to say is that we respect all your achievements in the Tenderloin—and beyond. And what we agree here will have significant consequences for all concerned. I expect you would like to devote your energies into making more money and we want to do the same. So we need to draw a line under what has happened and figure out the best way to live side by side either by not elbowing each other or by working together, sharing risks and the rewards."

"My biggest concern is to get access to my heroin. The rest is just cheap words."

"If tens of millions of dollars are of no matter to you, then I underestimate the respect you deserve. For the Lagotti family that is a considerable amount of money at stake if we can't agree a reasonable resolution to our difficulties."

Nikolay raised his eyebrows and widened his eyes a fraction. Clearly he wanted to get his hands on that kind of green.

"Our lottery operation in California is the beginning of the adventure, not the endgame. As more states create legalized gambling, we shall take advantage with our fake tickets: the numbers racket reborn for modern times. There will be enough profit in the venture to allow others to dip their beaks in the trough. If you work with us—supplying drivers, protection and boots on the ground—we could give you five per cent of the gross. But if you harm our people or our assets, then you will have nothing and can peck on the floor with the rest of the hens. The choice is yours. The time to decide your future is now. Before we leave the Palladium either you are working for or against our interests."

Nikolay's cheeks reddened and he sipped his long gone cold coffee. Mikhailov tried to refill his mug, but he told her not to fuss around him.

"Let us take a break for a short while and stretch our legs."

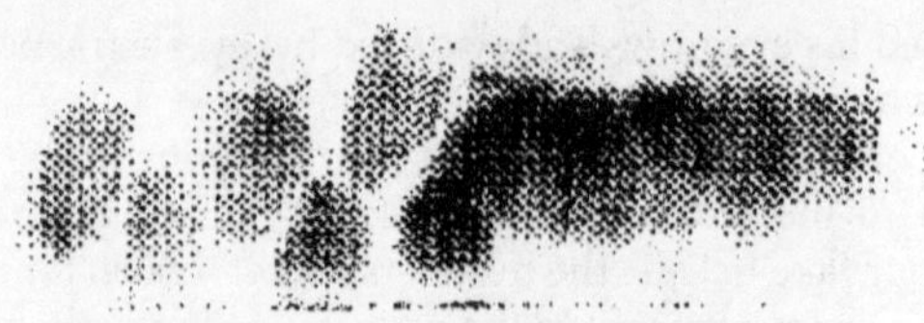

44

NIKOLAY STOOD UP, put his hands in his pants pockets and took two steps to stand to look out of the window. The sky was blue and Alcatraz was easy to spot. Alice poured fresh coffees, walked over and handed one to him. The others hovered near the drinks table, murmuring and chewing on cookies.

"You need to cut a deal with us and I understand that you may not think much of my brother—or me."

"He thinks he is somebody because he can get girls to fuck for money. That just means he's a pimp. He has ideas far above his ability and doesn't realize how small a man he is."

"Not everyone in my family shares Frank's view of you and you should remember that."

"That may be the case but when we last met, you showed me tremendous disrespect."

Alice's pupils dilated as she recalled that moment in her hotel room.

"There is a world of difference between wishing to do business with you and wanting to fuck. You failed to distinguish those two things. That's not about respect; it's a question of your judgment."

"You chastise me like your brother did."

"No, he believes the best method to get his way is to strong-arm a person. I operate by letting people understand their options and leaving them to decide which consequences they prefer. You are free to do whatever you want—within reason—but accept what happens next."

"Are you really willing to let me share in your numbers racket? How do I know you aren't dangling a juicy worm in front of me now just to squeeze a truce out of me?"

"Bottom line is that you don't, but my word counts for something and the offer is genuine. We want to work with people and you have shown your mettle. All these matters boil down to trust. You have met me and seen me operate. And now you must decide if what I say matches what I do."

"YOU TALK OF consequences and you threaten me with extinction. Those are not the words of a business partner. You make it hard for me to trust you when your family reneged on our last detail."

"Did I return to the Tenderloin?"

"I don't believe so."

"I did not. And if you are serious about joining us with the numbers racket, then you need to get past being offended by Frank. There are many people who take issue with his manners and you're at the back of the line. Instead focus on what it would mean to run the operation in California or beyond. That's the offer on the table—and to free up your narcotics pipeline in the short term. Keep your eyes on the prize, Nikolay."

Markov sipped and stared out the window some more while Alice continued to stand next to him. He was mesmerized by the sheer scale of the honey pot and that was central to their plan. If Frank had been in the summerhouse with the rest of the family and spent less time in Sam's condo, he would have known this too.

"Chuck the boy a bone and he'll stop yapping at your ankles. He wants to show what a great fella he is and I want a deal."

"AND WHAT MAKES your words more important than his in your family?"

"I'm older by four minutes…"

Nikolay smiled.

"…and I have the backing of the rest of my outfit. Don't underestimate me because I am a woman. Underestimate me because you only see a fraction of what I can do."

More silence and staring. If Nikolay had been more observant of his surroundings and less wrapped up in himself, he would have noticed that Alice had undone an extra blouse button before she went over to the window to talk to him. She understood how easy it was to play this chump and his eyes betrayed where his real focus lay. Sometimes all you needed was an attractive decolletage. Other times you had to threaten a man with death or poverty. Alice chose both options to hedge her bets.

"Your mother was more vocal at the last peace talks."

"She is doing her best to let others take the reins. Mama has worked hard all her life and deserves to enjoy the time she has."

"And who will take over from her?"

Alice smiled and shook her head.

"That's the kind of information we share with friends. When we agree a deal today, then I'll be happy to fill you in on our plans."

"Frank is a boy and Bobby is too old. Enough said already."

A grin ripped across Alice's face.

"If you know that, you appear to be a friend even now."

"Congratulations are in order and if this is true, then I apologize for my earlier behavior."

"Accepted, but not forgotten: not yet, anyway. Show me the man you can be at this table and then we shall discuss other matters further some other time."

She watched his eyes flit to her breasts and look at her face. Alice walked back to fill up her mug once more with gritted teeth and everyone shuffled to their seats.

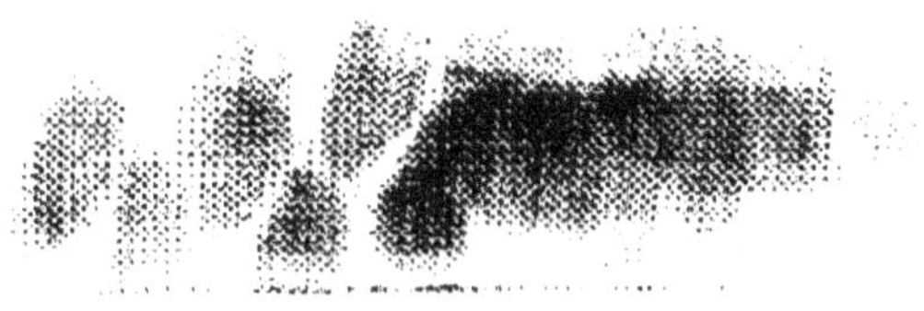

45

"SO HAVE YOU decided whether you will play ball?"

"Fuck you. I'll speak to the girl but not to a mook like you."

"What the hell did you say to him, Alice?"

"Nothing, Frank. Cool it."

"Don't you talk to me like that. You two are cooking something up between the pair of you."

Alice looked askance at Bobby, who stared back as confused as she was. Mary Lou continued to stare into space while Frank fumed. He stood up so quickly that his chair fell backwards onto the floor with a thud. Everyone watched as he muttered under his breath and stormed out of the room. Naldo picked up the seat and placed it without any fuss out of the way by a wall.

"My apologies, Nikolay."

"Sometimes children are best allowed out to play while the adults speak."

Markov cast a glance to Mikhailov who returned his look with a slight nod. All was good with everybody who remained, although Alice shifted her chair into the center with Mama to her left near the window and Bobby to her right nearer the coffee and cookie table. Once they had all settled down Nikolay waited a few seconds and then carried on.

"We were trying to agree how we can work together once you've opened up my narcotics supply."

"Indeed. We'll do that, but you have yet to say what you offer us in exchange."

"I shall open up the Tenderloin to prostitution for you if you enable me to join in your numbers racket."

"When we start in San Francisco, then you shall have fifty per cent of all the revenues you generate. For simplicity, we will keep our reps out of the city for the first twelve months. This gives your people ample chance to corner the market and means we can mop up any independent retailers who might have slipped through the net later on. The aim is to get every store on board: we are less concerned about who makes the sale as much as the product is sold."

"This is agreeable. And what about opportunities beyond the confines of the city?"

"Let's take one step at a time. Do well here and we will be happy to offer you other territories. If you need help with any other ventures, we ask —but don't demand—that you speak to us first. The more we work together, the greater our bond and that can only strengthen all here today."

Nikolay nodded and offered his open hand across the table. Alice stood up and reached over to seal the deal. And that was the point when the glass of the window was punctured by a bullet from who knows where.

THE SLUG WHIZZED through the air and into Mary Lou's orbit. She'd turned her head to stare out the window and the force of the bullet twisted her body round, whipping the blood departing the wound into an arc that caught Alice's cheek, shoulder and arm.

What was left of the shell spat out the other side Of her skull and into the wall. Mama's body tilted off the chair and headed down to the carpeted floor. The crack of the glass and the red-burst in the room caused Alice to hit the deck on pure instinct. Out of the corner of her eye, Alice caught the color scarlet near her Mama and saw a leg twitch.

Two more slugs entered the place. One landed in the mirror, next to the coffees and cookies, which shattered, shards of glass spraying out over Mikhailov and Bobby. The other bullet ricocheted off the coffee pot and pinged up into the ceiling. Alice kept her hands over her head as though that might protect her from a high caliber round.

Bobby wriggled over from his position past Alice and tried to cover Mary Lou's body to shield her corpse from the sniper. While trying to sink into the carpet, Alice swiveled around to survey the scene in the room and see who remained alive. In between table and chair legs, only Mama was lying still.

"Anyone else hurt?"

Naldo's voice of calm reason floated over the survivors. Without noticing herself do it, Alice grabbed the gun from her handbag, now nestling under a seat. Bobby's arms surrounded his wife, and he rocked her left-to-right with the first agony of her loss. His pain transformed him into a gripping, crying blob.

Alice glanced out of the window frame as though that would help her see the marksman. Then she stole another look around to see each of them holding weapons trained on the world outside the meeting room. Mikhailov had somehow got to the window and was bobbing and weaving, hoping to catch sight of the attacker. Alice saw Nikolay's lips move but she couldn't hear a word he said. She could tell by his expression he was getting increasingly frustrated. She swallowed and a wall of sound burst into her eardrums.

"What just happened?"

"We know nothing of this. My mother's been killed. You think I'd do that? To my Mama?

NIKOLAY SHOOK HIS head and stared out the window while barking instructions to Mikhailov in Russian. They glared at each other then both turned in Alice's direction. A grim menace took over their demeanors—no mean feat given what had just happened to her Mama.

Alice looked to Bobby who had grown silent and now had a piece in his hand, finger on the trigger. For one brief second, Alice tasted hate in her mouth and she blinked at Bobby, his expression exactly the same as when he'd torture someone. They both understood what to do next.

Bobby planted a pair of slugs into Nikolay: first the heart and then the head. As he squeezed the trigger to take out Markov, Alice sent a bullet in the back of Lara Mikhailov's knee who screamed with agony and rolled over to face Alice. That gave her the opportunity to slam two cartridges into Mikhailov's torso.

Sirens wailed in the distance and Naldo was the first to react.

"We gotta get outta here."

Insistence in his tone, he crawled to the window and stared outside.

"I'll cover you but we have to leave right now."

He shot aimlessly out the window to give Alice and Bobby a chance to crawl to the door and make their escape. No one returned fire and he figured it would be safe to exit himself. With Bobby and Alice no longer in the room, Naldo first went over to Mary Lou's body to check she wasn't carrying any incriminating documents. Then he emptied the contents of her bag and did the same. He stuffed papers and a gun into his jacket and fled the scene.

THIRTY MINUTES LATER, the three survivors sat in Naldo's car near the edge of town, traveling at five miles an hour below the speed limit, heading back to Palm Springs.

"Who d'you think ordered the hit?"

"It's down to who wanted Mary Lou dead. Nikolay?"

"He looked as surprised as we were. Perhaps New York got impatient."

"No. If the mob called for the hit, they'd have whacked the lot of us to give Markov a free run of the city."

"Then who? Some rival gang we don't even know?"

"Unlikely. It will be somebody known. Someone close. Usually, very close."

Alice stared at Naldo who appeared to think more than he was saying.

"Do you have a name?"

"Can't say for certain, but who is among us yet not here?"

"Frank?"

The word left Alice's mouth as the quietest whisper ever uttered by a human being.

"Anyone seen Isaak today?"

Silence.

"Doesn't mean he was gunning for your mother. He could have had Markov in his sights and plain missed. Worse shit has happened in my lifetime."

Despite wanting to cling to the wafer-thin possibility that Nikolay was the target, Alice realized deep in her heart that it looked like Frank had murdered her darling Mama.

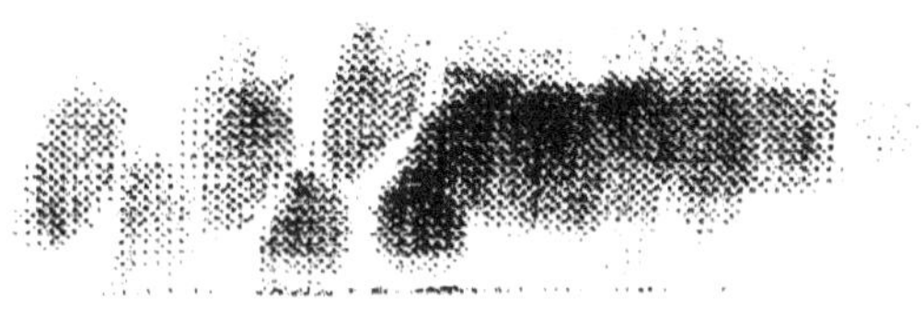

46

THE REMAINING PART of the day of the attack comprised bribing hotel staff and cops, constructing alibis and early thoughts about the morgue and a funeral. At home, Bobby and Alice sat in the living room trying to come to terms with the day's events but neither of them found that the least bit simple. Bobby was better at hiding his feelings, but even he would break down and cry regularly.

Naldo remained behind the wheel all the way to Oakcrest Drive and had done his best to leave the two alone since they got back indoors three hours earlier. But now the doorbell rang, which Naldo answered—Irma was in her room finding solace in prayer. He popped his head round the door to announce that Isaak was here.

"Where were you today? You were expected to be part of the security detail this morning."

"I've been in bed ill. When I was told about Mrs. Lagotti, I came straight over."

"And have you heard from Frank too? We haven't seen him since he walked out of the meeting shortly before some fuck blasted us with bullets."

Alice still couldn't bring herself to say out loud that Mama was dead. She detected an increased redness in Isaak's cheeks as she spoke. His eyes darted left and right and he could not maintain eye contact. That was when she knew he was the trigger man.

"Well, if you find him, remind him we're looking for him too."

"Sure thing."

"Can we get you a drink or some food? Maybe meds if you're still ill," interjected Bobby.

"A coffee would be good. It'd settle my stomach and ease my throat."

"Naldo, do you mind making him a pot?"

When the two bodyguards had moved to the kitchen, Bobby sat down next to Alice on the couch and whispered into her ear.

"We won't see that cocksucker again. I'll ensure Naldo deals with him after the funeral. There's no rush: we need to get the job done once he's less nervous."

Alice was pleased Bobby reached the same conclusion as her with greater presence of mind: she wanted to kill Isaak here and now.

FATHER CARMOODY SURFACED the following day, Saturday. He expressed his deepest sorrow for their loss and explained how Mary Lou had sought his counsel these past months.

"You are a Catholic priest? Am I right?"

"Yes, my dear."

"Are you aware of her early experience of the church and her views of the clergy in particular?"

"My child, your mother had a change of mind recently and wanted to let Jesus into her heart."

"You understand my wife suffered from dementia."

"Yes, my son. She spoke of how hard she found remembering the simplest of things and cried in my presence at not being able to recall the names of her own children."

Alice stormed out of the room: this man annoyed her, but she discovered over the coming days he inserted himself into their affairs. The only advantage of his existence to them was that he volunteered to liaise with the funeral parlor: arranging the release of the body from the pathologist, its transportation to Palm Springs and other more gruesome details neither Bobby nor Alice wanted to deal with.

The task they couldn't palm off to the priest was to contact everyone who knew Mary Lou to tell them what had happened. Given her dramatic end, news had traveled far across the country, but they took no chances: everybody needed a call. The only family Mary Lou had were Bobby, Frank and Alice, although somewhere her brothers and sisters might be still alive. No one had the desire to find them as Mary Lou turned her back on her kin when she left home.

FRANK APPEARED ON Sunday and refused to account for his whereabouts. Alice could barely stand to be in the same room as him and Bobby was taciturn even by his own quiet standards. Sensing the anger from his family, Frank left and visited Sammy instead where the welcome was warm and inviting, a red G-string the only thing standing between him and a willing bush.

By the end of the week, everyone stopped focusing on the cause of the funeral and fixated on the detailed organization of the church service and wake. Out of common decency, Bobby and Alice tried to include Frank in the decision making, but inevitably his was a minority voice on the rare occasions he left Sammy's bed. He wanted only the three of them there—and the priest if necessary—but Bobby understood Mary Lou was so widely known a small family affair was out of the question.

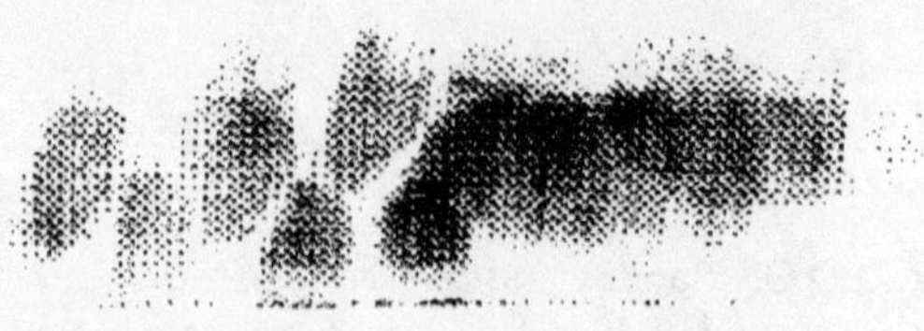

47

TIME TRICKLED BY until the day of the funeral. Alice awoke and felt guilty because for three seconds, she forgot Mama was dead. She cried yet again, got out of bed, showered and put on a black pants suit before heading downstairs for breakfast.

In the kitchen, Bobby was already sitting down nursing a mug of coffee, staring at a slice of granary toast supplied by Irma. Frank arrived and joined them to wait for the limousines, which were due at ten. The only noises were the clinking of crockery and the sound of Irma busying herself in the background.

The clock in the living room struck the hour and, in almost perfect synchrony, the doorbell rang as the limos were out front and waiting. There was one black stretch for Bobby, Alice and Frank with another for Irma, Naldo and a host of fellas. Bobby had nixed Naldo's suggestion to be in the same limo as the family for security reasons. The way Bobby figured it, if someone was going to whack him, they might as well do it today. While he didn't want to die, he didn't care if he lived. And he knew Alice was similarly inclined.

Outside the church were at least fifty mourners if not more—all come to send off Mary Lou. Frank wished they'd all just go away. He did not like his private grief being on public display. In contrast, Alice appeared heartened by the show of affection and respect afforded her mom by those attending. It showed how much Mama had touched so many lives during her brief visit to this crummy world.

Mama's Gone

THE SERVICE STARTED with a hymn and then the congregation stood and sat at the behest of Carmoody. After another song extolling the virtues of Jesus Christ, everyone sat and the priest began the eulogy.

"Mary Lou Lagotti, may she rest in peace, was a mother, a wife, a business woman. But above all she was a human being who died in tragic circumstances. She leaves behind two beautiful children—Frank Jr and Alice—as well as Bobby, her dutiful husband. She joined our community thirty years ago and she quickly developed into a fabulous contributor to our local charities. As her kids grew older, and her activities thrived, Mary Lou became a force for good in Palm Springs."

Frank disliked the hypocrisy of the man who met Mama only a few months before and knew nothing of her. He'd inveigled himself into Mama's life when she was at her most vulnerable. The guy's whole attitude sickened him to the core.

Alice remained too consumed with the pain of her loss and the reality of seeing her Mama's coffin in front of her. In that wooden box and its oak veneer was the body of her mother. Mama's corpse was almost within her grasp, but to acknowledge that meant Alice had to tell herself her mom was dead—and mean it—and that was too much for her to bear. So she cried again and waited for the juddering silent ache inside to subside enough to breathe again. And still the priest droned on while she curled up in her own thoughts.

AT THE GRAVESIDE, Carmoody issued a series of prayers and the coffin was lowered into the gaping hole awaiting it and the men used two shovels to heap the soil on top of the box. Bobby had the honor of throwing the first earth onto the wooden casket. The echoing thud as the earth slammed on the veneer sent a shiver down Bobby's spine. He focussed on the physical act of pushing the shovel into the mound of clay and dropping the contents into the abyss. He knew if he allowed himself half a second's thought about Mary Lou's corpse down in that pit he would break down completely.

When the coffin was no longer visible under the soil, Bobby, Alice and Frank walked away and back towards the church. Alice looked round for one last chance of seeing her mother and that was her undoing. The sensation of losing her Mama hit her knees and she collapsed to the ground.

Lagotti men grabbed an arm each and hauled her to her feet, half dragging her through the cemetery.

The wake took place at the house which gave those who couldn't make the funeral a chance to show their respect. Irma had asked permission to get three waitresses in to help her serve canapes and drinks. An hour in and the food was eaten although there was still enough hard liquor to last four more hours.

BY THE TIME the final guests departed, Bobby was left slumped in the living room with a tumbler of Scotch in his hand. Frank and Alice were seated on sun loungers.

"We're orphans, Frank."

"Because both our parents are dead?"

"Yep."

Alice knocked back the remains of her whiskey and soda.

"Let's sneak into the summerhouse like when we were kids."

Frank followed Alice inside as she switched on the lights.

"Give me a hug. We're all alone, kid."

Frank stepped toward her and Alice opened her arms and engulfed him in a sisterly embrace. She squeezed that huge torso and leaned her chin on one shoulder. Despite the momentary comfort of her brother's biceps, Alice snapped awake to remember why her Mama was dead and who was the cause.

"I know what you did, Frank."

"Huh?"

"At the peace conference. No idea why but you killed my Mama."

"What're you…"

Alice pulled out a knife from her pants pocket and slammed it into Frank's stomach, twisting the blade as she plugged him. He gurgled, clutched his belly with one hand and swiped at his twin with the other. His palm caught the side of Alice's head and she almost lost her balance, but then she removed the metal and stuck it in his chest…

The sound of glass breaking and the memory of her Mama's blood splashing onto her cheek…

Frank fell to his knees, grabbing Alice's arms, torso, anything to stop himself hitting the ground. She reached out and scrunched his hair with a hand, yanking back his head. Then she took the blade and pressed its serrated edge over his throat to cut him open from one ear to the other.

Alice slumped on the floor, bouncing off Frank's body as she collapsed and sat in the pool of his blood until the red liquid seeped into her undies and felt sticky and uncomfortable. She rolled onto her side, huddled into the smallest ball of humanity she could make and she cried.

Alice sobbed and sobbed until she could cry no more—for her Mama, for Frank and for herself. She picked up the knife and wiped it clean on Frank's jacket. Then she stood up, one foot either side of his corpse, just as Bobby entered the room in search of the children. He looked down at Frank then sighed. Alice Lagotti, head of the family, stepped away from her brother's body and held out a hand.

Bobby went towards her, bowed and kissed her cygnet ring. The stench of Frank's gizzards heavy in the air.

"Get this mess tidied up: we've got territory in San Francisco to reclaim and a deal to close with New York."

THE END

THANK YOU FOR READING!

Get a free novella

Building a relationship with my readers is the very best thing about writing. I send weekly newsletters with details of new releases, special offers and other bits of news relating to the Lagotti Family and Alex Cohen series, as well as information about my stand-alone novels.

And if you sign up to the mailing list I'll send you a copy of the Lagotti Family prequel, The Stickup. Just go to www.leopoldborstinski.com/newsletter-signup-book and we'll take it from there.

Enjoy this book? You can make a difference

Reviews are the most powerful tools in my arsenal when it comes to getting attention for my books. Much as I'd like to, I don't have the financial muscle of a New York publisher. I can't take out full page ads or put posters on the subway.

(Not yet, anyway).

But I do have something much more powerful and effective than that, and it's something that those publishers would kill to get their hands on.

A committed and loyal bunch of readers.

Honest reviews of my books help bring them to the attention of other readers.

If you've enjoyed this book I shall be very grateful if you would spend just five minutes leaving a review (it can be as short as you like) on the book's page. You can jump right to the page by clicking www.books2read.com/thecase

Thank you very much.

Leo

SNEAK PREVIEW

Check out this stand-alone Private Eye story, The Case…

I'd been in Vegas for a couple of days paid break to take photos for Eliza Rothstein, a jealous broad obsessed with the belief that her husband, Aaron, was shtupping a call girl from out of town. I told her not to worry and I'd check things out. Two hundred dollars a day plus expenses. Rothstein was rich and I knew I could get away with it. The thought I was taking Aaron's dough to break up his marriage didn't cross my mind. Besides, I knew Aaron wasn't shtupping a call girl.

He was shtupping Rachel, Eliza's closest friend, but I wanted a holiday and Aaron had taken Rachel to play the wheels in Vegas. So I came along for the ride. Aaron had set up a cozy apartment on the upper east side for the two of them, overlooking the park. If I hadn't wanted a holiday so bad, I'd have rented a place on the west side and used a telephoto lens. The case would have been that simple. Aaron was shrewd in business - he owned enough water utilities to drown the nation - but he let his dick do the walking whenever a blonde with big blue eyes and breasts to match came into his line of vision. And anyway, Rachel and Aaron were the worst kept secret in Manhattan. But Eliza was so dumb, she didn't understand why the guy who collected her trash was called Giuseppe. So I took the greenbacks and headed west.

Vegas is the only town where hookers and Frank Sinatra both feel at home, only they're surrounded by a million wannabes, hoping the next spin of the wheel will give them the big break. I didn't mind visiting it for a few days, but after a couple of weeks I missed the sun so bad my ulcer started playing up.

Aaron's money meant he could afford to stay at the Tropicana, the swankiest joint in Vegas. I was on expenses so I took a room on the fifteenth floor. By the time I arrived at reception, Aaron and Rachel were already tucked up for the night, so I wandered around the casino for some relaxation. I knew I wasn't going to bump into them because Aaron hadn't flown over here for the wheels, if you see what I mean. He was after some silky sheet action rather than blackjack and watered down Budweiser.

Anyway, I checked out the poker tables and watched a drunk lose his shirt at the wheel. Jeez, I could tell he was a loser from the moment I saw him. The lush was playing with his chips like a kid plays with his food. His first time at the wheel. Even the green baize felt his virginity every time he put the fifty buck chips on it. Pathetic. The kind of guy that gives a casino a bad name. And that's saying something.

After a couple of hours, I'd drunk enough vodka to knock out the ghosts and stumbled back to my room, number 1526. As soon as I put my head to the pillow, I was out until morning. By the time my eyes opened, the maid had already tried to clean my room. Fumbling for my watch, I saw it was half ten. I slouched out of bed and bumped into the shower. The water woke me up; I shaved and headed straight for reception.

Grab your copy NOW at www.books2read.com/thecase.

OTHER BOOKS BY THE AUTHOR

The Lagotti Family
The Stickup (Free Prequel Novella)
The Heist (Book 1)
The Getaway (Book 2)
Powder (Book 3)
Mama's Gone (Book 4)
The Girl in the Striped Bikini (Book 5, Short story)

Other Releases
The Case
The Death and Life of Penny Pitstop (Due 2019)

Alex Cohen
The Bowery Slugger (Book 1 - Due 2019)

ABOUT LEOPOLD BORSTINSKI

Leopold Borstinski is an independent author whose past careers have included financial journalism, business management of financial software companies, consulting and product sales and marketing, as well as teaching.

There is nothing he likes better so he does as much nothing as he possibly can. He has travelled extensively in Europe and the US and has visited Asia on several occasions. Leopold holds a Philosophy degree and tries not to drop it too often.

He lives near London and is married with one wife, one child and no pets.

Find out more at LeopoldBorstinski.com.